SEABEA CLOSE

K.J.RABANE

Table of Contents

[Layout of Seabeach Close](#)

[Chapter 1](#)

[Chapter 2](#)

[Chapter 3](#)

[Chapter 4](#)

[Chapter 5](#)

[Chapter 6](#)

[Chapter 7](#)

[Chapter 8](#)

[Chapter 9](#)

[Chapter 10](#)

[Chapter 11](#)

[Chapter 12](#)

[Chapter 13](#)

[Chapter 14](#)

[Chapter 15](#)

[Chapter 16](#)

[Chapter 17](#)

[Chapter 18](#)

[Chapter 19](#)

[Chapter 20](#)

[Chapter 21](#)

[Chapter 22](#)

[Chapter 23](#)

[Chapter 24](#)

[Chapter 25](#)

[Chapter 26](#)

[Chapter 27](#)

[Chapter 28](#)

[Chapter 29](#)

[Chapter 30](#)

[Chapter 31](#)

[Chapter 32](#)

[Chapter 33](#)

[Chapter 34](#)

[Chapter 35](#)

[Chapter 36](#)

[Chapter 37](#)

[Chapter 38](#)

[Chapter 39](#)

[Chapter 40](#)

[Chapter 41](#)

[Chapter 42](#)

[Chapter 43](#)

[Chapter 44](#)

[Chapter 45](#)

[Chapter 46](#)

[Chapter 47](#)

[Chapter 48](#)

[Chapter 49](#)

[Chapter 50](#)

- [Chapter 51](#)
- [Chapter 52](#)
- [Chapter 53](#)
- [Chapter 54](#)
- [Chapter 55](#)
- [Chapter 56](#)
- [Chapter 57](#)
- [Chapter 58](#)
- [Chapter 59](#)
- [Chapter 60](#)
- [Chapter 61](#)
- [Chapter 62](#)
- [Chapter 63](#)
- [Chapter 64](#)
- [Chapter 65](#)
- [Chapter 66](#)
- [Chapter 67](#)
- [Chapter 68](#)

Chapter 69

Chapter 70

Chapter 71

Chapter 72

Chapter 73

Chapter 74

Chapter 75

Chapter 76

THE END

About the Author

Dedication.

To my family

Acknowledgements
My Thanks go to

Rhys Briggs (Graphic Designer) for creating the cover of Seabeach Close.

Also To my *Tiny Writers* friends who have continued to support my work.

Tiny Writers

Pam Cockerill…Published children's author with Hodder and Stoughton. Now writing for the Amazon marketplace.

Robert Darke…Crime writer. And Photographer Books available on Amazon.

Iona Jenkins…Spiritual novels and poetry books available on Amazon. Latest novel T*o Sing with Bards and Angels* published by O-Book

Jan Marsh…Literary novels published by Amazon. Study guides available published by Coleridge Press

Ron Powell…RAF inspired novels, Biographies and Audio books also available from Amazon and Audiobooks.com

Layout of Seabeach Close

Detached, Split Level Houses.

Number 1…Ben and Felicity Frazer

Number 3…The Joneses. Emlyn, Gwyneth and Ian and their twins Bronwen and Bethan.

Number 5…Owned by DI Elis Williams and rented by DC Laura Davies.

Number 7…Owned by Charles Frazer, uninhabited but regularly cleaned by Molly Johnson.

The Bungalows.

Number 2…Norman and Alice Barker

Number 4…Sam, Jess and Daniel Evans

Number 6…Ted and May Finch

Number 8…formerly owned by The Coopers but now occupied by Henry and Janice Wilson and their son Jake.

The Beginning
The inhabitants of Seabeach Close

Chapter 1

It all started after The Coopers died in a car crash. If they'd still been alive, perhaps none of this would have happened.

The chain of events unfolded after we moved into Seabeach Close. I'd just celebrated my fifty-second birthday and Ted was coming up to sixty. The bungalow, situated on the South coast of Wales, was perfect. It had a sea-view and the beach and promenade stretched out in front of us like a gigantic blank canvas on which we could make our marks. The move was to be the start of a new life for us. We had savings and, with the sale of our last house, felt we were in a position to retire and enjoy a more relaxed way of life.

I remembered wiping away beads of sweat and thinking, what a day for a move! We were in the middle of a heatwave which had been sweeping through the UK a while back. But we continued to unload the car in spite of the heat and, while our cases stood waiting to be unpacked in the hallway, we opened every window in the bungalow feeling the sea breeze sliding towards us in a welcoming wave. Then, sitting in the kitchen, we drank the cool beers we'd picked up at the local supermarket on the way through the village.

When we'd spoken to our sons they'd agreed it could be a good move for us. In fact it was Will who'd suggested Wales in the first place. He'd said he'd looked into possible locations which he thought might suit us, and the village of Oysterbend had ticked all the boxes. He always had our best interests at heart even though he'd been living in San Diego with Beth for a while now.

Mark, our youngest, was busy working as a songwriter for a production company based in London and he usually rang once a week to see if we were okay. They were good boys who cared about us. Ted and I recognised they'd grown into men with lives of their own and taking early retirement from work could be just what we needed at this time in our lives. We weren't rich but we could manage. We were comfortable, in more ways than one.

'Relax Dad, have fun while you're still young enough to enjoy it,' Will had said, smiling from the laptop screen during a Zoom call from San Diego, not long after we'd unpacked and were getting used to living in our new home.

And for the first couple of years that was exactly what we did. We'd got used to the neighbours who seemed very nice. I was quieter than my husband but managed to make a few friends. Ted was a good mixer, a kind, thoughtful man, who wouldn't hurt a fly. That's why I was absolutely positive he could never have done it…whatever the police had to say to the contrary.

Chapter 2

First, let me explain the layout of Seabeach Close to you. It will make the story easier to understand and you can start to imagine what it was like to be living there. It is made up of two semi-detached bungalows with views of the sea from their large back gardens and four detached, split level houses facing them. These also have sea views but from the windows on the first floors.

As soon as I'd seen The Close I'd thought it was peaceful and Ted had agreed. There were no sounds of busy traffic just the distant cawing of the birds on the foreshore waiting to be feed. There was also plenty of space between the properties, not like some of the places we'd lived before, where every house seemed to be nudging its neighbours out of the way.

The nearest town from Oysterbend village was Newton Cross just five miles away and only reachable by a winding coast road, unless you had a boat of course.

As my story unfolds you will realise I'm a naturally suspicious person and often spent my time trying to find out as much as I could about our new neighbours. Looking back to what happened to us, it was perhaps just as well.

For a while we had no trouble worth mentioning. We got on with everyone, especially The Coopers who lived next-door at number eight. They were in their late fifties, older than us, but nearer to us in age than any of the other neighbours, which was why we'd gelled from the start, I suppose. They were also retired, full of fun and always ready with a bit of local news. I know I'd made up my mind not to listen to gossip but Avril Cooper had a way of telling a tale that took the sting out of the most outrageous story and besides it made sense to know as much as I could about them all in order to avoid problems later on.

Avril's husband Gordon was quieter and quite soon after we'd moved in he'd introduced Ted to his friends in the local gardening and allotment club. Regular meetings of the club were held in a shed, just outside the village, where the land was divided up into much-sought-after plots. Ted was thrilled and it meant I had some free time to potter about on my own, knowing he was happy and enjoying himself.

As I said, we got on well with our neighbours, at least for the first five years, until The Coopers died and the property was sold to the Wilsons. And that was when our problems really began.

If I'd only had a crystal ball! We could have sold up there and then and moved as far away from Seabeach Close as it was possible to go, which would have saved us all from the distressful events which were set to take place.

Chapter 3

I remember Ted was pottering about in the garden after a particularly bad winter. The shoreline had frozen solid and, although it was a pretty sight, had become treacherous to walk on. I'd always been aware that feeding the birds was vital to their survival but found trying to keep my footing on the ice quite difficult, in spite of still being only in my fifties and quite physically fit. But thankfully the overnight drop in temperature was only a brief remnant of winter's chill, which was slipping away like a boat from its moorings now, as it was spring.

I was cleaning the windows, and saw Ted removing some of the debris and generally tidying up the borders, when I heard it. The sound was so loud I could hear it from the kitchen at the back of the house. Leaving my duster and washcloth on the draining board I hurried into the bedroom. Peering through the blinds into the road I craned my neck in the direction of number eight to see what on earth was going on.

The new people, the Wilsons, had moved in the previous week and up until then all had been quiet. They'd nodded to us and smiled but we hadn't had a chance to speak to them properly as they always seemed so busy. From what we'd discovered the family consisted of the husband, Henry Wilson, who was a tall, handsome man with thick, dark hair and looked to be in his early thirties, his wife, Janice, who was much shorter than him and unremarkable by comparison with her husband, and their son, Jake. I thought Jake looked about the same age as Daniel, who lived at number four… fourteen or so I would say. He wasn't much like either his mother or his father, having a shock of auburn hair which I'd noticed fell into his eyes whenever he ran along the promenade at the back of the bungalows.

Ted, who'd guessed I'd want to know what was going on, came inside from the garden and after washing his hands, followed me into the front bedroom saying, 'Ha! I knew it!'

Standing away from nosing out of the window, I said, 'Look at the size of that lorry! What on earth's going on, Ted?'

I could tell by his expression that he had an idea. I'd been with him long enough to be able to read him like an open book. But, he was determined to keep me in suspense a while longer, so I followed him into the kitchen and waited as he put the kettle on, and taking his time arranged two mugs on a tray along with the biscuit tin.

I knew he enjoying seeing me trying to keep a lid on my frustration so I went along with it more often than not. Carrying the tray into the living room and placing it on a side table, Ted said, 'Come on love, sit down before you explode!'

I shrugged and played along by sitting opposite him and picking up my mug as if I wasn't really bothered.

'Looks like they're making a start on an extension,' he said.

'Oh, really?' Of course, I thought, that much was obvious. 'But, we haven't seen any plans, have we? I understood they had to submit plans for the neighbours to see first before building an extension?'

'Depends.' Ted rubbed his chin with the back of his hand. 'If it's just a loft conversion with a fanlight they don't necessarily have to consult the neighbours. Besides, if they're planning to add on to the other side of number eight there's plenty of spare land so it wouldn't be next to anyone who might complain.'

I didn't argue the point as Ted sounded so sure about it. You could say I was more of a worrier than my husband, being like a dog with a bone when a problem arose but I chose when to lose my rag and this wasn't worth getting worked up about. That was my first mistake!

'Okay then. Let's enjoy our cuppa first, and afterwards I think, as the sun has melted the ice on the foreshore, a walk along the beach is called for? What d'you think?' I asked, adding, 'It's still a bit chilly but the sun is out and so is the tide. As long as we wrap up warmly it will be better than sitting inside watching reruns of yesterday's bowls match on TV.'

Seabeach Close   K.J.Rabane

I wasn't sure whether Ted would consider a walk on a crisp, spring day better than sitting inside watching bowls, but he just nodded and drank his tea.

A while later, we left through the side gate where a path ran between us and number four. I could see that the overnight frost had lingered in places though, and the steps leading to the beach were still a bit slippery. We clung to the handrail and each other and, avoiding the ice, cautiously navigated a path onto the pebbles until we reached the hard sand which sparkled with tiny shards of ice crystals melting in the morning sun. I took a deep breath enjoying the feeling of the crisp, clean air, untainted by traffic fumes, entering my lungs, and followed Ted who was gingerly tapping ice from underneath his shoes before reaching up to help me onto the sand. Aware we were looking like a couple of oldies, I smiled.

'Not a day goes by when I don't recognise how fortunate we were to move here.' Ted caught my hand in his and squeezed it.

The frantic cries of seagulls circling overhead seemed, in hindsight, like a warning I shouldn't have ignored.

'We should have brought them something to eat,' Ted said, looking up.

'I will, later. Don't you worry.'

Seabeach Close   K.J.Rabane

We'd walked for about a mile along the sand before deciding to turn around and make our way back home. It was a regular walk of ours, out to the area known locally as The Point. We liked to walk across the sand whenever possible, in favour of taking the promenade route, as there were often a succession of joggers to avoid whatever the weather. I suppose we'd been gone for about an hour and a half, maybe a bit longer, as we'd stopped for a coffee in our favourite cafe on the way.

I saw it first, but then I suppose I'd been looking for it and Ted seemed to have other things on his mind. I'd had a feeling, ever since we saw the lorry unloading, that something of this sort was going to happen. But, it was still a shock. The roof of number eight had changed beyond all recognition. Scaffolding had been erected, and the workmen were busy throwing tiles into a skip.

'They haven't wasted much time,' Ted said, finally looking up as we reached the steps leading up from the beach.

'Looks as if they're going to remove the whole roof,' I replied, squinting up into the sunlight.

Ted was about to deny it when he suddenly stopped in his tracks. 'You could be right, at that. Certainly looks like it from here. But that can't be right surely, must be a bigger extension than I'd thought. Planning permission would definitely be needed for it if that's the case. Or perhaps they're just going to put on a new roof.'

'Nothing wrong with the old one.' I said. 'The Close hasn't been built that long. Number six was only five or six years old when we moved in, I'm sure of it. '

'Yeah, well, you know what people are like, more money than sense some of them. Anyway, love, let's get on I could do with a bite of lunch after that walk.'

Looking back, Ted had absolutely no idea that having a 'bite of lunch' would be the least of his worries. As I've said, The Wilsons moving in was the start of it all. How were we to know then, on such a beautiful, crisp spring morning, that our cosy little world was about to shatter into tiny pieces like a fallen Christmas tree bauble crunching under our feet?

Number 1
Ben and Felicity Frazer
Chapter 4

In the master bedroom of number one Seabeach Close Felicity Frazer yawned and stretched, as she watched a sliver of sunlight streaking through the shutter blinds coming to rest on her husband's fair hair and turning it to silver. Ben was still asleep. She sighed, not sure if it was with regret, boredom or love. He'd given her everything she could possibly want, hadn't he? A beautiful home, expensive foreign holidays, designer clothes the list was endless. He wasn't unkind and had worked hard to maintain their standard of living. So what was her problem? She'd had the other kind, and knew he was nothing like Clive Mitchell.

Okay, it was true he'd had help, every step of the way. His father had built up a thriving property development company and had bought the land on which Seabeach Close now stood. It was Charles Frazer's acumen which had been responsible for designing the houses, and it was *his* hard work which had paid for his son's education and expensive lifestyle. Although, to be fair Ben could have just sat back and lived like an over-indulged child, taking what was on offer. But, he'd worked hard in school and university and had a good law degree, in spite of a few hiccups along the way.

She wondered again why she felt so discontented. Ben loved her. But he'd been working for his father's company since he'd graduated and it had taken its toll on both of them. Charles didn't seem to understand or value his son enough. If he'd been lazy he could have taken all his father had to give and put his feet up, but he'd made sure he'd become a valuable member of the company. Surely it was to be admired? Felicity knew her father-in law could rely on Ben to find loopholes where other, less astute, lawyers had failed. So what *was* her problem?

She sighed again. She should have been happy, but there was one thing Ben had failed to give her and day after day the longing increased. She had only to see a pregnant woman pushing a pushchair, or with a toddler at her side to feel resentment growing inside her where a foetus should have been.

She heard her husband give a small grunt as he stirred.

'Hey! What's up?' He glanced at the digital display on their Home Assistant. 'It's still early, Flick…not tired?' Ben yawned and reached out for her hand.

'No. But I'm okay. The sun's up and I'm wide awake, so I think I'll go for an early run. You go back to sleep.'

'Right, well, don't forget your phone.' His voice was heavy with sleep and before she could slip into her running clothes she heard his regular breathing and knew he would sleep until the seven-forty-five alarm woke him.

Leaving the house and heading for the promenade she saw the couple who lived at number six heading for the steps leading down to the beach. The woman was holding a plastic carrier in which she usually carried bread for the seagulls. They were early risers like her, she thought, jogging on the spot as she waited for them to pass her.

'Nice morning,' Ted, said, as his wife muttered a curt, 'good morning,' before grabbing her husband's hand in a proprietorial manner. When they reached the steps, she saw them walking down towards the beach and heading for the shallows.

Smothering a smile, Felicity thought, surely the woman didn't think she fancied Ted? Jogging after the couple and keeping her distance, until they were well ahead of her, she reached the hard sand and began to run in the direction of the village. She'd planned to go as far as the square where the boats were berthed, then jog back along the promenade before it became too crowded.

Although it was still only spring the weather was good and she knew it usually drew the inhabitants from the town to visit the village of Oysterbend with its many attractions. It had a long sandy beach, a coastal miniature railway and an array of shops selling local produce and Welsh pottery, which meant on warm, sunny days the place was flooded with a steady stream of visitors.

Having left the beach she was approaching the harbour when she saw him. He was the sort of man you couldn't really miss, being a head and shoulders taller than most. His thick dark hair was worn longer than Ben's and curled onto his collar. She'd noticed him as soon as he'd moved into number eight but had never been faced with the opportunity to speak to him.

Feeling sweat prickling in her armpits and knowing strands of her pale blonde hair had escaped from her ponytail and were now sticking unflatteringly to her forehead, she turned on her heel and jogged towards the promenade. She passed him as he'd stopped to drink from a water bottle but didn't look in his direction. However, he caught up with her as she reached the back of the tennis courts.

'Hi. You live at number one, don't you,' he said, his breath coming in short gasps. He was wearing navy running shorts and a white tee shirt, his brown, lithe body even more impossible to ignore.

'Yes, *we* do,' she said, self-consciously stressing the we. She had no idea why.

She stopped to catch her breath as he held out his hand, 'Henry Wilson. We've just moved into number eight. Nice to meet you.'

His hand, warm and firm, closed around hers and she felt the warmth washing over her in a wave of recognition. There was something about this man. Could it be she'd met him before? She didn't think so, but there was definitely *something* familiar about him.

'Yes, er you too, I hope you don't mind, can't stop,' she said, picking up her pace once again and running towards the path leading into Seabeach Close. Out of sight of him she felt foolish and unaccountably embarrassed, still unable to shake off the impression this wasn't the first time she'd met Henry Wilson.

Ben was getting into his car as she reached the house. He looked handsome and polished, not a hair out of place, completely professional. It was one of the reasons she'd been drawn to him in the first place. But she'd soon discovered first impressions can often be misleading. She knew Ben had a secret his appearance could not disguise, a secret which would not go away however hard he'd tried. And however hard he'd attempted to hide it from her.

But, this morning in bed, as he'd reached forward to kiss her she was aware the attraction she'd always felt for him was beginning to fade into familiarity and she shivered at the thought. It was then she realised where she'd seen Henry Wilson before and his connection with her husband's past.

Number 3

The Joneses

Chapter 5

'Dad, can you take them over the beach? They're driving me mad. Spring Bank Holiday! Some bloody holiday, Ian working all the hours God sent, and me up to my eyes and…'

Emlyn laid his trowel down on the grass at his side. 'Calm down Gwyneth, love. Of course I'll take them,' he said. 'Bethan, Bron, get your buckets and we'll be off to collect some shells. First one to find an oyster-shell can choose which place we'll go to for our ice-creams - Bryant's or Joe's.' He knew he was on to a good thing as the beach was littered with oyster-shells thrown up by the tide and neither of his granddaughters would favour Bryant's over Joe's.

Gwyneth caught his arm and whispered, 'Thanks Dad, but watch what Bron eats. Not too many sweets, now.'

'Stop worrying about her. Big boned is all she is. There's always one twin bigger than the other. It's a known fact.'

Gwyneth shrugged and said, 'So, that's what it is, is it Dad?' Then, telling the girls to behave, she walked back inside and up the stairs to the kitchen.

Seabeach Close   K.J.Rabane

Breathing a sigh of relief at a moment of peace and quiet Gwyneth made a much-longed for cuppa thinking this one she'd drink uninterrupted for a change. Then sitting on the window seat in the living room she looked out over the rooftops opposite towards the sea. She could smell the salty air drifting up from the shore and slipping in through the living room windows and smiled. Busy or not it had been a good move. They had struggled in the small terraced house on the main road leading to Newton Cross, car fumes, nowhere for the girls to play and miles away from the beach. Then her father had suggested they sell both their houses and move in together. She'd talked it over with Ian who'd thought it might be a good idea, as long as they could find something suitable which was large enough and which they could afford. She knew he liked her father and got on well with him. He'd said he could see it working out for them all. He'd even tentatively thought about the new properties overlooking the sea, in Oysterbend. They'd discussed it with Emlyn and had worked on the figures before finally deciding they could probably afford it if the sales of both houses went through as planned.

Gwyneth had never in her wildest dreams, thought they would be living in a house like number three Seabeach Close but they'd managed it and now life was good. Through the bay window she could just see her father and the girls picking up shells from the sand. What a difference to closing the windows in order to escape the exhaust fumes from the busy road, accompanied by the constant noise of heavy traffic.

Just as she was relaxing and thinking about starting the cleaning she heard the rumble of a large lorry entering The Close and coming to a stop outside number eight. She watched as the rear door of the vehicle opened and two of the largest glass panels imaginable were being carried around to the back of the bungalow. These were soon followed by a contraption comprising of what looked like a folded down balcony made of metal and glass. There had been work going on opposite for a few days now but she'd assumed it was because they were still in the process of moving in. She was curious as to what they were actually going to do to number eight now.

She speculated, as she sipped her tea, where the contraption was going to be situated and took a certain amount of comfort from the fact that whatever they did with it there was no possibility of it obstructing their view of the sea.

As she watched, a car draw up and parked in the driveway of number eight. Then a woman and a teenage boy emerged carrying Superstar plastic bags from the local mini-market. The woman was pleasant looking but nothing special and obviously not a match for her husband in the looks department, she thought, putting her cup down on the windowsill to watch.

He'd been the first one she'd seen, not long after they'd moved in. Ian had made her laugh by saying he looked like a cross between Idris Elba and Bradley Cooper, either of whom she wouldn't have minded coming home to. But then, thinking about it, she knew without a doubt she wouldn't change Ian for either film star or the man who'd just moved into number eight, even it they begged her on bended knees, which was unlikely to say the least.

As soon as the thought had occurred to her, Henry Wilson jogged into The Close his tee shirt clinging to his chest with sweat. Watching him as he stopped to speak to the men who were unloading the lorry, she thought, it was just as well she loved her Ian to bits. Then drinking the last dregs from her cup and walking back into the kitchen began to prepare the potatoes for their evening meal.

Picking up the kitchen knife, Gwyneth became determined to put all fanciful thoughts concerning her new neighbour well and truly out of her mind.

Number 5

Detective Inspector Elis Williams

CHAPTER 6

Frustrated and annoyed Elis put down the phone. Trouble at number five again! It was becoming a pain in the butt lately. When his Mam and Dad had retired and moved into Seabeach Close he'd been happy to have them near enough to keep and eye on as they were having a few health problems. Melanie had been a great help when his mam died, he had to give her that, even though thinking of her now with any shred of fondness had become an alien concept. Then his dad had a stroke shortly afterwards and Melanie had got fed up of waiting for him to propose and had swiftly found someone more suitable. Someone whose job didn't have him getting up at all hours, staying late and unable to say when he'd be finished. She wanted the stability he couldn't give her and so he'd stood back and watched her walking away with regret but little else. He'd always known she wasn't 'the one' and doubted whether such a creature even existed.

At first, after his dad died and he'd been left the house, he'd thought maybe he'd move into number five it, was too big for him but the views were spectacular and the house had only been built a couple of years of ago. Although, after considering the prospect, he'd soon decided against it. He liked his town apartment which was near enough to the station so he could grab a few extra hours of sleep when the occasion arose. It was also only a short drive of five or so miles from Newton Cross to the village of Oysterbend and Seabeach Close.

He'd decided renting the property would be a better option and would provide an extra income, but to date the mess some of his tenants had created and which had to be put right, had eaten into most of the benefits he'd acquired from such additional funds.

Thankfully there wasn't much going on in Newton Cross at present, apart from the usual druggies who, when they got to court, were usually fined and sent on their way. Frustratingly for him they were often back on the streets before he'd had time to leave the court and get back to work. He'd see them collecting in doorways and scuttling out of sight whenever they suspected they were being watched.

Leaving the station and driving along the coast road until he reached Seabeach Close, he noticed a skip outside number eight. He'd heard it had been sold and idly wondered who had moved in, not that it was of much concern to him, as *he* didn't have to live there. After parking in his driveway Elis slid the key into the lock and held his breath wondering what would be waiting for him this time. As soon as he stepped inside, the smell hit him. The hallway was littered with detritus, the aftermath of the party the neighbours had complained to him about, as soon as he'd got back from his holidays. The pleasure of two weeks putting his feet up and relaxing in a cottage in France had instantly evaporated as he was brought back to reality with a jolt.

The bedrooms, apart from being untidy looked to be more or less undamaged. He took the stairs to the first floor and opened the sitting room door. It was in a state. He closed his eyes, took a deep breath and tried to assess the situation calmly. Again it was the smell that hit his nostrils before the sight of the beer cans, bottles and cigarette butts littering every surface. Lying on top of the coffee table, were the obvious signs of drug-taking apparatus, the folded foil, a couple of plastic supermarket loyalty cards alongside a faint strip of white powder, a spoon, a syringe and the stubs of a couple of spliffs. He moved to the window and opened it wide, releasing the fetid-weed-scented air into The Close.

Taking his mobile from his pocket he rang the now familiar number. 'Gwyn, it's Elis…yeah…deep clean it is. Soon as poss. Ta.'

There was no point in trying to trace his previous occupants. They'd fled the nest days ago if this was anything to go by. It felt like he'd never had a holiday he thought closing the door on the mess and going into the kitchen. Ignoring the sight which met him there, he put on the kettle, found a jar of coffee and washed a mug clean in the sink, then drank the hot black liquid as he waited for Gwyn's cleaning company van to arrive.

This had to stop, he said out loud, the words bouncing back at him in derision from the bottom of his mug. He knew he could always sell the place, but was still reluctant to do so. With property values in the area being what they were it made sense to keep it, if only as an investment.

Afterwards, leaving Gwyn, and a couple of lads from his firm cleaning up, and having told him to post the key back through the letterbox when he'd finished, Elis drove back to the station.

'You Okay, Boss?' Laura asked, as he sat down opposite her and sighed.

'Yeah, just number five again.' As he'd answered her a thought suddenly struck him. A month ago Laura Davies had transferred to Newton Cross from Cardiff. She was staying in a shared flat with a couple of students and he knew she wasn't happy there. She was a steady type, not given to the all night parties, which her flat-share companions held every weekend. The rent on number five would be too steep for a single person to afford and besides it was a big house for one occupant…but the germ of an idea was growing and he needed time to think it over.

The case they'd been working on was almost wrapped up, just the paperwork remained. He had a court appearance booked for the following day to give evidence in the Maunder case, so he spent the afternoon sitting at his desk going over some of the finer points to make sure he didn't slip up on any of the details.

When he'd finished he walked past Laura's desk and noticed she was staring at her computer screen.

'What's up, Constable?' He asked with a smile. 'Looks serious.'

'Sorry. It's nothing, sir…just…well, it was quiet and as it's nearly time for me to knock off, I…' She looked embarrassed.

'Okay spill the beans,' he said, glancing at the screen.

'Flat hunting,' she said.

'Right, no, okay, carry on. It's fine. I'm having an early night anyway. Sergeant Jenkins is holding the fort tonight.'

When he'd been deployed to Newton Cross after passing his DI exams, he'd been over the moon on two counts. To get a Detective Inspector's post so soon after graduating was one thing, to get the town close to where his elderly parents were living was even better. However, he couldn't deny it was a bit of a dead-end post work-wise. Nothing much happened which would necessitate his expertise as most of it was routine policing.

Seabeach Close   K.J.Rabane

As he walked towards his apartment he couldn't stop thinking about the problem of number five. Once inside, he called to his smart Home Assistant to put on the lamp and play Miles Davies, poured a glass of chilled white wine from the half-full bottle in his fridge then sat down put his feet up. Jazz always cleared his head and made him focus on the matter at hand.

Laura was too good an opportunity to miss. In some ways she was the answer to his prayer. She could look after the place for him…she was neat, if her appearance was anything to go by…no all nighters, he was as certain as he could be of that… there was just the rent to be decided.

While he was thinking about how to get around the question of the rent his phone rang. It was the Chief Superintendent from the Cardiff force. Their conversation was short and to the point. There would be a full briefing in the morning but he'd outlined the reason he needed to see him and his team urgently. Elis put down his phone, a slow smile spreading over his face, it seemed his problem over the rent issue with Laura might be easily be solved.

Number 7
Molly, the cleaner.

CHAPTER 7

Reaching up to open the kitchen window, Molly Johnson inhaled the fresh salty air. Then turning away, lit a cigarette and was struck by a bout of nicotine induced coughing, after which she picked up her glass of orange juice liberally laced with vodka, and sat down to admire the view. She wasn't interested in the seascape unfolding over the rooftops of the bungalows opposite, her gaze was focused primarily on the man who had recently moved into number eight. Even from here she could see he was a good looker, the first one to live in The Close, with the possible exception of Ben Frazer at number one. But Ben was too fair and insipid for her taste. She recognised her failing and had to admit, she had a fondness for 'bad boys'. It had always been her undoing.

Molly hadn't really seen this one up close but she planned to remedy that as soon as possible. Watching him, as he bent down and picked up a concrete slab from the driveway like it was a bag of feathers, she sighed. She liked a man who could handle himself but hadn't been able to find one who could compare in any way to Ethan. Why had she suddenly thought of Ethan? That was years ago.

Seabeach Close   K.J.Rabane

The man she was watching was what her mother would have called 'tall, dark and handsome' although her mother had always warned her that handsome is as handsome does, especially when she came home with yet another handsome looser. In those days, she thought idly, she'd had her pick of them. Although her mother had been right all along, if her past was anything to go by. Looking back she knew none of them were any good not even the ugly ones who'd tried their luck. And through necessity she'd sampled a few of those too.

Her thoughts returned to the man opposite. Pity he was married with a kid. But then he might fancy a bit of the other on the side, if so inclined. His wife wasn't any competition in the looks department, that was for sure. She was verging on plain.

Glancing in the mirrored glass of the cooker door Molly tried to hold in her stomach muscles but had to admit to defeat. At thirty-two she was showing the first signs of becoming overweight. Her hair was starting to show a few strands of grey and there were definitely crow's feet at the corner of her eyes. She'd seen the first indication years ago but had liked to think they were just laughter lines. Thinking about it now she'd had nothing to laugh about then though, nor lately.

Returning to her thoughts about the new inhabitant of number eight, she said out loud, 'Wouldn't fancy you in a fit girl. Would he?' As she pondered over the answer, she picked up the cleaning cloth and flicked away a week's worth of dust, which was almost non-existent. Then with a sigh she held up the bottle of vodka and poured the remains into her glass. This time she ignored the orange juice and drank it down in one gulp.

Feeling the alcohol picking up her mood she walked into the living room and opened the window to let in some fresh air. He was standing in the driveway again. As she opened the window he looked up, and their eyes met for just a fraction of a second. Molly gasped and took a step back. She wasn't mistaken and she knew he'd recognised her too.

Remembering what had happened almost ten years ago her pulse began to race. Unable to quite believe what she was seeing, she looked again but his back was turned to her. Nevertheless, there was no doubt in her mind, the same broad shoulders, the same black hair. She held her breath remembering how it had felt to run her fingers through his hair and to lay beside him while he slept.

So, what was he doing here? He was a living reminder of a past which she'd tried to put behind her and to forget it ever happened. Waiting until he walked around to the back garden of number eight, she reached over to close the window desperately hoping he hadn't recognised her but somehow knowing with a blinding certainty that he had.

Okay, her life wasn't brilliant but it was better than she deserved. How could she continue to work in this house now? What if Charles Frazer found out about her past? Her hands began to shake. This was the best job she'd had in a long time, it was money for old rope and there was the other job Frazer had found for her as well. Anger began to overwhelm her. Why should she run? She'd done it before and look where it had got her.

Going back into the kitchen Molly lit another cigarette. The nicotine rush calmed her immediately, which was why she couldn't give up the habit. Thinking more clearly about the situation facing her she decided…no, she wouldn't run this time, absolutely no way! She'd make that plain to him and as soon as possible. She was here to stay, whatever plans he had to the contrary. Then suddenly a germ of an idea began to grow and by the time she'd stubbed out her cigarette she knew exactly what to do.

Number 2
Norman and Alice Barker

CHAPTER 8

In the first bungalow opposite the detached, split levels houses, Norman Barker glanced over at his wife who was busy knitting dolls clothes for their granddaughter.

'Okay, I know,' he said, smiling at her before picking up the small black pouch on the side table, removing his hearing aid and slipping it into his ear, then positioning the tiny box behind it, he arranged his hair so it wasn't so noticeable. Norman wasn't a vain man but he hated the paraphernalia associated with encroaching age. He could see them all from his living room window…the oldies carefully walking along the prom, walking sticks at the ready, making for the next available seat in order to sit and watch the world go by.

He was seventy-one and had retired years ago. But, he made sure he kept fit by working on his allotment and taking a daily walk from his bungalow to the harbour or in the opposite direction out towards The Point. Alice sometimes joined him but more often than not made an excuse. Although she was a few years younger than him, just lately, due to arthritis pain, she'd been forced into a more sedentary life by accepting her lot and resorting to knitting for their grandchildren or watching the world go by from behind their net curtains. On fine days she would sit on their favourite bench waiting for him to join her after his walk. Arthritis was in her family and she'd been struggling to even walk to the bathroom some mornings, especially during the winter months, which was why he'd crossed the line and become a criminal. But spring was in the air and the temperature, although cold in the mornings, was sure to warm up nicely by eleven when they could walk towards the cafe.

As Norman planned their morning's activities the living room was suddenly filled with a high pitched screeching sound from his hearing aid as he adjusted it. Alice looked up from her knitting and smiled at him.

'Thanks love. I know you don't like wearing it but it does make such a difference, believe me. Some days I feel quite hoarse from shouting and repeating myself.' Her smile softened the criticism, which was, or something similar, issued frequently.

Norman nodded, returning her smile. Sitting in a chair alongside his wife, he picked up the morning paper as a shaft of sunlight sliced its way through the slats of the venetian blinds. He blinked, stood up and walked over to the window. But before he could adjust the slats he gazed out over the sand to the sea, which was sparkling in the crisp morning light. 'It was the right decision to sleep in the front of the bungalow and live in the back, wasn't it, love?' he said, glancing back at her for confirmation as if it were needed.

'It was, love,' his wife replied mechanically, and he knew she'd heard him mention this many times since they'd first moved into Seabeach Close. But that was the way of things with encroaching age, they'd heard each others stories many times before and recognised this was part of the fond memories they shared, along with the book and the box, which was well hidden in the loft space.

'Those new people at number eight are at it again,' he said. I can hear them working on that roof of theirs from here. What it must be like for May and Ted living next door to them I can't imagine.'

Alice smiled and Norman waited, but could see her biting back the words…it was only because he was using his much-neglected aid that the noise was so obvious…and then pointing out yet again what a difference it made. This repeated conversation had run its course and he could see by her expression that she'd decided it should remain unsaid, some battles being better left for another day.

Number 4
Sam, Jess and Daniel Evans

CHAPTER 9

Daniel Evans slipped his arms through the handgrips and manoeuvred himself out of the shower until he was able to reach his wheelchair. Propelling it towards the mirror he picked up his comb and slid it through his wet hair. Then squeezing a blob of gel onto his hands massaged his scalp, whilst spiking up his hair into peeks at the front, until he was pleased with the result.

In his bedroom, he saw his mother had laid out his clothes as usual and smiled. At last she'd realised he could manage on his own without having to dress him. He was nearly fifteen and having his mother dress him was something he was determined to avoid at all costs.

When he was satisfied with his appearance Daniel guided his wheelchair into the hallway, calling to his mother who was in the kitchen

'I'm off for a run, Ma. See you later.'

His father was in the garden fixing a new lock on the shed door. 'Take care,' he said, without looking up, as Daniel opened the garden gate and negotiated his wheelchair into the lane leading to the promenade. His upper arm strength was good, which was why he used this chair in favour of the motorised version he used when shopping in the Newton Cross Mall.

The promenade was thankfully devoid of tourists, it being early in the season so Daniel picked up speed feeling the wind threading through his hair and blowing it back from his face. He felt alive, able to forget his disability and to concentrate on what he could do rather than what he could not.

Reaching the halfway point to the harbour he felt a thud against his chest and, gasping for air, realised someone had kicked a ball up from the beach which had landed smack on him. About to throw it back he saw a head emerge over the sea wall followed by a body, as a boy climbed up towards him. Recognising him as the new lad who had moved into number eight and whom he thought might be about his own age, Daniel said, 'Hi. This yours?'

'Yeah, thanks. Thought it was a goner for sure.'

'You've just moved into number eight, haven't you? I think I've seen you practising with the basketball net in your garden. You're good.'

The boy's face reddened, as Daniel added, 'If you fancy throwing a few nets and feel like some competition I'm a member of the gym in the village. It's where I practise in-between fixtures.'

The boy frowned. 'You play basketball?'

'Yeah. You never heard of wheelchair basketball?' Daniel laughed to ease the boy's embarrassment.' It's okay, don't worry, I'm better at it than I look. I'm Daniel by the way.'

'Jake.'

'Well then, what do you say? Fancy coming up the gym?'

'What now?'

'Yeah, good a time as any and you've got the ball. Shame to waste it.'

Jake grinned, nodded and jogged alongside Daniel until they reached the village.'

CHAPTER 10

I'd like to think I'd been worrying about nothing and the new neighbours at number eight were just adding a loft room but I was beginning to feel this was going to be something more intrusive. The building work seemed to go on for ages. Ted and I usually liked to sit in the back garden to enjoy the peace and quiet of an afternoon but all that had changed now. Not only did we have the noise of building work to contend with every day, but there were the parties!

I'm not a spoilsport, no one could call me that, and I've enjoyed many parties over the years but these were different. For a start, the age of their visitors was far younger than either of the Wilsons. They'd asked us to call them Henry and Janice, by the way, but I still thought of them as the Wilsons. I suppose I was protecting myself against becoming too friendly as I'd a strong feeling we might have to become firm with them not only about the building work but the noise, *and* the sound of the music playing at full volume. They didn't seem to appreciate that we were semi-detached and a bit of consideration on their part wouldn't have been out of place. This was a quiet neighbourhood and I, for one, didn't appreciate the sudden change.

Ted did try his best to get along with them without causing any problems but if I'm honest I can't say I did the same. It was because I found them irritating in the extreme and possibly, thinking about it now, didn't try to hide my feelings. Call it self protection if you like but I was beginning to regret the loss of The Coopers in more ways than one.

The night of the Wilsons' Spring Bank Holiday party was a case in point. The weather was good, in fact it was unusually warm for the time of the year, even after seven o'clock in the evening when the sea breezes could make sitting out a little chilly. Their 'friends' started to arrive early just as we were putting our garden chairs away in the shed for the night.

I'd gone inside to make us a drink when Ted poked his head around the kitchen door and said, 'We've just had an invitation, love. The new folk, next door, want us to go in for drinks. What do you think?'

'I'm making us a drink now,' I replied, irritably.

'Come on, love, we've got to show willing. Be good neighbours and all that.'

I could see that Ted was put in an awkward position and didn't want to make things uncomfortable for him. So, with a sigh, I shrugged and followed him through the back gate carrying a bottle of supermarket plonk, and into next door's backyard, which seemed to be already full of people.

They'd erected a gazebo amongst the rubble of the building work, one of those green material things which stands on stilts. I had to be very careful I didn't fall or trip and I told Ted to watch his step too. It's not as if we're both that old. I don't want to give you the wrong impression here. It's just that the last thing we needed right now was to break something. Besides, they could have made an attempt to sort out the mess before having a party. In my opinion it seemed pure madness not to do so. What was the hurry anyway? Why couldn't they have waited until the building work was finished? There was the whole summer ahead of them to have parties! It was beyond me... didn't make an ounce of sense!

As far as I could make out, there was a crowd of youngsters in groups drinking beer. I recognised some of them as locals who I'd seen on the beach and in the village. One group were gathered near 'the bar,' which had been hastily erected under the gazebo. Then I saw Henry Wilson walking towards us carrying our drinks. He handed Ted a bottle of beer and me a glass of what he said was champagne. He hadn't even asked us what we wanted to drink, just assumed we'd like what he'd brought us. Before I took the glass from him I gave him our bottle, and he muttered a quick thanks then called to his son to take it into the bar area, without even giving it a second glance, which, as it turned out, was just as well.

'You probably know most of the people here,' he said, smiling the sort of smile that spoke volumes. I'd seen it before, arrogance and self-assurance dripping from him like butter melting in the sun. I felt it slide over me and shivered. The unspoken words, "I know I'm handsome just waiting for you to realise it," floating towards me with every breath he took.

'We've asked everyone from The Close to join us, together with a few of our new friends, so that we can all get to know each other,' he said. 'By the way, Janice has laid out some food in the kitchen. So, if you're hungry go inside and help yourself.'

'Thanks,' Ted said, 'we will.'

I didn't reply but had to admit it *was* champagne and a good vintage at that.

We'd planned to stay for just an hour and a half at the most but the evening seemed to fly by. I thought the champagne was probably responsible, but on reflection it *was* pleasant to mix with our neighbours and I got into a very interesting conversation with Alice Barker, the elderly lady who lived at number two. She was busy talking about her granddaughter and it made me realise I was longing for Will to call and tell me his wife was pregnant. They'd been married for a few years now and his business was thriving. However, I couldn't see it happening any time soon as he hadn't even hinted at starting a family. And as for Mark, well, he was too busy in the music business to think about settling down.

I glanced over at Ted who was now in conversation with two of Henry Wilsons's 'so-called' new friends. They appeared to me to be in their late teens, early twenties and I did wonder what my husband found in common with them but then Ted was used to boys of his own and I know he'd missed seeing Mark, since we'd moved down here.

As it turned out I hardly noticed the time slipping by and had a longer conversation with Emlyn and his daughter Gwyneth than I think I'd had since moving in five years ago. Ian, Gwyneth's husband was baby-sitting the twins apparently. He's a skilled carpenter and I'd no idea he was working for Charles Frazer.

The Frazers had obviously either declined the Wilson's invitation or had other fish to fry. Or, maybe, a get-together with the neighbours was considered to be beneath them. I hadn't been able to take to Felicity, Charles Fraser's daughter-in-law. There was no real reason for my dislike. On the surface she seemed pleasant enough. I just had this strong feeling that she was trouble with a capital T and my instinct was usually good in such things. Looking back I feel I'd probably been right about her too. She'd been only too keen to put her spoke in it with the police, even though she was in danger of exposing a problem which lay much closer to home. She should have been concentrating on her husband, not Ted.

Anyway the food was good, in fact it was delicious and I was in the middle of eating a sliver of quiche when Janice Wilson came over to talk to me.

'What do you think of it?' she asked.

'It's really tasty,' I replied, meaning it. 'Although I'd only taken a small piece, in case it was unpalatable.'

'I'm so glad you think so. It's dairy free and not to everyone's taste. But I'm lactose intolerant and there are often so little alternatives which actually taste good.'

'I can sympathise. I have to watch dairy too, which was why I didn't take a larger piece, and I know what you mean about finding delicious alternatives,' I said.

'I'll give you the recipe, if you like,' she suggested, with a smile, then became quite chatty. To my surprise I found myself warming towards her, even though I'd been determined not to get involved with the Wilsons. As I've mentioned there was no reason why I should feel like this, but after The Coopers I was wary of them and once again my initial intuition was correct.

But I never did discover the whole truth about Henry Wilson and I doubt whether any other people did either.

Number 5
Detective Constable Laura Davies

CHAPTER 11

Laura walked up the garden path and opened the door of number five Seabeach Close. Once inside, she looked around and sighed with satisfaction, unable to quite believe her good fortune. When her boss had explained, why he was willing to let her stay in his house at such a reasonable rent, it finally made sense. At first she'd been doubtful, wondering if he'd perhaps wanted more from the arrangement than he'd been willing to disclose. It just seemed too good to be true. It wasn't as if she wouldn't have welcomed his attentions, far from it, but under such circumstances she'd have felt extremely uncomfortable, almost as if he were letting her stay there at a ridiculously low rent in order to capitalise on his investment whenever he choose.

She remembered how she'd been down that path once before, in total innocence, believing everything she'd been told by Todd Baxter. But Chief Superintendent Todd Baxter had other ideas and was in a position to manipulate her. Now, she looked on it as a learning curve and an experience she was not likely to repeat.

However, it seemed she'd misjudged Elis's intentions entirely and was now able to relax in comfort and enjoy the peace and quiet of living on her own. He'd explained that, apart from their agreement, all he wanted was for her to keep the place tidy and to make sure to lock up when she left the house each day.

In the bedroom cupboard on the ground floor Laura hung up her clothes and began to sing the chorus of a song that had been like an ear worm in her brain all day. Then she tied her chestnut brown hair away from her face into a pony tail and catching sight of her reflection in the cupboard mirror decided she looked happier than she'd been for ages.

Later, relaxing in a warm bath with a glass of chilled white wine and an audiobook, she decided that her move to Oysterbend from Cardiff was the beginning of a new chapter in her life and one which she was determined to enjoy and to forget about the Todd Baxters of this world.

Laura's parents, who lived in Devon, hadn't been keen when she'd told them of her intention to become to be a detective. Her father hadn't liked the idea at all. He kept stressing, that by choosing such a career, she was leaving herself open to experiencing the rougher side of life and could be putting herself in danger. She told him not to worry, she was a big girl now and had to make such decisions for herself. Then her mother became convinced that no nice, young man would want to date someone who could never be relied upon to turn up on time for a date due to work commitments.

In spite of her parents concerns she had stuck to her resolve and when she'd graduated from police training college in Bridgend had decided she liked the thought of living in South Wales and had applied for a job in Cardiff. Her parents were even more unhappy about her decision to relocate as they were convinced Devon was a much more attractive proposition than moving to South Wales. Thinking about it now, she decided they'd only had her best interests at heart. Being an only child they'd tried to shield her from any problems before they arose but she needed to make her own mistakes…to stop feeling smothered by the comfort blanket in which they'd wrapped her. Such a life, although safe, was not how she wanted to live. She wanted to make a difference and wanted to make it on her own.

Her mobile rang just as she was stepping out of the bath. It was Elis. 'Hi, everything okay?' he asked.

'Yeah, more than okay, thanks to you, Boss.'

'Excellent. I don't want to spoil your first night in Seabeach Close but the Super's been on the phone and there's a meeting planned for eight-thirty tomorrow morning. I'm afraid this is serious, as I briefly outlined to you earlier. Alec is back from his holiday so we'll be at full strength and it seems we're going to need it. Can't say more now…see you in the morning. Oh, by the way, Laura, make sure you park in a side street and come in the back way to the station, and remember, don't mention your occupation to anyone,' he added.

It had to be serious, otherwise he wouldn't have phoned, as she was normally in the station well before half-eight. So, it looked as if he was preparing her for what was to come. She wondered what all the secrecy was about too but decided not to think about it until tomorrow and to have an early night. In the kitchen she made a hot drink then went downstairs to her bedroom.

The following morning, driving towards town, Laura knew that whatever was going on Elis would likely be the one in charge. DCI Chambers was still on sick leave and not expected to return anytime soon.

When she arrived, she parked as instructed and made her way to the incident room via the back entrance. The first thing she noticed was the absence of the usual buzz of conversation. Taking her seat alongside one of the seconded constables from West Wales, whom, she noticed, looked as if he'd been up half the night, she waited for the briefing to begin.

Superintendent Manning, a tall thin man with a bald head, looked to be in his mid-forties and kept blinking as if his contact lenses were troubling him. Behind him on the incident board were photos of three men and two women. The faces were slightly blurred and not easily distinguishable. But they were told it was all they had to work with at the moment. Laura listened as Manning outlined the purpose behind the meeting and what was to be expected of them and it was only when he'd finished briefing them, and Elis had shown him out, that the room filled with the buzz of conversation. It was obvious everyone had been surprised by the contents of the briefing. Some were actively moaning about the increase in work and the anticipated long hours it would involve, but Laura felt excitement washing over her like a refreshing shower of rain after a drought. This was what she'd hoped for when she'd joined the force.

Later, having lunch in the canteen, she looked around hoping to see Elis. Perhaps he could give her some more information regarding her role in the investigation but he was nowhere to be seen. Returning to her desk, a while later, she saw he was eating lunch in his room. Through the plexiglass screen he raised his hand and beckoned to her to come in.

'Well, what d' you make of the briefing, then?'

'Bit of a shock. Operation Creeping Jenny! Must be serious if the investigation involves us working in conjunction with The Met. It was a lot to take in. I'd no idea the problem was so widespread, especially in our vicinity. I'd thought we were handling the usual problems, just a few of the local drug pushers, the ones we regularly arrest who spread weed around the community like bags of confetti.'

'Mmm,' Elis looked at her thoughtfully, then replied. 'It will mean a lot more work, of course, but it will also be a chance for us to make a real difference and that's got to be a good thing where drugs are concerned.' He frowned then leaned forward in his chair, said, 'You've got the point of the meeting and the importance of our role in the investigation?'

Laura nodded and he continued, 'Although we understand, by international standards, it's a small role, it's nevertheless vital…an important cog in a much larger wheel.'

'I understand, sir.'

'Excellent! So, as such, I'm sure you are aware of the secrecy involved?'

Laura gave another small nod. 'Right, well I've had a chat with the Chief Super and we've agreed that you should have a particular role to play in this.'

Shifting from one foot to another she waited to hear what this role might involve, her pulse racing.

'Take a seat, Laura. From now on you'll no longer come into the station but will be working from the house in Seabeach Close. So, in effect, you'll be working undercover until this operation is completed.'

When he'd initially explained why he wanted her to live in the house and why the rent was so reasonable he'd been a bit vague and only said it would involve police work and she'd be told more soon. Although she'd been waiting for this briefing, it had been much more than she'd anticipated. So, not wanting to show her surprise and trying to appear professional, Laura didn't respond until he'd continued to explain what her role was to be in more detail.

'One of the reasons we've chosen you is because you recently transferred from Cardiff and it's unlikely that anyone, five miles away in Oysterbend, would know you're a police officer. Even if they've seen you entering the station, you're not in uniform and could be working in a different capacity altogether, which is another reason you are a perfect candidate for undercover work.'

Elis glanced at his phone which had pinged with a text message. Then he said, 'As you know this is no small time drug dealing op we're talking about but one on a much larger scale. There are links to the main dealers operating in London and Birmingham. The Met are hoping to break the distribution chain by discovering who the secondary dealers are and who is responsible for the expansion of their network throughout the UK.' He frowned and passed a folder across the desk to her. 'Apparently there's good intel that one of these dealers, who is vital in spreading the network throughout the coast of South Wales, is operating in our area. When you go back to your desk, read the contents of this file then return it to me and go home.'

'Right, I understand, sir she said, again. 'And I'll do my best.'

He bit his lip and nodded. 'I've no doubt you will, which is why I suggested you for this in the first place. Your anonymity is important but so is your interaction with the villagers. Listen to gossip, keep alert to anything which sounds suspicious but be aware you could be putting yourself in a dangerous position if it becomes known that you're an undercover officer. Look for any signs of a new dealer operating in the area, other than the known local perps. But remember these criminals are no pushovers. So take care to maintain your undercover identity at all times. I can't stress this enough.'

Aware that he was waiting for her to comment further Laura took a deep breath. 'I've not connected with anyone in the area yet, as I've only just moved into the house. And, as you mentioned, I'm an unknown quantity to any of them.' She hesitated and before she could continue, he said,

'I know you will do your best, Laura. But if you ever feel threatened you must ring my mobile straight away. Besides, I have a legitimate reason to call at the house as I'm the owner so it won't seem unusual. But, I will limit these visits to avoid suspicion falling on you. We'll work it out between us as to how to go forward. Contact will always be via mobile, never the landline. Do you have any questions?'

'Er, yes, just one. If I'm not going to be working as a police officer, surely people will expect me to be doing something in order to be able to afford the rent.'

She saw Elis give a slow smile. 'It's all sorted. You'll be working from home selling greetings cards online. I've seen some of your drawings and doodles by the way.'

Laura raised her eyebrows.

Seeing her expression, he nodded and said, 'Yeah, I know, but I *am* a detective.'

She felt her cheeks burning and pushed a strand of hair behind her ear. 'Surely you don't expect me to design greetings cards though?'

'No, not at all. You don't have to worry on that score. We'll arrange all that side of it. You won't actually be selling any yourself obviously, but your online profile will tell a different story. However, your ability to draw will be invaluable in terms of a cover story. It will give you the opportunity to sit sketching while keeping an eye on what's happening, without anyone becoming suspicious.'

'I see. I just hope my doodles bear close inspection then,' she replied with a grin.

'They will, I'm sure of it. Remember, I've seen you at work and you don't miss a thing, which was the primary reason why it was my suggestion for you to take on this role rather than Dennis. Don't get me wrong, Constable Jones has his good points but I can't exactly see him being unobtrusive.'

For the first time since Laura had joined the force she felt useful. It was one of the reasons she'd asked for a transfer from Cardiff in the first place, but it wasn't the only one, Todd Baxter, being a case in point. She'd also been underused in the city, her intellect being submerged under a mound of paperwork and where she'd been made aware that WDCs took a secondary role to the men. And after she'd put Baxter firmly in his place, her job had soon diminished into little more than a filing clerk.

As she drove away from the station, she thought about her insistence that she wouldn't let Elis down. But she was going to discover that in future keeping her promise to him would be far harder than she'd ever thought, in fact it had been impossible.

CHAPTER 12

I overslept after the party at number eight. The sound of the phone ringing eventually waking me and Ted being nowhere to be found.

It was Mark. 'Hi Mum how are things going? Dad around?'

'No, I've only just woken up myself. I think he must have gone out for a walk. He's probably feeding the birds.'

'Right. Everything okay is it?'

'Er, yes.'

'What?'

'Nothing.'

'Come on, Mum, out with it.'

'Nothing, love. It's just me being silly. We went to the party, next door. The one I mentioned in my text last night. And well I'm not sure everything is okay there.'

'Why?

'It's just…well…I can't quite make out Henry Wilson. You know me when I get that feeling.'

Seabeach Close   K.J.Rabane

'I do! Anything I can do to help?' I heard his anxiety by the tone of his voice and a sharp intake of breath, so had second thoughts.

'No, it's nothing. Forget it. I suppose it's all the noise from that damned extension. Now it's finished it's become like he's spying on us. Dad thinks I'm making a fuss about nothing though and he's probably right. Hang on a minute that sounds like him now.'

I heard the buzz of conversation in the background followed by Mark saying quickly, 'Right then, got to go, tell him I said hello and don't forget to let me know about next door. I don't want you to start worrying, especially if I can do something to help.'

'Will do. Thanks for ringing, Mark. Love you.' I put down the phone but couldn't help wondering if perhaps I should have told him about the guy in the red shirt after all.

Later that day I saw a small blue car drawing up outside number five opposite. From our bedroom window I watched as a young woman opened the front door and went inside. I'd seen her at the house a couple of days ago, and thought maybe she was looking the place over to rent. As I watched, she reappeared moments later, opened the boot of the car and removed what looked to me like a small artist's easel and some boxes of paints. She then made a few extra trips during which she unloaded some hand luggage before finally lifting a large suitcase out of the back seat and wheeling it inside.

Seabeach Close   K.J.Rabane

Ted was in the kitchen washing up. I told him what I'd just seen and he replied, 'Seems like we're going to have another new neighbour then, love.'

'Let's hope it's only just the one this time, not like the noisy crowd who moved in there before,' I said.

I was still feeling a bit uneasy, partly because of the guy in the red shirt. It wasn't what he'd said but there was something shifty about him and he was looking at Ted, in particular, with an odd expression on his surly face. The thing was, we'd had some trouble in London which was one of the reasons we moved to Brighton, and the way he was inspecting Ted in detail reminded me of what happened before. And I didn't like it. I didn't like it one bit.

There was no need to upset Ted about it though. He loved living here and after all I could've been mistaken. But he seemed like a bully to me. Perhaps I was overreacting which was understandable in the circumstances.

It had happened when Ted had been working in the local Garden Centre just before we moved. A fight broke out. All he'd done was to try and break them up but a man wearing a red shirt had insisted that Ted had started it. The police were called and Ted was given a caution…which made us both furious! He hasn't got over it to this day. So, I decided I wouldn't tell him about the man I'd seen last night, it would only remind him of it all. But, on reflection, I think maybe I should have mentioned it to Mark, because it might have changed the outcome of what was to follow. But for now I decided to forget about next door and focus on our new neighbour who had moved into number five.

Number 5

Detective Inspector Elis Williams

CHAPTER 13

After he'd made sure Laura was settling in to number five Ellis began to feel guilty at not being able to tell her the whole truth. However, there had been nothing he could do about it. His instructions had been clear and his hands were metaphorically tied by red tape.

Operation Creeping Jenny was controlled by the officers in The Metropolitan Police Force. Newton Cross and the surrounding area was only a small part of the investigation. Small, but essential if they were to stamp out the distribution link operating in the South Wales area. He cupped his hands behind his neck, leaned back in his chair, and frowned. This case needed careful handling. Word spread fast in a place like Oysterbend, which was one of the reasons why Laura's identity had to be protected. She was a first class detective, young it was true but he trusted her implicitly. She'd not been responsible for what happened to her in Cardiff and he didn't want anything to go wrong for her this time.

It was fortunate that Laura could live in his house in Seabeach Close for a number of reasons, first because he could keep a close eye on her and second, and more selfishly, because he was totally fed up of clearing up the mess after yet another batch of useless tenants.

His mobile rang and he glanced at the display. It was his superintendent, who although in his mid-fifties had already decided to put his feet up and let others do the work for him.

'Well?' He was a man of few words

'It's done.' Two could play at that game, Elis thought.

'And she understands?'

'She does.'

'Fine.'

The phone signal clicked off in his ear and Elis sighed. Drug gangs had been operating in Newton Cross for years. But they were small-time thugs in the scheme of things - marijuana E's and amphetamines, nothing like the hard stuff and not on such a vast scale. Previously, the dealers had been easy to spot hanging around outside clubs or in side streets. A particularly favourite patch of theirs was outside the train and bus stations. The Newton Cross force had been continually frustrated by the process of bringing them in, getting them to court and waiting until they were replaced or released, when it started all over again like an unstoppable tide.

But this was different. These people were in another league altogether and the end result was death at the worst or the routine destruction of lives, which in his book was murder, in all but name. The Met, knew where the big operators were based in London and this latest operation meant they were treading carefully in order to make sure there were no slip ups. So, to avoid alerting the main distributors there would be no arrests until they could swoop down on the whole network. The part Elis and his team were to play was to identify the link in the chain without the big boys becoming suspicious. It needed careful handling, one slip up and it would be like knocking down a standing pile of dominoes and toppling them backwards from South Wales to London.

An operation as large as this was unheard of in Newton Cross and he was aware how important it was to his future career in the force.

Number 4
Sam, Jess and Daniel Evans.

CHAPTER 14

Pressing the button on the car's dashboard Sam Evans watched in his rear-view mirror as the boot ramp was raised and his son successfully negotiated his wheelchair from the car to the pavement.

'Thanks for the lift Mr Evans,' Jake said, opening the passenger-side door and pulling his school bag out behind him.

Sam heard Jake and Daniel as they continued their conversation about what they were going to do after tea, and was glad that the Wilsons had moved into The Close. Jake was the same age as Daniel and the boy was polite and obviously missing his friends in London. Having a shared interest in basketball had thankfully been the catalyst drawing them both together and for that he was grateful.

Before his accident Daniel had been a promising scrum-half playing for the Newton Cross rugby fifteen and Sam had even dared to imagine him playing for Wales one day. But during training the unthinkable had happened and after his accident his son had been left paralysed from the waist down. It had been a difficult time for Sam and Jess as they'd watched their son learning to cope with his disability whilst feeling totally helpless to make it go away. But Daniel had surprised them both with his determination not to let the accident shape his future. It had been one of the proudest moments of Sam's life to see him excel at wheelchair basketball and to watch him holding the Newton Cross cup high in the air when his team won the championship as his school friends cheered him on.

Later that evening, having heard Daniel getting into bed, he knocked at his son's bedroom door and went inside for their regular bedtime chat.

'So, enjoy your evening with Jake?' he asked, sitting in the chair by the bed.

'Yeah. I raced him along the prom and we ended up in the village square, then had a coffee in *Pelosi's* with the rest of the gang from school.'

'I saw the pair of you shooting a few hoops in the backyard before the light went. He seems like a nice kid.'

'Yeah, he's okay. Doesn't much like living in Oysterbend though.'

'Really? Why's that?'

'Well, for a start he misses his mates, and for another thing he doesn't get on with Henry Wilson.'

'Lots of teenagers go through a spell where they're arguing with their father about everything. It'll pass, you'll see.'

'It's not like that, Dad. He didn't want to come down here in the first place, but his mother had met Wilson and the next thing he knew they were all moving, whether he liked it or not.' Daniel said, frowning.

Sam raised his eyebrows. 'So, Wilson's not his father then?'

'Nah, his dad died a couple of years back. He took it badly and I think maybe he just can't bear the thought of his mother being married to another guy. But, guess what? They made him change his name to Wilson too! He tried to kick up a fuss but his mum got upset so he kept his mouth shut in the end.'

'Poor kid.' Sam sympathised.

'I tell you what though, he did say something funny tonight. He said his mum had only known Wilson for a month or two before they married and they'd decided to pack up and come down here right away. Can you imagine how shocked he'd been? He said he didn't even have enough time to have leaving bash with his mates.'

'Yes, I can,' Sam agreed, stroking his chin thoughtfully.

'He also said it wasn't like her at all. I think it was one of the reasons why he doesn't like Wilson. He thinks he conned her into it. His mum was the type who took time to make decisions, especially life changing ones. It wasn't like her to jump into things so quickly. It was as if he'd hypnotised her or something.'

'Wilson's a good looking guy though,' Sam suggested.

'Yeah, but she hasn't had a serious relationship since his dad died, apparently. Jake told me she'd always said no-one could replace him. It's one of the reason he thinks it doesn't make any sense. He's convinced Wilson's got some sort of hold over her. She would never have done it all so quickly if it had been up to her. '

Sam bit his lip and tried to hide a smile. What did teenagers know about love? The expression 'being madly in love' couldn't be nearer the truth. People did the strangest things when in the first flush of a love affair. Daniel would soon understand, when it happened to him. The thought took shape and made him frown, as he realised it would take a very special girl who would be willing to share her life with his son.

'I expect he'll settle down soon though.' Sam stood up. 'Wait till the summer weather kicks in and he can swim in the sea, surf the waves and enjoy living in Oysterbend like the rest of us. He'll soon forget his misgivings about his stepfather I'm sure.'

Kissing his son good night and closing his bedroom door he sighed. Henry Wilson had certainly given him the impression that Jake was his son and that everything in the garden was rosy. In fact he'd been at pains to do so.

Walking into the kitchen he wondered what Jess would make of this latest little piece of news.

CHAPTER 15

It was Ted's evening for meeting his friends from the gardening club. They all had allotments, except Ted who'd been put on the waiting list. Today they were meeting at a plot where Vernon, one of the gardeners, had a shed complete with a fridge stocked with beer. I knew he'd been looking forward to this meeting all day. His face was wreathed in smiles as soon as he'd woken up, and he couldn't do enough for me.

'You sit down, I'll do that.'

'Fancy a cuppa.'

'It's going to be another fine day. Put your feet up and I'll run the cleaner over.'

He was like a kid with a new toy which was yet another reason I felt pleased we'd moved to the area.

A warm evening breeze crept in through our kitchen window and I took a deep breath, inhaling the salty air. Deciding to go and feed the seagulls, I filled a plastic carrier to the brim and made my way to the beach. The sun was beginning to dip lower in the sky and casting a few stray shadows onto the sand. But the air was still warm, as the birds flapped and screamed around me. I took my time throwing the bread towards them as they all needed feeding.

Walking in the direction of a rocky outcrop, every stray one having been fed and who were now thankfully leaving me alone, I sat down and relaxed. I loved this time of the day when I could take a breather, along with a few stragglers as we watched the evening shadows together.

After a while I stood up and walked towards the steps leading up to the promenade. I stopped to enjoy the view for a while then turned back to the steps. But before I began to climb up from the beach I glanced up the roof of number eight. Large glass panels glinting in the setting sun had been opened onto a viewing balcony. Assessing its position, once more I became concerned about our new neighbours being able to spy on Ted and me quite freely, as we sat in the garden or walked along the beach. I'd mentioned it to Ted when it was being built but all he'd said was why would anybody bother to look at us. Nevertheless, I liked and valued my privacy.

The phone was ringing as I opened the back door. I hoped it was Mark as I hadn't heard from him for a while. It was.

'Hi Mum,' Then he added mechanically, 'Dad about?'

'No love, gardening club meeting.'

'At Vernon's shed, I suppose.'

'That's about the size of it. He's been looking forward to it all day. They've been there since half four and I don't expect him to come home much before ten on an evening like this. He really enjoys some time out with the boys.'

I heard Mark's laughter when I mentioned 'boys.' It was a hoarse, throaty chuckle and my insides twisted.

'You're still smoking then.'

His sigh drifted down the phone towards me'

'Don't go on now, Mum. Just wanted to say Rita told me she'll meet you on the prom as usual on Thursday.'

'Tell her it's my day for Tesco and I'll meet her at half eleven.'

'Will do. Must be off now, busy, busy, you know how it is. Glad you're okay, give my love to Dad. I'll try to ring next week same as usual.'

But today wasn't the same as usual I hadn't heard from him for two weeks and I'd been worried. Anyway, at least I knew he was okay now, and if I'd mentioned my concern to Ted, he would only have said I was fussing again. Well, one of us had to be the worrier and planner in this relationship. And the role had always sat firmly on *my* shoulders.

When Ted came home a while later I was in the sitting room reading. I told him about Mark's phone call and he gave me a knowing look, saying, 'Happy now?'

I closed my book, said I was, and asked, 'Well, how was the gardening club meeting?'

'Good. Vernon's daughter's had her baby…little girl. So we had to wet the baby's head naturally.'

'I could tell.' I smiled.

'Haha can't put one over on you, can I love?' He sat down beside me and took my hand in his. 'Now then, when I was walking back home, along the prom, I noticed a light on in next-door's loft room. When I came closer I saw it was Wilson and he definitely looked as if he was spying out of that new balcony of his with a pair of binoculars. I thought, maybe you had a point, because although, it might have been my imagination I could've sworn he'd been watching me walking back down the prom. But, why I would be of any interest to him is a mystery.'

I shivered. So, I'd been right all along. I knew the extension would mean trouble.

'And you're calling me nosy?' I said, trying to make light of it. I didn't want Ted to think I was being overly fussy, where these new neighbours were concerned, because I'd already made my feelings clear about the loft extension. It wasn't worth him starting to worry too. But, to be perfectly honest, I'd thought they were an odd family right from the start, especially Henry Wilson. There was something definitely not quite right about him. It was as if he was an actor playing a part and the thought made me feel distinctly uncomfortable.

I decided it might be as well to keep ourselves to ourselves in future, as far as the Wilsons were concerned. There would be no more parties at number eight, however many invitations they gave us.

Number 1
Ben and Felicity Frazer

CHAPTER 16

The office still smelled new even though his father had acquired the building, which was situated ten miles away from the town of Newton Cross, nearly two years ago. Ben Frazer yawned, glanced at his watch and frowned at the growing mound of files his father had thrown onto his desk.

'Really Dad?'

'Yeah, really. I need you to find a loophole. I could lose a great deal of money on this project. The land deal has to succeed before I can build the new estate overlooking Limecove Bay.'

'Okay, but you know Flick isn't going to be pleased. I was supposed to take her to that new place on Hudson's point tonight. I've been home late every night this week and I did promise her.'

'Felicity will have to understand if she wants to continue living the lifestyle you've made for her, or should I say we've made. Besides, I remember her and her mother living in that two up two down on Slade Street, which was the rougher end of Birmingham.'

Ben watched his father leave his office, back still straight, hair still thick, even if it was now heavily flecked with grey. He was still a good-looking man in spite of being in his sixties. He remembered the affairs and his mother's tears. Thankfully his father's libido had waned over the years and his appetite for forbidden fruit had disappeared, but unfortunately his mother hadn't lived to see it. When he was alone, Ben picked up his mobile and with a heavy heart rang his wife.

As he'd anticipated she wasn't happy at the prospect of him working well into the night. Over the last month or two he'd been afraid he was beginning to lose her. He'd felt her gradually pulling away from him. It was nothing he could put his finger on but it was there nevertheless. And it was something more for him to worry about. As if the pressure of work wasn't enough! It was little wonder he'd gone looking for help in the only way he'd known possible.

Felicity put down the phone and taking a deep breath dragged a comb through her pale blond hair before pulling it away from her face into a rough ponytail. All her friends at the tennis club were talking about the new place. She saw frown lines creasing her forehead as she glared at her reflection in her bathroom mirror. Now it looked once again as if Ben had disappointed her. It wasn't just missing out on a meal in a new restaurant. She wasn't that shallow. It was the loss of the close bond they used to share. There was a time when she would have been the most important person in his life but now it was a combination of work and his father.

She'd never felt so lonely. Her true friends were in Birmingham and the ones she'd met at the tennis club weren't real friends at all. They were mostly only interested in one thing…how much money they could make and how much they could spend. There were times when she wished they could run away from Seabeach Close and live in a small house somewhere, far away from Charles Frazer's empire and his hold over his son.

Pulling on her running shorts and vest, she slipped her feet into her trainers and left the house. Jogging along the path between the bungalows which led to the promenade she thought she saw a light on in the loft room of number eight and soon became aware of someone standing at the window peering through binoculars, as a few stray sunbeams bounced back at her from the newly erected glass balustrade. Then she straightened her back, stretched her muscles and jogged past the bungalow in the direction of The Point.

The sky was clear, but a few evening shadows were starting to lengthen on the path. The promenade was lit by strings of fairy lights which cast coloured patches of light along her route. Glancing to one side she could see the tide creeping in over the sand towards the woman who lived at number six. As usual she was feeding the seagulls. Felicity hadn't taken to the woman, who seemed to make it her business to get to know everyone in the vicinity, and this evening was no exception. A couple of guys were talking to

Seabeach Close   K.J.Rabane

her at the waters edge, the three figures being silhouetted against the darkening sky as they chatted, their heads bent. Ha, she thought, with a spoonful of self-pity, even she has a better social life than I do.

Felicity had been running for ten minutes or so when she heard the sound of trainers slapping on the concrete path behind her. These were quickly followed by a figure overtaking her. As he passed her she recognised that it was her new neighbour, who was soon out of sight as he disappeared around the bend in the path.

The Point consisted of a couple of cafes, the new restaurant and bar and overlooking them a hillock where stood three viewing benches. Reaching it she could see he was there before her, muscle stretching and jogging on the spot. Felicity wondered whether to ignore him and carry on or stop and talk.

'Hello. What kept you?' he said, with a grin, taking the decision out of her hands. 'Nice evening for a run.'

'Mm it is,' she replied breathlessly.

He pointed to the nearest bench which had a view of the sea and the lighthouse. 'Fancy a chat and a breather?' he asked.

She nodded and sat down, her heart rate racing not only from the run. 'Okay. But I can't stay long.' The words floated away from her on the evening breeze which had suddenly spring up.

Seabeach Close   K.J.Rabane

Henry Wilson was a man who had the kind of looks most women couldn't ignore, added to which she now knew was a rich, deep voice of the kind to send a shiver down your spine. Realising she was thinking like a love-sick teenager and wondering what could possibly have prompted her to think so, other than the obvious, she focused her gaze on the horizon as if the view was the most important thing on her mind. It gave her the opportunity she needed to think more clearly.

'We haven't really had a chance to get to know each other, have we? You're married to Charles Frazer's son aren't you?' he said.

'Ben, yes.'

'Of course… Ben,' he replied slowly, Then added, 'I spoke to him the other day and he mentioned that his father had built Seabeach Close. As you know we've only just moved down from London and are still settling in. Nice place though, quiet and relaxing.'

'Has your son got used to moving to a new school yet? It must be quite a change for him?'

She was aware she was searching for something to say and felt it showed. But her embarrassment didn't last as he replied,'Jack? Sorry, Jake…yeah, yeah he's made a few new friends.'

Felicity hesitated and raised her eyebrows before she spoke. How many people forgot their son's name, she wondered? But she had so much to think about in

Seabeach Close K.J.Rabane

her own life at the moment she couldn't spend time analysing what was probably just a slip of the tongue.

'Oh good,' she replied, with an air of finality. Must get on or I'll need to warm up again.' She stood up.

'Hey, don't go yet, we're only just getting to know each other.' He looked up at her, and smiled. 'I tell you what, why don't we stop off at that café on the corner and grab a coffee. Take a breather? The run can wait for a while. What d'you say?"

It would have been a simple thing, just to make an excuse, say she had to get back, and to make it sound plausible but before she knew it she'd agreed and was following him towards the Cosy Café.

It was, in fact, nothing like its name implied. But it was a café and the coffee wasn't bad and there was the additional attraction of refill cups being available at no extra charge. It also served until late during the spring and summer months, which was about all it had to recommend it.

As they sipped their drinks, Felicity found it was impossible not to be affected by him. Mesmerised by his dark eyes, which, she noticed, had a glint of amber in the irises, she became unable to look away. Thankfully he didn't seem to notice and carried on talking about some of their neighbours in The Close. Eventually, she could feel herself beginning to relax. Although he'd only recently moved into the area it seemed he'd got to know most of his neighbours. He gave her the distinct impression he was a people person, who liked to chat and had no hidden agenda. At least that was her first opinion of him, only time would tell if it was the right one.

'So, your husband works for his father and you said he's a lawyer? Must be handy having one in the family.' He called to the waitress to top up their mugs.

'A bit too handy at times,' she said, hearing the bitterness in her voice. 'We were supposed to go to Mario's tonight. I've heard so much about it lately. It's the new place just around the corner from here. But then Ben had to work…a last-minute thing. It happens a lot lately.'

'Must be frustrating. For both of you, I mean,' he added, and she felt tears collecting at the corner of her eyes. She knew they'd been prompted by sympathy and was annoyed at herself.

'Hey, are you okay?' He put his hand on her arm, and she couldn't stop the tears spilling down her cheeks.

The words wouldn't come and he didn't force her. Finally, pulling herself together, she blew her nose into a tissue and muttered, 'It's…don't take any notice of me, I'm fine.'

'Anyone can see you're not fine, Felicity. So, if ever you need someone to talk to, please give me a ring. Whatever you say, you should know it will be just between us.' He slipped his hand into the pocket of his running shorts, asked for her mobile number and pinged his details to her phone.

'Thanks,' she whispered. 'I mean…for… But it's late. I must get back before Ben comes home and wonders where I've got to.'

'Well, if you're sure you're okay, I'll take a run up the hill and back through the cuttings,' he said, leaving her glancing at his details on her phone. Then, before she could think any more about it, she deleted his name and typed *Penny* into her phone's memory alongside his number. Was she already beginning to think she would use it? And why wouldn't she want her husband to see she had his number? Well, the answer to that was obvious, she thought, as she stood up, left the cafe, stretched her muscles then jogged back towards Seabeach Close.

Number 3
The Joneses

CHAPTER 17

Emlyn watched as Bronwen made short work of her double-cone ice cream, the remains clinging to her lips like sea-foam. Bethan, however, had only scratched the surface of hers, savouring every morsel as if it were the finest caviar. The difference between the twins was plain to see, especially when it came to food, Emlyn thought, smiling indulgently.

'Hey, steady on Bron', he said, for form sake. 'Plenty of time, cariad,'

But Bronwyn had finished and was in the process of licking her fingers whilst wandering off to stand near the low seawall overlooking the sandy beach. Emlyn walked towards the waste basket, his back to the twins, and slid his empty ice cream carton into the bin, just as Arthur, from the Chess Club, was about to do the same.

'How's things Em? Haven't seen you at the club lately. Too busy with the allotment I expect. It's certainly the weather for it, that's for sure.' He turned to glance at the twins. 'Looking after the grandkids I see. They're growing up fast, just like mine. Our eldest is taller than me and he's only sixteen. '

Seabeach Close   K.J.Rabane

Arthur had always been one for stating the bleeding obvious, thought Emlyn. Besides it was no wonder his eldest was taller than him as he was only five foot five himself. 'I'm fine, ta Arthur,' he replied. 'Aye, it's my day for spending the morning with the girls. Gives Gwyneth time to catch up on the housework without them running about the place messing it all up. She'll be glad when they get back to school next Monday, I don't mind telling you. The month of May has too many school holidays for her liking. '

Arthur nodded. 'I envy you though. Mine live in Scotland now. Only time I see them these days is on Zoom on the computer. Not the same as in the flesh but better than nothing…' Arthur suddenly stopped talking, as a shrill scream made them both turn around.

Emlyn hurried back towards his granddaughters, his pulse racing.

'Bamps! It's Bronwyn she's been eating some sweets she found on the wall and now she's crying and making a funny noise,' Bethan whimpered.

Bronwen had a faint film of white around her lips, which Emlyn soon realised was definitely not made of ice cream. Both Arthur and he were so shocked they stood as if glued to the spot for a moment as Bronwen started to shake uncontrollably. Then, as if a spell were suddenly broken both men sprang into action. Feeling helpless Emlyn tried to put his finger into Bronwen's mouth to make her sick, whilst being unsure whether he was doing the right thing. He'd seen two round pink pills on the wall behind her, which could look like sweets to a child. Picking them up, he stuffed them into his pocket with hands which wouldn't stop shaking, then asked Arthur to ring 999 for him.

When he'd finished talking to the operator, Arthur said, 'The ambulance won't be long Em. Shall I take Bethan back to the house?'

Emlyn nodded, 'Tell Gwyneth what's happened and say I'm taking Bronwen to hospital will you Arthur?' Then turning to Bethan, who was whimpering at his side, he said, 'Go on home with Uncle Arthur now love. I'm going to take Bronwen to the hospital for the doctor to make her better.'

Holding Bronwen close to him as he waited, Emlyn felt the minutes stretching into hours, each second longer than the last, until he finally heard the sound of a siren wailing, as the ambulance took the coast road from Newton Cross towards Oysterbend. The sight of Bronwen being in such a state was an image he knew he would never get out of his mind, however long he lived.

'Won't be long now, cariad. The hospital will soon make you better, you'll see. Be a brave girl for Grandpa now love.'

When the ambulance drew to a halt in the square he saw two paramedics pushing a stretcher and rushing towards him. With a sigh of relief he quickly explained what had happened and then followed alongside them, as they hurried towards the ambulance. Once inside, he sat with Bronwen's, holding her hand and feeling useless as the paramedics asked him again to explain what had exactly occurred, whilst the siren screeched and the blue lights flashed as they raced towards Newton Cross General.

When they arrived at the hospital Emlyn followed as Bronwen was wheeled inside and the paramedics rushed her into the Accident and Emergency Department.

It seemed an age to him before he saw Gwyneth and Ian hurrying towards him. Trying to explain to them first hand what had happened was difficult. Trying to comfort them by saying she'd be fine now, even more difficult, when he wasn't certain of the outcome himself.

Gwyneth, her face streaked with tears and her voice just a croak, managed to say, 'It's got to be something serious, Dad. They don't use a blue light for nothing,' She wiped her tears away with the back of her hand, then buried her face in her husband's shoulder and sobbed uncontrollably.

Ian patted her back. 'Hush now. Try not to worry, sweetheart. They'll let us know what's going on as soon as they can.' He raised questioning eyebrows at Emlyn.

Unable to say the words they wanted to hear, Emlyn asked instead, 'Is Bethan alright?'

'She's at Alice and Norman's. They'll ring us if there's a problem,' Ian replied, as Gwyneth turned towards her father and blew her nose into Ian's handkerchief.

'It's the not knowing I can't stand. I'm going to …'

'Hang on love. Let the doctors see to her first. They'll come and get us when they can. Try not to worry, they know what they're doing.' He knew he was sounding more positive than he felt and hoped his daughter wouldn't see though his subterfuge.

Again, every minute that passed seemed like an hour to Emlyn, until a doctor finally came to see them. He was a tall, thin man with fair hair and wearing blue hospital scrubs. He showed them into a room at the side of the reception desk, then introduced himself, 'I'm Doctor Thomas. I've been looking after Bronwen and she's responding well.' He turned towards Emlyn and said, 'I understand your granddaughter was standing by the seawall when it happened? Can you tell me exactly how she could have got her hands on the amphetamines?'

All three looked at him in bewilderment. Gwyneth's jaw dropped open as she gasped. Ian got to his feet and Emlyn stuttered, 'I don't understand… did, did you say amphetamines? Drugs? He shook his head, unable to believe his ears. 'Our Bronwyn got hold of drugs… is that what you're saying?'

'I'm afraid so. The police have been informed and are waiting to take a statement from you, Mr Jones.'

Gwyneth choked back tears as she rocked back in forth in her seat in distress, pushing away Ian's hand as he tried to comfort her.

Turning to Gwyneth and Ian, Doctor Thomas said, 'I know this is a very worrying time for you both but please try and understand, your daughter's going to be fine. She's been given something to counteract the hyperactivity effect of the amphetamines, and she'll be staying in overnight so we can keep an eye on her. But it's just as a precaution. I'm sure she'll be ready for you to take her home in the morning with no ill effects. But, if you would like to stay overnight, please feel free to stay in the rest room attached to the children's ward, not as comfortable as a bed, I'm afraid, but the best we can do as we are dealing with an RTA and struggling for beds at the moment.' He turned back to Emlyn and smiled. 'Your prompt action has no doubt contributed to there being no further damage, Mr Jones.'

'Can we see her?' Gwyneth asked.

'Of course.' He stood aside and opening the door said, 'Nurse Hopkins, would you take Bronwyn's parents to the ward please, and show them where they can spend the night?' Then turning to Emlyn, he added, 'Could you come with me, there's a police constable waiting to talk to you about the incident. It's just along here, sir.'

The room was only a short distance away and the doctor stopped, turned to him and said, 'When you're finished, you can find your granddaughter on Ward 4 on the first floor, Mr Jones. There's a lift at the end of this corridor.'

'Thank you Doctor, he replied.

Then stepping inside Emlyn saw that Dennis Evans was waiting for him. 'What a turn up for the books, Den! They're saying our Bron got hold of drugs. Drugs…on the seafront in Oysterbend? What's the world coming to?' He shook his head, baffled beyond belief.

'So, you've no idea where she got them from then, Em?' Dennis pressed the record button on his phone.

'Now, what do you think, lad? One minute she's eating one of Joe's ice-creams, the next she's crying and shaking like Bernie Jenkins after a night on the pop.' Emlyn bit his bottom lip. Then pressing the heel of his palm against his forehead said, 'They must've been there, on the seawall, just waiting all along. Anyone could've picked them up.'

Dennis sighed and nodded as Emlyn continued, 'I saw a couple of what looked like pink smarties on the wall by Bron and slipped them into my pocket but wasn't sure if that was what she'd eaten. I gave them to the doctor on duty when we arrived.' He suddenly shuddered at the thought. 'It was he who said they were amphetamines.' Emlyn's hands began to shake at the thought and he thrust them firmly into his pockets.

Dennis sighed again and switched off the recording. 'Well, that's all I can tell my boss then, along with this recording. I'm just glad that Bron's okay, Em. Try not to think about what could have happened. It doesn't bare thinking about.' He stood up. 'It's possible someone from the station might want to have another talk with you, after I've explained the situation, just to clarify some details. Nothing to worry about though.'

Emlyn, making his way to the ward felt anger bubbling up inside like molten lava. If the police didn't come to speak to him he have a few words of his own to say to them. Starting with Elis Williams!

Number 2
Norman and Alice Barker

CHAPTER 18

Alice watched the seagulls swirling in the breeze, sunshine dappling their feathers as they swooped to shore. It was promising to be another fine day and as Norman was going to his gardening club she decided to take her knitting bag and go for a walk along the prom. She'd intended to sit on the bench their favourite one, not far from the shops. It was the one with the brass plaque which read… *To Ivor who like to sit and watch the waves.* She had no idea who Ivor was but could empathise with the sentiment.

She'd only been sitting there for a short while when Emlyn Jones stopped to talk to her.

'Norman at the club, is he Alice?'

'He is Emlyn.'

'Just on my way there myself,' he said, glancing up at the sky. Looks like the weather is going to hold.'

'We were so sorry to hear about Bronwyn.' Alice put her knitting down in her lap. 'But she's getting better now? I saw her playing on the beach with her dad and Bethan yesterday. Full of beans she was.'

'She is, Alice. But I can't deny it shocked the life out of us all.'

'I'm sure it did! It comes to something when children aren't safe in Oysterbend.' She shook her head. 'I hope the police are doing all they can to stop these young druggies hanging about the place. We've seen them lying in the shop doorways when we go shopping in town.'

'You're quite right. It's a disgrace. I was talking to Elis about it the other day. He was stopping off at number five. Anyway, I took the opportunity to stress how disgusted we all are about the druggies and something should be done about it.' Emlyn looked down at his shoes, his mind returning to the day Bronwen found the pills near this very bench. 'He told me the police are doing all they can to get them off the streets in the area. He said they had it all in hand and not to worry, they wouldn't rest until the problem was solved. But he did have the sense to agree with me and not try to fob me off.'

'Well, I hope they do! This time.' A frown creased Alice's forehead. She didn't feel at all comfortable about being a hypocrite, but it had to be done.

'By the way,' Emlyn said, looking out over the bay, 'Elis has got a new tenant. I've seen her in the garden, just to say hello, like. She seems quite tidy, not a bit like the last lot, thank goodness.' His mobile began to ring so Alice picked up her needles once more, as Emlyn gave her a quick wave and walked off towards the shops.

Seabeach Close					K.J.Rabane

She'd been knitting for ten minutes or so when she saw Henry Wilson, their new neighbour, jogging from the direction of the cuttings. He stopped to catch his breath when he saw her.

'Lovely morning, he said. 'I've just run back from The Point, so would you mind if I sat and had a chat for a while. We haven't really had a chance to get to know each other since I moved in.'

He held out his hand, 'Henry Wilson, and you're Mrs Barker? You were at our party, not long after we arrived. But I'm afraid I didn't get to speak to everyone who was there that night. We had quite a crowd turn up as things turned out. '

'Alice, please, call me Alice,' she said. 'So, how are you settling in?'

'Fine, thanks. We love it here. Thankfully Jake is getting used to his new school and he's made friends with Daniel at number four.'

'That's good. Daniel is such a nice, kind boy. And your wife?'

For a fraction of a second Alice thought he looked as if he didn't know who she was talking about. She saw him hesitate and then realising, replied, 'Yeah, eh yes, she likes it here too.'

Alice nodded. 'That's good. It does take a while to settle into a new place.'

'I've often seen you sitting on this bench, knitting.' He turned to face her and smiled, and she had to admit he had the kind of smile that would turn your knees to jelly. If, of course, she'd been young enough to appreciate its effect. 'It's such a popular place to sit I expect you collect quite a few people who stop to chat from time to time too.'

Alice nodded. 'I do. I usually sit here when my husband is at his gardening club and yes people are very friendly and often stop for a while.'

'That's good. I've already noticed Oysterbend seems to be a friendly sort of place.' He stood up, flexing his legs. 'Right, well, mustn't stay too long or my muscles will start to cramp up. It was nice to meet you properly, Alice. I hope we have a chat again soon.'

'I'm sure we will,' she replied, wondering how he'd managed to notice, that she was in the habit of sitting on this particular bench in such a short time. She wasn't sure whether she liked the idea. Either, he was a very observant young man, or he was just plain nosy, she thought, picking up her knitting once more.

She didn't want to dwell on the prospect of their private life being unravelled by a stranger, not now when their past had been well and truly hidden from view since they'd moved into Seabeach Close, far enough away from Newport and the court case. And, certainly not now, when they had their own reasons for making sure they weren't being spied on by their neighbours.

Number 1
Ben and Felicity Frazer

CHAPTER 19

Ben Frazer glanced at his smart watch and saw he was going to be late. The old man would be on his case again. This latest land deal had been trouble from the start. He'd tried to explain the pitfalls to his father but he wasn't ready to listen. He was getting worse the older he got, there was no doubt about it, thought Ben, as he negotiated the rush hour traffic.

Driving towards the company's premises ten miles north of Newton Cross he felt the pulse in his neck begin to race. This constant daily pressure was getting to him. It was having an affect on his marriage too. He could tell Felicity was unhappy but could do nothing about it until this latest deal went through. Pulling into his parking space he tapped his smart watch and checked his blood pressure. It was just as he thought, it was higher than was healthy. He hadn't been running with his wife for weeks. It was time he focused on something other than work. Picking up the water bottle from its cradle he took a swig, removed a small container from his pocket and tipped two white pills into his hand which he raised to his mouth, then swallowed. He'd been able to get away with telling Felicity they were paracetamols in the past, but his father was no fool which was why he only took them before he started work.

He was aware he was playing with fire. Amphetamines were the last thing he should be taking with raised blood pressure. But he needed help to get through the day, especially when he'd had a sleepless night. He'd taken them on odd occasions before, whenever he'd felt he needed them and didn't see there was a problem. He chose to ignore what happened during his university years and afterwards.

'Here you are last! I haven't got all day to wait for you my lad. We've got to get over to Fosters straight away.' His father said tapping on his car window. Ben wound it down, thankfully having replaced the pill container in his pocket.

'Traffic was crazy on the road to Newton Cross. You know what it's like.'

'SO, get up earlier,' Charles Frazer exclaimed.

The day was starting much as he'd thought it would. Ben felt the buzz of the speed and, leaving his car in the parking lot, followed his father into the waiting limo.

He'd first started to take uppers when he was in university. He'd just met Felicity when he was on holiday in Devon and was hoping he could persuade her to come and stay with him in his flat for a while as she still hadn't found a suitable job locally, after qualifying as a graphic designer. He'd passed his law exams with flying colours and was eager to learn how his father's business worked so he could represent him in the future. But, it had been harder than he'd thought. The firm's business interests were more complicated than he'd expected and he felt out of his depth but unwilling to show it. However, at first, his father had seemed proud of his efforts, although failing to understand the pressure he was putting him under. And, as the years passed and the business had expanded, the pressure, had increased to the point where it felt like a boil waiting to burst. And lately, so had his need for his 'little helpers.'

Marrying Felicity was the best thing he'd ever done and for a while he'd managed without the drugs. She'd helped him and supported him through his period of withdrawal but he knew the toll it had taken on their relationship. She didn't need to know he'd slipped back into addiction. He could just about explain it to himself and knew there were no words he could say which would satisfy Felicity.

The Birmingham end of the company was winding up, as his father had decided to move to Wales. There were plots of land for sale from Cardiff to Oysterbend at a fraction of the cost of land in England.

Charles Frazer had bought the plot on which Seabeach Close was built and, as a late wedding present, had given the keys of number one to them both with undisguised pride. It was the largest property in The Close and had the best view. Ben had begun to feel more relaxed about the prospect of working with his father in Wales, and his future with the woman he loved, far away from all the temptations big city life had to offer.

Everything had been fine for a while. He'd cut back on the pills. There had been days, weeks even, when he hadn't needed them at all. But that was until the land at the Fosters Shopping Mall had come up for grabs. He'd tried to dissuade his father from getting involved, knowing the pitfalls but it had been useless and had fallen on deaf ears. And now his fears were being realised and he'd had to resort once more to taking something to get him through the day on a regular basis. He chose to put out of his mind the infertility issues which had arisen. He'd been told his problem could possibly be drug related, after having had a private consultation, but hadn't dared to talk to Felicity about it knowing she'd hit the roof.

As for obtaining what he required in Oysterbend, he couldn't believe how easy it had been. He'd imagined himself hanging outside some dodgy club to get the drugs. But, speed, coke, E's and more besides were here on his doorstep and it hadn't taken him long to discover exactly where to get them.

CHAPTER 20

The weather was getting warmer by the day. The forecasters on TV were promising a heatwave. Ted and I were looking forward to a summer relaxing in the back garden and walking along the beach. But, it didn't turn out quite as we'd expected.

It started with the parties next door, as I'd suspected it would. They always included everyone from The Close in their invitations. No doubt hoping the neighbours wouldn't complain if they were there themselves. Ted was tempted to go but I said no, definitely not. I wanted to stay well away from Henry Wilson. I knew he was trouble. I could smell it a mile away. So we put up with the noise and with the comments from our friends and neighbours as to how charming Henry was and what a delightful family they were.

Delightful on the surface they might be, but I knew all along it was just a front and was wary about getting too close to them. I suppose it was because I spent a lot of time on the beach feeding the birds, chatting to people and walking along the prom that I noticed more than the rest. I knew he was watching us all. But, I couldn't discuss it with Ted. He'd say I was getting paranoid. Although, when I'd mentioned it to Mark he told me to be careful. He'd listened to my concerns and like me didn't feel comfortable with what I'd told him. Besides, what did we know about their family other than what they'd been willing to tell us?

The feeling didn't go away, however hard I tried to rationalise it. I felt there was something not quite right about them. I'd felt it from the start. On the surface they appeared to be what they'd said they were, a husband, wife and a child. But I could smell it…just because it looks and smells like a rose…it doesn't necessarily mean it is one.

It was the week before the children finished school for their summer holiday break. I was feeding the birds on the seashore when Wilson approached me. I happened to be alone at the time as Ted was in town.

'No Ted with you today?' he asked. I turned away, ignoring his question and not wanting to give him the satisfaction of knowing where my husband was, besides I thought it a stupid question. It was more than obvious Ted wasn't with me! But then I thought better of it.

'Ted's changing our books at the library in town,' I said.

'Those birds seem to know when you're coming to feed them. It's like they're waiting for you,' he said.

Huh! I thought they're not the only ones.

'I suppose you've made quite a few friends since you've been here,' he continued, 'everyone seems so very friendly. Makes quite a difference from living in a big city, don't you think?'

'They *are* friendly. Very,' I replied, unwilling to enter into a lengthy conversation with the man.

'Yes. I've noticed you often have help feeding the birds. People stopping to help I mean. I suppose they have more time to stop and chat in a place like this. The pace of life is so much slower than where we used to live.'

'Nothing escapes you. Does it?' I answered, a trace of sarcasm lingering with the salt on my tongue. I certainly wasn't willing to point out we'd been living in Brighton before we'd moved here. It was none of his business.

'Not a lot,' he said, quietly, and I shivered at his tone of voice. Paranoid I might be but the way he said it had definitely sounded like a threat to me.

So, I decided, the time had come to try and be at least a bit neighbourly, if only to satisfy Ted and keep Wilson off our backs. They were new to the area after all. It made sense to at least try to connect with them, if only on a superficial level.

'Your son will be on holiday from school soon. Are you going away anywhere nice?' I asked, thinking two could play at the 'being nosy' game.

'No, no just staying put. We've had a lot of expense renovating the property since we moved in. Besides, why would we feel the need to go away when we have such a lovely beach on our doorstep.' He spread his arms out and smiled.

'True,' I replied. 'Ted and I feel the same. Although, we might have a break soon… catch up with our son for a couple of days.' It wasn't anything he couldn't find out for himself, as we had talked about visiting Mark soon, although I thought it might be something I'd do alone, as I could do with a break and Ted was settled with his friends and his hobbies.

There was something disconcerting about Wilson though and I was beginning to wish we hadn't been so forthcoming at the party we went to after they'd first moved in. He seemed to be the type of man who never forgot things, even the minutest detail. And I've met that type before, busybodies, who store up information like a computer hard drive just waiting to spill out personal details whenever they think it necessary, whilst keeping their own business close to their chests.

I threw the remaining bread out to sea as the birds swooped down on it with a flurry of flapping feathers accompanied by the sound of high pitched screeching, then I screwed up the empty bag and popped it into my pocket.

'I'll walk back with you to the prom,' Wilson suggested.

I couldn't find a reasonable explanation as to why I didn't want it to happen so just nodded. At least the bus from town was just pulling into the Oysterbend stop. I could see Ted's green baseball cap as he marched along the prom towards us.

Wilson looked him up and down as he approached, and then said, 'So no books take your fancy at the library then?'

'Library?' Ted replied, adding, 'oh, no, nothing today.'

When we were inside Ted turned to me, 'Library?'

'It was the first thing I could think of to tell him.'

'Why would you need to tell him anything?'

'I just didn't want the man to know everything we're doing.'

Ted began to laugh. 'You'll be the death of me one day,' he said with a grin. 'Now then, let's have a cuppa and forget about Henry Wilson. After all, I've only been at the chess club. It's not as if I was masterminding a drug ring or organising a mafia-style killing.'

I wish it had been as easy as Ted suggested but the man was not so easily forgotten. And Ted's jokes were irritating me this morning.

Seabeach Close K.J.Rabane

Number 7
Molly, the cleaner

CHAPTER 21

Molly Johnson had visited *Cute Cuts* in Oysterbend yesterday afternoon, and her hair still looked pretty much as it always did. The home colour she'd used had left the ends dry and brittle, so she'd had a trim. But it hadn't made any difference really. *Cute Cuts* wasn't known for its expertise but it was cheap. She had to admit she'd let herself go after Ethan. Leaving the salon she realised the time had come to change all that, she would start by losing weight. It would come off if she worked at it. It might take a bit of time but the body-shaping underwear she'd bought in town a while back would help for now.

The following day she'd dressed more carefully, putting on a pair of cotton jeans and the new yellow top she'd bought in the cut-price boutique, next to the hairdressers. The jeans were of a stretchy material and clung to her ample backside like a second skin. The top was low-cut and made of a light flimsy cotton. There wasn't a lot she could do with her hair except to tie it back in a knot, trying to mimic the one favoured by Felicity Frazer. The result wasn't perfect but anyone who saw her going to work would have raised an eyebrow or two. Fully made-up and without her usual trainers and baggy jogging bottoms she looked nothing like she usually did, as she walked towards Seabeach Close.

After inserting the key into the lock and before closing the front door of number seven, she glanced over her shoulder across the road to number eight where all was quiet. There was no sign of him today, nor any of his 'family'.

It took her less than half an hour to vacuum and dust the whole house. Then, thinking, as she often did, that Charles Frazer must have money to burn, she made for the kitchen on the upper floor. He could easily have employed her once a month instead of every week, as there was no one to mess up the place. Molly knew this was the easiest and most convenient job she'd had in years, no travelling expenses, nobody to tell her what to do. She was her own boss as soon as she closed the front door behind her. Although, she *was* aware it could change at any time if Frazer wanted to sell the property. But, there seemed to be no possibility of it at the moment, so she was prepared to make the most of the situation, while it lasted.

Seeing Ethan had been a shock and made her realise he could make things very difficult for her. There was always the chance that Frazer was keeping the house as a long term investment or even for his retirement so she felt she could relax a bit where that was concerned. That's if everything stayed the same. She considered the prospect, then opened her large handbag and removed a half bottle of vodka. It wasn't just number seven of course. It was vital she kept things on an even keel with Frazer as there was the other stuff to consider. He'd made it possible for her to build up quite a nice little nest egg over the years.

But, what was Ethan doing suddenly turning up in Seabeach Close? Why now? Why here? She remembered seeing him in a prison cell ten years ago. It had been enough to make her think seriously about where her life was going then and whether she wanted him to be part of it in the future.

So, he'd changed his name, but then so had she, well sort of. Talking to the neighbours she'd found out that he was now calling himself Henry Wilson. But changing his name hadn't made a scrap of difference. She would never forget a face like his, not when it had been resting on her pillow night after night for months. She wondered what he was thinking now? There was no doubt he'd recognised her too. So, how would he play it? Would he pretend she'd made a mistake if she confronted him? Was it safer for both of them if she allowed him to keep up the pretence of being Wilson? A thought occurred to her then. If that was the case, it could work in her favour and she needn't worry. But, she'd have to talk to him about it and soon.

Downing a measure of vodka followed by a mug of strong black coffee she walked into the sitting room, still carrying the mug. She'd topped it up from the coffee machine in the kitchen, wishing she had half of the appliances in Frazer's state-of-the-art kitchen instead of the ones in her dilapidated cottage. Molly glanced again at the bungalow opposite then sat on the window seat cradling her mug in her hands, whilst mulling over the problem of her one-time lover. Before long she saw him drive up in his car and park outside his bungalow. Standing up she rushed downstairs towards the front door still holding her mug. She couldn't hide from him for ever. She needed to know how this was going to work. Not knowing was driving her mad.

Walking quickly down the path, she was standing on the pavement waiting for him as he got out of the car. He looked across at her, smiled, and then raised his hand.

'Another nice day,' he said. Then closing his car door firmly behind him, he crossed the road towards her.

Molly's heart began to race. He hadn't lost any of his good looks. He was wearing shorts and a tee-shirt and there was no doubt both showed his taut muscles to good effect. As he got closer she started to panic - this wasn't a good idea - she should go back inside - pretend she didn't know him. She still had time to bury the past.

'I don't think we've met,' he said, holding out his hand. 'I've just moved into number eight with my family. I'm still getting to know all the neighbours - Henry Wilson - good to meet you.'

Ignoring his outstretched hand, she muttered, 'I clean the house for Charles Fraser.' Why had she said that? Why hadn't she let him know he was fooling no one with this stupid pretence?

'Oh, I see. That's why I haven't seen you around before. Must be hard, cleaning on such a hot day. Anyway, I mustn't stop you from your coffee break.' He indicated the hand still holding her mug. 'No doubt we'll see each other again.'

Molly watched him walking away, her thoughts in turmoil. So that was how it was going to be, was it? Over her dead body! Her mother had been right all along as far as he was concerned. Handsome is as handsome does was particularly true in his case.

In some ways the thought made it easier to cope with the problem. It strengthened her resolve to find out what on earth he was doing in Seabeach Close and why he was pretending he'd never met her before? No doubt he thought he could get away with it, if he kept up the pretence. But professing to be married with a child, was his biggest lie yet. There was no way she could let him get away with it this time. This time she had her business interests to protect.

Although they'd had a shared history, it *was* in the past but could not lie undisturbed if she was to protect her future. However, there were still so many questions left unanswered where he was concerned.

This time she wanted answers and was determined to get them one way or another.

Number 5

Detective Constable Laura Davies

CHAPTER 22

Laura was in the kitchen when she saw Henry Wilson walking across the road to talk to the cleaner at number seven. She was curious about him. In fact her job was to be curious about all the inhabitants of Seabeach Close in particular and the village in general. She knew she didn't have all the facts, but her boss had insisted that she had been given enough information in order to become effective in her brief.

Wishing she shared his confidence, Laura picked up a sketchbook and pencil and headed for the beach. It was nearly noon and the sun was already burning her cheeks so she made for the shelter of a rocky overhang, sat down and began to sketch a few outlines on her pad. Adjusting her sunglasses to have a better view of the beach and promenade she began her surveillance.

Up to now she'd just observed the inhabitants of the neighbourhood but, she'd decided, the time had come to start interacting with them. So, glancing down at her pad and then out to sea she added more details. Having her cover story ready, if anyone stopped to talk, she put her pencil down and watched the woman who lived in one of the bungalows as she fed the seagulls. It wasn't long before Laura saw she was joined by an older woman who started to help her. Seeing an opportunity to interact with them, she tucked her sketch pad under her arm and walked over to them. As she approached, the older woman screwed up her own carrier bag and smiling at her companion walked back up the beach. Above Laura's head the birds screeched as they circled and swooped towards the bread.

'Hello, she said. 'I've just moved into number five. I saw you and your husband feeding the seagulls the other day. I'm Laura by the way.'

The woman turned towards her, screwed up her eyes against the sun and said, 'And I'm May. And yes, we often feed them. We have plenty of stale bread and they're always hungry for it. It's nice to meet you, Laura.' Then she added, 'and as you can see I've had some help this morning too.' She smiled while nodding in the direction of the woman who'd now reached the steps leading to the promenade. 'So, how are you settling in?'

'Fine,' Laura replied. 'It's a lovely house and the neighbours seem friendly enough.'

May frowned 'Yes, well, some of them are. No, that's not right, most of them are,' she said, glancing at Laura's sketchpad. 'I see, you're an artist?'

'I like to think so, although it's mostly for my own enjoyment,' she added quickly, 'but my real job is designing greeting cards, which I sell online.'

'That sounds interesting. You must let me have your business card. I'd like to see some of your designs. The selection in the local supermarket isn't up to much, as a matter of fact.'

Anticipating her cover story would need to be backed up Laura removed a small card holder from her bag and handed a card to her. This part of the cover story had been set in motion by her boss. All she knew was that one of the tech boys in the station had organised a website in her name, and an artist had been employed to provide the 'print on demand' stock.

'You don't find the house too big for you then?' May asked.

Laura was prepared for this question. 'Well, it is a little larger than is necessary to be honest, but the location was just too good an opportunity to miss. Having the beach so near is very inspirational in my line of work, I find.'

May nodded, glanced at the card and said, 'I see, it must be…yes. Thanks for this. I'll take a look at your site when I get home. Right, well I'm off. It's getting a bit too hot for me. Nice to have met you. No doubt we'll meet again.'

Watching her as she walked back along the beach, Laura saw her stop to talk to a young man wearing shorts and a yellow tee-shirt. Turning away she decided to walk along the sand in the direction of the village. Lunch in one of the cafe's with a sea-view would be good. It was also a perfect way to keep an eye on the villagers she argued, not entirely believing her thinly veiled excuse for a cuppa and a cake.

As it turned out it was the perfect time to meet the woman who lived in the house next door - the one who had the twins. Elis had told her about the twin who'd swallowed the amphetamines and had ended up in the hospital. It was the opening she needed.

The girls were playing with a small sandy coloured dog as their mother sat at a table outside the café. She was drinking coffee, the remains of her lunch and those of the children still resting on the table in front of her.

The woman smiled as Laura approached her. 'Hello there, I think you live next door to me? I've just moved into number five. I'm Laura,' she said.

'Yes, I saw you'd moved in. I'm Gwyneth. And those two tormenting our new puppy are Bronwen and Bethan. I've been meaning to come over to see if you needed anything but things have been…'

The twins weren't identical, Laura noted. Although facially quite similar one was much bigger boned than the other, the smaller one looking very like her mother. Laura could only assume that Bronwen looked more like her father. They were dressed alike in pink shorts and pink and white candy striped tops. Their fair hair being tied back by pink ribbons.

'How is your daughter now? I saw the report of the incident on the local news. What a terrible experience it must have been for you all.'

'Oh it was…terrible…unimaginable!' Gwyneth sighed. 'But she's fine now thanks, although I don't mind telling you it was a terrible shock. That's why we got the dog really. She's been on about having one for ages. We thought it might take her mind off what happened.'

'It certainly seems to have worked, judging by all the fun she's having,' Laura said, whilst glancing around at the seats all of which were taken. 'I thought I'd stop for some lunch but I hadn't realised it would be so busy.'

'It's the warm weather. It's always the same. Why don't you sit here?' Gwyneth indicated the empty chair at her side. 'I've almost finished.'

'Oh no, I'd feel like I was driving you away. You stay. I can go back home for lunch.'

'Nonsense! But if you'd feel any better about it, I'll order another cup of coffee. The kids seem happy enough and I'd welcome a chat.'

'In that case I will, thanks.' As the waiter approached, Laura added, 'but please let me pay for your coffee,' Laura said.

As they chatted and watched the children playing, Laura felt at ease with Gwyneth, who appeared to be open and straight forward, although she was still aware appearances could always be deceptive. In her experience not everyone was what they appeared to be at first sight and it could be a mistake to form an opinion too quickly. However, establishing a friendship with this woman might be beneficial in the future, in more ways than one, especially as she was nearer to her age than some of the other inhabitants of Seabeach Close.

'I was wondering if perhaps you'd you like to pop over to mine for coffee sometime? I know so few people here and it would be good to get to know you better,' Laura suggested. '

'I would, thanks. But, hey, I go to my Yoga class at ten tomorrow morning. Why don't you come along too? It's for beginners and I've only been a couple of times myself. We haven't been in Seabeach Close for long either. We used to live a couple of miles north of Newton Cross before we moved here. So I decided to start Yoga to get to know some of the locals myself.'

'I'd like that. But I thought you'd lived her for ages. You seem to know everyone really well.'

'That's mainly through my Dad. He used to live in a cottage in the village before he moved in with us and he knows loads of people, and so we've got know some of his friends.' She picked up her cup and drank, her eyes still trained on the twins. 'I'm glad you've decided to come to Yoga though. There are a few women around our age who come. Felicity at number one does occasionally. But I think, she's taken up jogging lately so we might not see much of her.'

'Thanks Gwyneth. Not sure I'd know what to wear though and don't you have to have a mat or something?' Laura tried to look vague, knowing perfectly well she'd joined a fitness club in Bridgend when she was doing her police training.

'No problem. I've got a spare mat and you can just wear something loose.'

'I can do that.' Laura grinned.

'Great. We can walk to the church hall if you like. It will only take us five minutes or so. I'll be waiting for you at our front gate at, let's say... ten to.'

'Sure. I'll be there. Thanks again.'

Gwyneth drained the remains of her coffee and stood up as the waiter arrived to bring Laura's lunch. 'Right, I'll leave you to enjoy your meal in peace. I'll see you tomorrow morning then,' she said, 'Come along girls we're off home now.'

All in all this had been quite a productive morning, Laura thought. She now had a connection in the village which would be an even better cover.

Later, inside number five, she opened up her laptop and made up a new file headed VILLAGERS, then proceeded to make notes on everyone she'd come into contact with earlier.

Waking early the following morning, she saw sunlight streaming through the blinds she'd failed to close the night before. She'd been exhausted and had fallen into a deep sleep as soon as her head hit the pillow. She stretched her arms, flexing her muscles and feeling the blood pumping as she slid out of bed and did a few press ups on the carpet. At least she had a reason for mixing with Gwyneth and the members of the local yoga club. It was a start. Undercover work was new to her and although her boss had said he was confident she would do a good job, she was conscious of the fact that she was still a novice and had a lot to learn.

In the kitchen she popped a slice of bread in the toaster and switched on the coffee machine. Then, balancing her breakfast tray on one arm, opened the door into the living room and went to sit near the window.

In the garden of the house opposite Henry Wilson was planting flowers in a large terracotta pot. She watched him as he patted the earth around the flowers and then attacked the cherry tree pruning it vigorously. The closer she looked it became obvious he didn't have a clue what he was doing. It wouldn't have concerned her in the least, except for the fact that when she'd been talking to Gwyneth earlier she'd mentioned her father was thrilled that an expert horticulturalist had moved into number eight. She might not have noticed his lack of expertise either, if it hadn't been for the fact that she'd grown up with a father who had run a large garden centre and who knew all there was to know about trees and plants.

Laura had spent most of her childhood sitting alongside him as he'd shown her how to replant seedlings and propagate plants which was why she could tell Henry Wilson was definitely no expert.

'So, what *was* he up to?' she said out load. The question lingering a moment longer on her lips. After she'd finished eating she drank her coffee wondering if she should take a walk over to number eight and play the innocent. She could say she'd heard he was just the man she was looking for as she needed some advice on what to buy for her father, who had retired and thought he might like to take up gardening.

Perhaps she should run it past Elis first though? Then she shrugged. 'Why on earth would I do that? He's given me a job to do. I can't keep running to him for advice.' Aware she was now both talking to and answering herself, she stood up and carried the tray back into the kitchen. Glancing at the clock, she decided there was time to have a quick shower, pull on a pair of leggings and a loose top and then go to meet Gwyneth.

Having decided not to discuss, with Elis, her intention of directly interacting with Wilson, she left the house unaware that he would have instructed her to leave well alone at all costs.

CHAPTER 23

I thought the woman who had moved into number five seemed pleasant enough. Young and pretty which will make a change from the noisy, untidy bunch who'd left in a hurry a while back. Yesterday, I saw her going to meet Gwyneth and they were obviously going to Yoga, as she'd handed her a mat. No doubt we'd see a lot more of her during the coming weeks. I'd often thought I might like to join a yoga class myself but hadn't done anything about it and thought maybe it was a bit late in the day for me now. Although, I must stop thinking like that. Sixty was no age these days, and looking at Ted who was five years older and fit as a fiddle, I really shouldn't make age a yardstick to stop doing anything I wanted to do. With this thought in mind, I filled my carrier and topped it off with a layer of the stale granary bread Ted had refused to eat toasted, as he said it stuck to his back teeth.

The forecasters on breakfast TV had said the weather was going to improve and a heatwave was on its way. In some respects I was looking forward to it. More time to spend on the beach, more time to feed the birds, more time to keep an eye on the inhabitants of number eight. You might think boredom was looming if I had so much spare time to 'spy' on my neighbours but you'd be extremely far from the mark.

I was never bored. Spying on number eight was a necessity, not a pastime. And, I was determined to get to the bottom of what Henry Wilson was doing in Seabeach Close.

With hindsight I know I'd been right from the start. But at first it was just this odd feeling and as it grew my interest in Henry Wilson became something of an obsession. The more I saw of him the stronger the feeling grew.

On the surface, he appeared to be convivial, helpful, and a happy family man. Whether it was to do with his family situation, which I found a bit odd for some reason, or the fact that he appeared to be extremely interested in the goings on of his neighbours, I wasn't sure. Also, his relationship with his wife seemed forced, never spontaneous. Perhaps they were a couple who kept their loving gestures for the privacy of their own home but they didn't look like a pair at all and I never saw him connecting with his son either. Jake spent more time with Daniel at number four than he ever did with his father.

I'd heard that Wilson worked from home as a sort of gardening expert with an Internet company called CLICK ON US...ALL YOU NEED TO KNOW ABOUT PLANTS. Ted had checked it out and said it was quite impressive. But in my opinion he didn't seem to spend an awful lot of time working. He was either jogging on the prom, walking along the beach or sitting at his loft window, binoculars glued to his eyes obviously spying on his neighbours. At least that's what I *thought* he was doing.

Ted said I was making a fuss about nothing and that he was probably just interested in the birds flying around the bay of which, we knew first hand, there were many differing species. But I was sure it was because he had a particular interest in another type of bird altogether, well, one in particular. I'd seen him talking to Felicity Fraser on a number of occasions and she was a very attractive young woman, who spent at lot of time on her own. I know there might be no harm in it, but I've noticed a few other things too. For instance, they would meet up early in the mornings and jog in the direction of The Point. It happened most days and they were gone for quite a while, longer than was necessary it seemed to me. I began to wonder what Ben Fraser would think of it *and* Wilson's wife Janice? I haven't mentioned this to Ted either, because I can imagine what he would say. But my 'overactive imagination,' as Ted liked to label it, had proven to be spot on in the past. He couldn't deny it. It was a fact.

Then there was that son of theirs Jake, well he doesn't look much like either his father or his mother. There was certainly no hint of a biological link between Wilson and the son. Jake's skin was whiter than white, the sort which was usually accompanied by ginger hair just like Jake's. So, perhaps the link with his father would be a latent one and Jake followed his mother biologically. I was going around in circles and beginning to think perhaps I *was* making too much of this after all. Nevertheless, I was determined to keep and eye on them all, just in case.

It was raining, thick drops splashing against the window, the sky darkening by the minute. Ted was watching bowls on TV in the living room.

'I'm just off to feed the birds,' I called to him, putting on my raincoat.

From the living room I heard him reply, 'I hope those seagulls know how lucky they are to have you, my love. Not many people would struggle out in the rain to feed them. Take care.'

The shower had turned into something more substantial by the time I reached the shoreline but I could tell my efforts weren't wasted. After I'd finished feeding them, I stuffed my carrier into the pocket of my raincoat and decided to walk back to our bungalow through The Close, as the grass border was muddy near the prom and I'd have to cross it to get to our back door. Walking towards our front gate, I saw Laura, our new neighbour at number five. She was standing at the side of her car, rain dripping from her hair onto her shoulders. She had the bonnet up and was looking completely baffled.

'Hello, Laura?' I said, 'We met the other day on the beach. Having trouble, are you?'

Oh, hi, yes. I'm afraid I am. It's this old banger. It's very temperamental, always letting me down. I know

I should get rid of it but buying a new one is so expensive.'

'I could take a look at it for you,' I offered, the rain having stopped.

She frowned, raised and eyebrow, hesitated, then said, 'Um yes… if you like.'

I laughed. It was the usual reaction I got when I tried to put into practice what I'd learned over the years, so I felt I had to give her some sort of explanation.

'When we first moved here I went to car maintenance classes in the village hall, mainly because Ted hasn't got a clue what's under the bonnet of a car and I thought it might come in handy in the future.'

Laura sighed, obviously relieved. 'Oh, I see. Yes, that's great, if you don't mind. I'd really appreciate it. I was going to meet someone in town. But it looks like I'll have to ring and tell him I can't make it.' I saw she was blushing.

'Don't do that. Let me have a quick peek first, just to see what the damage is. I wouldn't want you to miss out on your date.'

She blushed again, saying quickly, 'Oh it's not like that. I just don't like letting anyone down.'

She reminded me of Will when he was young and going out on a first date. He'd do anything not to let on how important it was. I suppose I warmed to her then. It made me realise how much I missed my eldest boy and wished he lived nearer.

Less than ten minutes later I'd sorted out the problem and watched her driving away from me with a degree of self-satisfaction. I was glad I'd been able to help. After all, having Laura in The Close was a distinct advantage as far as I could see. She lived almost directly opposite to number eight. I wondered if she'd had any misgivings about our new neighbour? Once I got to know her better I'd ask her what she thought of him.

Number 5
Detective Constable Laura Davies

CHAPTER 24

Laura drove away from Seabeach Close still smiling to herself. She couldn't believe that the middle-aged woman across the road, who'd seemed so unremarkable, had been so helpful. Passing the police station in Newton Cross she took a sharp left up a side street, then a right and pulled into the back entrance of an apartment block. Having first messaged her boss to say she was on her way and after pressing the intercom button to say she'd arrived, she heard the click of the outer door and let herself inside. The foyer had marble floor tiles and orchids in pots, although she wasn't quite sure if they were real or fake. A staircase with a silver metal handrail curved upwards at the side of a lift. Elis's apartment was on the top floor, so ignoring the staircase she made for the lift and pressed the appropriate button. When she arrived he was waiting for her at the open door to his apartment.

'Sorry if this seems a bit cloak and dagger,' he said, as she stepped inside. 'But I know you realise it's necessary. There's coffee brewing if you'd like a cup?'

Laura sat down on the large corner sofa, as in the open-plan kitchen area Elis poured coffee from the machine into a couple of white bone china mugs. As he did so, she glanced around and realised she would never have imagined him living here. She could have visualised him in a utilitarian, no nonsense flat, clean and tidy but that was about all, just like the one her brother had, before he met Sally. However, the interior was cleverly furnished, no clutter and sparse furnishings, which might have appeared cold and uninteresting if handled badly. But, it was quite the opposite. The grey corner sofa was comfortable with just a couple of pale blue scatter cushions arranged at intervals. The oak flooring was highly polished with a large grey and blue rug positioned at its centre. She was also aware the place was spotless, not a speck of dust in sight, but then this was more than likely due to a cleaning service.

The only drawback she could see was the lack of a view from the large windows which led onto a narrow balcony, as the block was in the centre of town. Nevertheless, she could imagine the advantages of being able to walk to work in favour of driving. No doubt Elis would move into number five eventually, she reflected, unable to understand quite why anyone wouldn't want to live in a house which had the view she saw from her window every morning.

'So, you've got the file for me?' Elis asked, handing her a mug and sitting down opposite her.

Laura placed the mug on a side table and opened her handbag to remove the USB stick. As she handed it to him, she said, 'And, this is the way you want me to compile all my files in the future, no downloads, is that right?'

'Right. It's important not to risk the chance of a hacker discovering the connection between you and your police work. I'll copy this to my PC, which is secure. It won't be logged on to the police computer network just for now either.'

'To be honest I still feel a bit as though I'm operating in the dark.' Laura picked up her coffee mug, took a sip and then continued, 'I do understand why all the secrecy is necessary and can handle it, no problem. But there's very little I've actually been told about this operation, and there are times when I'm not really sure wha*t is* expected of me, other than keeping an eye on the neighbours to see if there's anything odd going on. Which without knowing exactly what I'm supposed to be looking for makes me feel anxious that I might slip up and miss something important. '

Elis sighed. 'I know, it's not ideal.' He stood up and walked over to the window. 'As you already know our part in Operation Creeping Jenny is to discover the distribution link and who is responsible for spreading the drugs throughout our area and further west. There's strong intel that Oysterbend is the focal point and I'm afraid that's all I can tell you at the moment. I know it's not what you want to hear but there it is.'

'I understand. So, as you outlined before, it's essentially a watching brief? Nothing's changed?'

Initially Elis didn't turn around to face her but she could hear his sharp intake of breath. When he finally turned around, she saw him raise his shoulders and shake his head slowly from side to side. 'I wish there was more I could tell you. But…'

'No problem,' Laura jumped in. 'I was hoping maybe you had some idea as to whom I should concentrate on, which might make it a bit easier, but I get the picture. I'll spread my investigations wider. In fact I've already made contact with a neighbour who has got me to join a local Yoga class and I feel that might open a few doors.'

'For now, at least, carry on as we discussed. Get to know them all and file a report to me every week. I'll arrange a different meeting place next time. We have to avoid arousing suspicion where you are concerned.'

'Ok…ay.' She said again, drawing out the word. 'I'll do my best.' Realising she wasn't going to get more information from him, Laura stood up. 'Back to it then, I suppose.'

'Remember, it's vital that you maintain your cover story, otherwise it could compromise things at our end.'

Laura stood up. 'Of course, sir. I'll be in touch with regular updates.'

'Fine. But, if there's anything urgent and you need to contact me. It can be arranged like this.' He stroked his chin. 'Ring my mobile and say there's a leak at the house and I'll come over carrying a bag of tools. The codeword is *leak*. You can disguise it anyway you like to avoid suspicion, especially if someone is within hearing distance. I'll just need a reason to call at the property.'

'I understand,' Laura replied. 'If I think anyone is curious I'll tell them how good my landlord is at fixing things.'

'Ha! If you only knew!' Elis laughed. 'I don't know one end of a screwdriver from the other.'

He walked with her to the lift then, back inside his apartment, watched from the window as she drove away. Afterwards, he couldn't stop thinking about the situation that had caused him to avoid telling her the whole truth. He'd had no choice in the matter, even though he'd explained he trusted her judgement in the matter. But, having repeatedly discussed it with his superiors he soon got the message…they were adamant that she should not be told…yet…maybe never.

Walking back to the station he decided he would need to keep a close eye on her himself. He owed her that at least. No matter what his instructions were, he wouldn't place her in danger, without backup.

It was unfortunate that the operation was being led from The Met. They had no idea how different the village and the town were from a big city. There had been substantial drug raids in the past in South Wales which had been concluded successfully. But they'd been mostly led by the Cardiff force who understood the close-knit communities and how they worked. This was quite different of course but only up to a point and he could see problems arising from not putting Laura totally in the picture. By the time he reached the station he'd decided on a plan of action, but one which he would not discuss with his superiors.

Number 7
Molly the cleaner

CHAPTER 25

Molly was determined that it was time she did something more about her appearance. Her previous attempt was inadequate to say the least but she had lost a few pounds since seeing Ethan at number eight and he was the driving force in her latest decision. It was all part of her plan to protect her future. But, he wasn't the only reason, just the catalyst. She'd simply got fed up of looking in the mirror at a woman who looked older than her years, when by using some of her hard earned cash she could make a few changes to improve things.

She'd often walked past *Oscars* on the High Street. The salon was stylish but expensive. As Molly pushed open the door she wondered why she hadn't done this before. Living on the streets had made her determined to never sink that low again. It was why she'd needed the extra work Fraser had provided. It was why she'd saved and, apart from buying the odd bottle of vodka, had never been extravagant. This was the exception and she was determined to enjoy the experience.

At the desk sat a perfectly groomed girl with a cut glass accent. 'May I help?' she asked.

'I've an appointment with Sue, at ten-thirty,' Molly said, aware she'd unintentionally dropped her native welsh accent.

Sue appeared, wearing a white dress and looking like a nurse rather than a stylist. 'Miss Johnson? This way please.'

Molly followed and was seated in a chair with a view of the High Street. The windows were tinted and of the kind where it was possible to see out but still be unobserved by passers by.

'You said on the phone you wanted a re-style…cut and colour?' Sue said, handing her a glossy book. 'I'll have Nadine make you a drink whilst we go through some of the styles I think might suit you.' Sue sat alongside her.

Eventually, while Molly relaxed drinking Earl Grey tea from a fine porcelain mug, Sue smiled, 'Now then, what d'you think of this, as a suggestion?' She turned the book towards her and Molly saw a glamorous young woman, her face framed by a caramel coloured, sharp cut bob, the angled ends of which sat an inch away from her shoulders.

'I love it,' Molly said. 'But I can't see me ever looking like that.'

'They all say that.' Sue stood up. 'You just wait and see.'

The stylist handed her a fashion magazine whilst she set about mixing the hair colour they'd chosen,

Molly relaxed as piped music filtered through the sound system. Glancing out of the window which gave a view of the street, she saw shoppers hurrying by unaware they were being watched.

Then after her hair was washed she felt the colour being applied and when this was completed was handed yet another cup of tea, this time accompanied by a small plate of tempting pastries, which she declined, thinking she was determined to change and continue as she meant to go on.

'I'll be back in twenty minutes to see how the colour is developing,' Sue said. 'But if there's anything you need, please just press the bell and Penny will see to it.'

Left alone, Molly found her gaze drifting towards the window and the passers-by again. Her attention was suddenly caught by Elis Williams who owned Number Five. He was a man in his mid-forties with sandy hair and a ready smile. He was also tall with broad shoulders and she'd heard on the grapevine that he'd been going to get married but the relationship had failed, mainly due to his job apparently. She'd thought him a distinct possibility once, but had stayed clear of him when she'd realised he was a detective. Getting involved with the police just wasn't an option, however attractive and available he might be.

Later, as Sue was drying her hair she saw him again. He was walking towards a man who was standing in a doorway reading a paper. Intrigued, she watched, as the man folded the paper and stuck it under his arm. It was then she realised it was Ethan, or Wilson as he was now calling himself.

The detective had stopped to talk to him and Molly desperately wished she could hear what they were saying. Nevertheless, it wasn't difficult to see that Elis was furious. His whole manner indicating there was an argument in progress. After a while she saw Ethan turn to walk away. But, Elis put a hand on his shoulder to stop him. More words were exchanged, then she saw Ethan shaking off his hand, as he headed in the direction of the market.

Molly wondered what the connection could possibly be between them but then remembered a prison cell in south London ten years ago. Making sense of it all was a different matter though. Something was going on and you could bet your life it was to do with the man known as Henry Wilson moving into Number Eight.

'Wow!' Sue exclaimed having returned and brushed out Molly's style, 'So what do you think of your new look?'

Molly looked away from the road and back to the mirror. For a brief moment she didn't recognise herself. Could a new hair colour and cut have made such a difference? The colour was flattering, the caramel shade softening her features and taking away the brassy tones she'd achieved through using home colouring kits. The colour also suited the cut which was sharp and fashionable and she wished she'd had it all done long before now.

Leaving the salon she decided not to stop at having a new hairstyle so headed for the local department store where there was a flash sale in progress. In the make-up department she had a makeover from one of the girls, overeager to sell the products on her counter, and ended up with a small cardboard carrier stacked with all she would need to continue the look at home. Afterwards, she headed for the outlet next to Marks and Spencer where prices had been slashed on last year's designer brands, determined to carry on her intention of spoiling herself. It was about time, she reasoned. No one else was going to do it for her.

With a spring in her step, she headed back to her car and was searching for her car keys in her bag, not looking where she was going, when she walked straight into the new inhabitant of number eight.

CHAPTER 26

'Surely you're not going to feed the birds today, love? Ted said, peering at the raindrops sliding down the window pane.

'Someone has to, and besides I need a bit of a walk. You stay and watch the cricket on the box, love. I'm okay on my own.'

To tell the truth I was glad to get out. I needed to talk to Mark without his dad listening. I hadn't heard from him in over a fortnight and I was beginning to worry. Ted would only have said I was making a fuss about nothing and the boy was now a man not a child, who needed to check in with his mother at every whipstitch. But he didn't understand. Besides a mother's instinct is usually the right one and I'd learned to trust mine.

In spite of the weather there were still plenty of people about, wrapped up in see-through plastic ponchos or raincoats, looking like slabs of meat zipped into freezer bags. On the beach I saw the usual all-year-round swimmers, who were there even in bad weather when ice crystals formed on the seashore. It was obvious a summer shower like this would be no deterrent to them.

It had taken time but most of the locals seemed to recognise me now and some would help me to feed the birds, even the younger crowd, who often stopped to chat. Having finished my task, I folded up my Sainsbury's carrier and put it into the pocket of my raincoat. Then walked towards the steps leading to the prom.

The woman was sitting on the third bench along, oblivious of the rain. I thought about joining her but decided it would look odd, me sitting in the rain, when I lived such a short distance away.

I should say something though, as I was passing.

'Not much fun in this, is it?' I said.

'No. Weather looks set for the day too,' she mumbled,

So I stopped, and said, 'Yes, nothing new is there? This rain will be here for a while I should imagine. Bad for the businesses, who rely on the good weather too.'

'Right.' she sighed, stood up and said, 'Just as I thought. You think it's in for the day?'

'It's often like this during a summer in Wales,' I replied.

'I was going to have a snack, brought it with me but ended up putting it in the bin,' she said.

I waited as she walked away then put my own carrier in the bin, as it was still soaking into my pocket. Then, satisfied I'd managed to do as I'd intended in spite of the rain, I headed back to the bungalow where I hoped Ted had put the kettle on. I still hadn't heard from Mark but, in spite of Ted's instructions decided I would ring again later.

The note was on the kitchen table. It read;-*Had a phone call from Emlyn. There's an unscheduled meeting of the allotment society this morning, I won't be back until teatime. We are having lunch in the ship, so I'll just need a snack for tea. Love Ted.*

In a way it was just as well. At least I had the rest of the day to talk to Mark uninterrupted by Ted's asides.

When I eventually did get through to him he sounded in a flap. 'What is it Ma? I'm up to my neck here and things are not going well on the distribution front. Our American backers have pulled out so we have to stick to our core bases. But then that's this business for you.'

'I'm sorry to hear that, love. Is there anything I can do to help?'

I heard his short bark of laughter which he managed to stifle as he said, 'No, no, you're okay, Ma.'

'Okay, well if you're sure. I'll be off to Asda then.'

Mark grunted a reply and I realised he wanted to get off the phone. So I picked up a new carrier bag and headed for the supermarket in the village.

I was halfway there when I suddenly realised what I could do to help Mark. It wasn't much in the scheme of things but nevertheless it was worth a try. Taking my mobile from my pocket I looked at the time and realised it was still quite early but then Will was an early riser like me, so I rang him.

He seemed surprised to hear from me. 'How did you know, Ma?' He asked.

'Know what?

'That you're going to be a grandma,' he said.

To say I was shocked would be an understatement. I was both shocked and thrilled and couldn't wait to tell Ted the good news.

'That's fantastic! Congratulations to you both, love. I can't wait to tell Dad the good news. How *is* Beth, any morning sickness?'

He put my daughter-in-law on the phone and we chatted for a while and then Will finished off by asking about Mark and was the business going well.

It was the opportunity I needed. 'Bit worried about him, love. But I've an idea which might help. I just wanted to run it past you, if you have the time.'

In the background I heard the sound of the doorbell and laughter.

'Go ahead. Looks like the news has got around and I've got the rest of the day free. Beth's best friend and her sister have arrived and when they get together I usually close the door on the Den, knowing I'll be left to my own devices for a while.'

He laughed and I was struck by the fact that everything was working out well for him in the States. He was happy and that made me happy, all that was needed from me now was to make sure Mark was in a good place and I could relax at last.

When we'd finished talking I put my mobile back in my pocket, and set off with a spring in my step. The rain had stopped and sunshine was filtering through the clouds. Puddles gleamed with reflected colours and the rain-dappled sand glittered like newly minted coins. It looked like everything was going to turn out fine after all, including the weather.

Number 1
Ben and Felicity Frazer

CHAPTER 27

Felicity watched the sun coming up on the horizon as her husband's car backed out of the drive. She waved to him from the window, relieved she wouldn't have to play a part any longer and could have the rest of the day to be herself.

She'd been for a run earlier but unfortunately hadn't seen Henry Wilson. So, she slipped into the new backless cotton sundress. which hung limply in her wardrobe waiting for an opportunity to be worn, like a wallflower at a dance. She thought she would walk along the promenade into the village and have a coffee and a cake overlooking the coastal path and put her husband and her new neighbour firmly out of her thoughts where they belonged. She decided to forget about men in general and the trouble they caused in particular.

Even though it was early there were a few holidaymakers sitting outside the café eating breakfast. Changing her earlier intention she ordered a fresh orange juice, toast and honey whilst watching the members of the rowing club practising for their upcoming regatta. The tide was high and lapped against the rocks, the repetitive, hypnotic sound helping her to relax and forget her husband and his troubles.

She saw early morning joggers making their way along the prom, but her resolve was faltering, as disappointment at not seeing her new neighbour began to set in. She felt his loss unaccountably twisting at her insides like an ache, whilst simultaneously recognising it to be a ridiculous and dangerous emotion. They were both married and he'd given her no indication whatsoever he was attracted to her. He'd only been friendly, the rest was purely in her imagination, born out of frustration at the way her love for her husband was waning. Determined to get a grip on her emotions or end up making a fool of herself, she looked away from the promenade and focused on the coastal path snaking towards the village from the headland.

On the path, Felicity saw two figures walking towards her. At first she thought it was Henry Wilson and his wife but as they drew nearer she could see he was with her father-in-law's cleaner. It took her a while to realise it was Molly though. She was amazed at her transformation and wouldn't necessarily have recognised her, if it hadn't been for the way she rolled her hips from side to side. She was wearing figure hugging jeans and a white cropped top and she'd done something new to her hair. The whole effect, even from this distance made her seem much younger.

Feeling a wave of jealousy washing over her, she watched Henry bend towards Molly, their heads almost touching. Then she saw the woman shrug, turn away, and march off leaving him alone on the path.

Still mulling over in her mind what she'd just seen, she looked up from her plate and there he was, standing right in front of her.

'Having an early breakfast? Mind if I join you?'

Feeling flustered, she replied, 'Er, no, of course, please do.'

'It's just that Janice has gone to Cardiff to do some much needed clothes shopping, or at least that's what she told me. And, well, I couldn't be bothered to make breakfast.'

She wondered whether she should mention having seen him with Molly but decided against it. She didn't want to sound as if she'd been watching them or that she was curious about what she'd just seen.

Taking the dilemma out of her hands, he said, 'I've just been speaking to your father-in-law's cleaner. I did wonder if she could do a few days for Janice and me, as the house is in a bit of a tip after the builders left.'

'Oh, right.' Felicity replied, with undisguised relief which she hoped he hadn't noticed. 'So she'll be cleaning for you too then?'

He chuckled wryly. 'In fact quite the opposite, she sent me away with a flea in my ear saying she had more than enough to do cleaning Number One without tidying up my mess.'

'That sounds like Molly,' she replied.

'Actually, I'm at bit of a loose end for the rest of the day. I wonder, if you're not busy, would you fancy a walk around the coast to Captain Crabbe's Cove for lunch and maybe an afternoon swim?'

Felicity felt her pulse racing and before she could think of a reply, he added, 'We could pick up our swimming gear on the way?'

It was as much as she could do not to jump for joy but managed to just nod and say, 'Yes. Sounds good.'

Opening her front door she ran upstairs two at a time, thrust clean underwear and a towel into a beach bag, put on her bikini, shorts and tee shirt and left the house. It did briefly cross her mind to wonder how Ben would feel when she told him how she'd spent the day and who with?

Number 3
Emlyn Jones.

CHAPTER 28

Having found he had a rare day free Emlyn decided to walk up to the allotments. He'd had a word with Ted the day before and they'd planned they should meet up at his shed to have a chat and maybe a cool beer, curtesy of the small fridge Emlyn had installed not long after he'd been allocated his plot.

It was a fine, clear day and he could do with a breath of fresh air and a chat. Everyone else was making the most of the good weather it seemed. Gwyneth and Ian had gone out for lunch, the kids were in school and he'd caught a brief glimpse of Miss Jenkins, their teacher, taking them into the woods for a nature trek, when he'd been picking up his morning paper. He'd also seen Felicity Fraser and the new bloke from number eight walking in the direction of Crabbe's Cove.

Taking a short cut at the back of the bungalows at the start of his walk, he'd noticed Daniel and his new friend Jake knocking a ball around in his back garden. He sighed with contentment and inhaled the fresh morning air, which carried with it the promise of good weather to come

Seabeach Close   K.J.Rabane

As he'd continued to walk along the promenade and into the village square he'd also seen May, who was feeding the birds on the seashore, as usual, and even Norman and Alice were relaxing in deckchairs in their back garden, although falling asleep was probably nearer the mark.

Living in Seabeach Close with his family Emlyn felt he was one of the lucky ones. It was a peaceful, relaxing environment in which to spend the last chapter of his life.

He had hoped he could have a word with Henry Wilson upas he'd heard he was an expert horticulturalist. But he could see plants were not exactly on his mind when he's seen him with Felicity, earlier. They certainly made a striking couple, she being as fair as he was dark. In fact he'd always thought that Felicity and Ben Fraser looked more like brother and sister than husband and wife.

As he approached the allotments he could hear someone talking and saw Ted wasn't alone. Two young guys were with him and, although it was still early, they were drinking from cans of beer and much to his annoyance throwing down the empties on the grass border. At first glance Emlyn thought the young men were friends of Ted's but on closer inspection they just looked like a pair of layabouts who didn't belong anywhere near the carefully tended plots.

When he saw him, Ted raised his hand and to his relief the beer-swilling pair sauntered away.

Opening up the shed Emlyn pulled out a couple of folding chairs, and picking up the discarded cans from the ground he placed them in a plastic refuse bag, saying, 'Fancy a cool one, Ted?'

'That would be great. It's warming up no end, a perfect excuse, if ever we needed one.'

'No need of an excuse. What happens on the allotments, stays of the allotments,' Emlyn grinned, aware of his double standards regarding the youths who were now leaving through the gate leading into the lane.

'Hope I didn't scare those two off, Ted. Friends of yours are they?'

'What? Oh no. Remember the old chap who used to have the plot next to yours? They were his sons and they said they'd decided to come over to take a look so as to tell their old man how it's getting on. Apparently, he's missing the place but too infirm to come and see for himself,' Ted said, taking a can from Emlyn.

'Really? Thought they might be causing a bit of a nuisance, at first. Looked a bit on the rough side to me.'

'No, they were okay.' Ted wiped his forehead with his handkerchief. 'But then you can't always go by looks I suppose.'

'True. As a matter of fact I was wondering about the new chap in number eight earlier. He's supposed to be a dab hand at gardening, or so I've heard. Might be worth asking him to join the club?'

Ted shielded his eyes against the sun and replied, 'Can't see him being interested, Em. We're small fry compared to him. I think he's some sort of expert. But I suppose we could ask him to give a talk to the club, if you like.'

'That's sounds like a plan, Ted. Good idea. We should bring it up at the next meeting.'

Having eaten their packed lunches, talked about when Ted was likely to get his own plot and nodded off in the afternoon sunshine, they packed away the chairs and noticed the sun was creeping lower in the sky as they left the allotments and walked back home together.

Reaching the steps leading up from the beach they saw May talking to the young men who'd been at the allotments earlier. Then, seeing them both, she climbed up the last few steps and joined them.

'Everything okay?' Ted asked, taking her arm.

'Of course. It was such a nice afternoon I went for a walk as the tide was out. Then, I tripped on some pebbles, can you believe it, and those two helped me up.' She pointed to the young men who were now kicking a ball about on the sand. Seeing Ted looking at her with concern, Emlyn heard her say, 'Stop worrying. I'm absolutely fine! I should have been looking where I was going, love…that's all.'

Saying goodbye and leaving them on the prom, Emlyn walked back to The Close feeling the loss of his wife so intensely it was almost unbearable. It was no doubt prompted by seeing Ted and May and the closeness they shared. It would never go away, he knew that, Megan would be with him for as long as he lived but he owed it to his family not to become a maudlin old git.

Bronwyn and Bethan were playing in the front garden. As he approached they jumped up from the grass and ran towards him, 'Hey Bampa, come and see what we found on the beach today.'

In Bethan's outstretched hand was a small pipe, a piece of tin foil, and a plastic spoon.

Seabeach Close K.J.Rabane

Number 1
Felicity Frazer

CHAPTER 29

Warm sand caressed her body as Felicity relaxed into it. The sea, a shimmering sheet of glass in the afternoon sun, and the sound of the ripples lapping on the shore had lulled her into a doze. They'd eaten crab salad and drunk a bottle of wine in the cliff top diner before making their descent to the cove, and the wine was beginning to take its effect. As her eyes closed, she sensed Henry sitting with his back against a rock, watching her.

Captain Crabbe's Cove, a hidden gem known mostly to the locals, became reachable by means of a narrow, steep and overgrown path. So, at this time of the day there were just a few couples heading homeward and leaving them alone on the beach.

'Sorry, I must've dozed off,' Felicity said, propping herself up on an arm and turning to face him. 'Can't believe I did that.'

'No problem. I've been enjoying the view.' He stretched and yawned. 'By the way, how are things at home now? Any improvement?'

'Not so as you'd notice. He's still working long hours and comes home shattered. I've told him to speak to his father about it but he says this contract is crucial and he can't let it slip away from him. Apparently, it's vital to the business. An excuse I've heard many times before, of course.'

'That's big business for you, I suppose,' he replied and leaning towards her, added, 'thankfully mine is small fry by comparison.'

Felicity moved to a sitting position, her back resting against the rock alongside him. His brown body and muscular legs were impossible to ignore, as was the strong physical attraction she felt towards him. Trying to think about something else, she said, 'What made you decide to come and live in Wales? It's not as exciting as living in London surely?'

'Ha! Believe me, excitement is not all it's cracked up to be. There's something to be said for the quiet life and living so near to the sea has a lot going for it.' Suddenly changing the subject, he said, 'The last time we met you said Ben was suffering from mood swings. Any improvement on that front?'

Felicity bit her lip aware he seemed to want to focus on her problems rather than talk about himself. She wanted, in fact she needed, to talk to someone but was feeling a strong sense disloyalty by discussing her husband and unloading their problems on to him. 'Things haven't changed,' she said quickly. 'But then he *is* working very hard and I shouldn't complain.'

'Fair enough, but if you ever need a friend…I'm here for you.'

Seabeach Close   K.J.Rabane

Sympathy was not what she needed at that particular moment. Frustratingly she felt tears on her cheeks and wiped them away with the back of her hand.

If he noticed, he didn't comment, but instead said, 'Fancy one last swim before we walk back?' He was holding out his hand to pull her to her feet. Then still keeping her hand in his they ran down the empty beach to the sea and jumped headlong into the waves. He was a strong swimmer and she not so much but he adjusted his pace to meet hers until they lay on their backs and floated for a while.

All was quiet, except for the gentle swish of the tide, which felt to Felicity, as if a sheet of silk was sliding over her body. His hand reached for hers again and they lay with their fingers touching, letting the current gently move their bodies back and forth, until she felt Ben and his problems slipping away on the tide. There was only this cove and the man at her side, nothing else mattered. It was perfect. Peace had been something she'd craved these last few months and now she wanted to hold on to it and never let it go.

After they'd dried off, dressed, and were walking up the steep path, Felicity began to dread the thought of leaving him. She wanted to wrap each moment in cotton wool to savour, when she was alone at home. Becoming suddenly submerged by emotion she blurted out, 'Do you think Ben might be taking drugs?'

Henry stopped on the path and put a hand on her arm. 'What on earth makes you say that? Do you have any evidence?'

'No, not exactly. It's just, well, I've been reading it up on the Internet and he does seem to be displaying some of the signs. I thought…you know…what with him working long hours…perhaps he's started taking drugs to keep him awake? He's done it before. It was a long time ago, when we were students. It's not as if he's always taking drugs, addicted or anything…' Aware she was back peddling and sounding defensive, she stopped.

Henry moved his hand to her shoulder. 'Listen, if you suspect he's taking drugs you should search your house. There's sure to be some proof somewhere. If nothing else it will put your mind at rest and at least you'll know for certain and can decide what to do about it.'

'I will.' But the words were whispered, and the breeze blew them away as they walked on.

The nearer to the village they came, she began to feel more positive. Now, she had a plan of action, where Ben was concerned, in addition to which she had a friend in whom she could confide. But was she kidding herself? Could she ever be just 'a friend' to Henry Wilson?

They parted company on the promenade, Felicity somehow knowing her intention, of keeping their relationship to friendship alone, would be harder to achieve than to imagine.

Chapter 30

I was still worried about Mark but didn't want to bother Ted about it. So, I thought I might suggest going up to London for a visit. Ted was busy with the allotment, although it wasn't officially his plot yet and so I rang Mark to see how he felt about me coming up for a day or two. I said I wouldn't stay at his flat, as I knew he liked his space and I didn't fancy sleeping in his spare room.

Later that afternoon I had a chat with Ted and told him I was going up to see Mark and I'd book into the Strand Palace for a couple of nights. I was beginning to feel quite optimistic about the trip. I might even have afternoon tea at the Savoy. I could do with a treat, I decided. It was ages since I'd made any contact with the friends I'd left behind when we moved, maybe I'd give some of them a call. We could meet up in our favourite restaurant for lunch.

Ted was all for it. In fact he greeted it with undisguised delight, which took the wind out of my sails a bit, I must admit. But he knew I was missing Mark and would never put obstacles in my way if I wanted to do something. He never had. Besides, he probably realised he could spend more time up at the allotments and laze about every afternoon with the rest of the members of the club, chatting and generally putting the world to rights.

So, as Mark was fine with the idea too, I made plans for the trip. First, I saw to it that the fridge was stocked with meals for Ted during my absence, each one labeled with details on how to microwave them. Next, I packed a small case with all I'd need, making sure it was light and easy to manage. I also reminded Ted not to forget about feeding the birds.

On Thursday morning he drove me to the station where I caught the train to Paddington. I'd forgotten how much I enjoyed train journeys. Without having to concentrate on the road, I sat back to watch the passing scenery. The once-green fields and hedgerows, which had flourished only a week or so ago were now rapidly turning to the colour of straw. We'd seen the first signs of this during our walks in the countryside surrounding Oysterbend.

The weather forecasters had been banging on about how we were set for a heatwave to rival the summer of nineteen-seventy-six. It was all down to global warming they said. Back then streams, which during the winter months had overflowed into the surrounding countryside, had become thin ribbons of water snaking through desiccated woodlands towards shrunken rivers. I was too young to remember it but I have a vague memory of my father and I seeing a river which had almost dried to a stream and for some reason it had stuck in my mind.

As we neared London I saw, with a sigh of relief, that thankfully the River Thames still wound its way through Windsor unchanged, as were the cruisers lining the riverbanks. Feeling a pang of nostalgia for the life I'd once led I shrugged. That was then and this was now. Moving on didn't mean the end of the line for us, I thought, as the train slowed reaching its destination.

At Paddington Station I was surprised to see Mark waiting for me. I'd planned to take a taxi to my hotel and then ring him in the hope we could meet up for dinner later. He looked thinner than when he'd waved us goodbye on our last visit six months ago. There were deep shadows under his eyes and I began to worry that he wasn't eating enough or getting enough sleep and then decided my days of being an overprotective mother were over. He was a man and wouldn't appreciate me fussing over him.

'Hi Ma, how's things? Dad OK?' he asked, giving me a hug.'

'Dad is fine. Everything is great at our end,' I said. 'Have you got time to catch up now or shall we meet later?'

'Now might be good' he said taking my case. 'I thought we could have lunch rather than dinner. I've got a few people to see later.'

'That suits me too. Why don't we go to my hotel and I'll treat you to lunch there?'

At The Strand Palace we took the lift up to my room. Alone in the lift with him I asked about his work problems.

'Slightly better now. We've made a few new contacts, so things are looking more positive. But I'm not kidding you, it's been a hard few months.'

I didn't need a crystal ball to see that, I thought. In my room he went into more detail about what had been happening and I felt it did him good to shift the burden onto my shoulders, if only briefly. Afterwards, I suggested we put aside his work problems and just enjoy each other's company for a bit.

'Yeah. It's nothing I can't handle, don't worry. I've just been offloading to you, like I used to do as a kid. Everything will work out fine,' he said, as we entered the dining room and were shown to our seats.

Later, drinking strong black coffee after finishing our meal, he asked, 'How are you getting on with the new neighbours at number eight? Have things improved since the party?'

'Hard to say really. I think I like her, not sure what to make of him though, and I've heard rumours his online business isn't quite what it seems.'

'Really? Why?' Mark sat up straighter in his seat.

'He's supposed to be a horticulturalist giving advice online. But Dad has his suspicions that he's not quite what he seems in that department.'

Mark began to laugh

'What's so funny?' I asked.

'Is that all? I thought he was a contract killer at least, by the look on your face.'

'Well, you know me. Dad is always saying I'm making a fuss about nothing. But this time it wasn't me. You know what he's like, no one knows more about gardening than him. So, I didn't automatically dismiss his concerns '

'Maybe the guy's just a bit out of his depth. Lots of people think they'll make a fortune online but very soon their sites collapse through lack of interest.'

'So you think Wilson's okay then?'

'Wouldn't have a clue, but with you two living next door…I'm sure, if there was anything odd going on, you'd find out about it pretty damn quick.'

I didn't know whether I should be affronted, but decided, under the circumstances he was probably right. In some ways it was reassuring to know that Mark thought we were so on the ball.

Having satisfied myself that he was eating enough and was okay, I kissed him goodbye and went up to my room to change. In the shower I pondered over our future with optimism. Both our boys were doing well. And I was now reassured about Mark, after our conversation. So, I could relax and enjoy and the rest of my well-earned holiday.

The following day I booked afternoon tea at the Savoy and in the morning spent a leisurely walk around Covent Garden. I'd arranged to meet a few friends at the wine bar in the morning and Mark said he'd meet me for lunch I so had a few hours to kill before we met up.

Seabeach Close   K.J.Rabane

The opera singers were, as usual, serenading the holidaymakers. So, I sat down outside a cafe and ordered a coffee and a scone, whilst listening to the free performance.

I was drinking my second cup, and relaxing in the sunshine, when I saw him with another man. They were deep in conversation and what happened next shook me to the core. Now, I understood my first instinct hadn't been far wrong. Henry Wilson was definitely not what he seemed. Should I ring Mark and tell him what I'd seen? But as I took my mobile out of my bag, sense made me think again. A different approach was what was needed this time. If Mark and Ted thought I was making a fuss about nothing I'd get nowhere.

But suddenly the pleasure of the day had changed and I knew I'd have to watch Wilson more carefully than ever in future. He was lying to us all. What I'd just seen had made it more than obvious. But what lay behind it all was the question uppermost in my mind. And I was determined to find the answer one way or another.

Number 5
Detective Inspector Elis Williams

CHAPTER 31

Elis glanced at his mobile which had pinged with a text message. It was from Laura.

Sorry to bother you, he read, *but I have a leak in the downstairs toilet.*

The codeword was all he needed to spring into action. The message was clear. He left the station, reached his car, with the tool-bag permanently stashed in the boot, and drove through Newton Cross and out onto the coast road leading to Seabeach Close.

Laura met him at the front door of number five, holding a sink plunger in her hand. He bit his lip to stop his mouth from stretching into a grin. Following her upstairs into the kitchen, he put his tool-bag on the floor. A rich aroma of coffee drifted towards him and when they were seated at the table cradling mugs of steaming hot coffee, he said, 'So what's the problem?'

'I'm convinced all is not what it seems at number eight. I can't put a finger on it but I'm certain Henry Wilson isn't the person he's making himself out to be. For a start, my dad's a keen gardener, in fact he's an expert. Henry Wilson has a website, where he's giving advice to subscribers, and on which he describes himself as a horticulturalist. I've been watching him and know that it's a lie. He has absolutely no idea what to do with plants. My dad taught me enough to know what I'm talking about. So, what is he really doing here and why the false online persona? I know he seems to spend a lot of his time talking to his neighbours, which is fine, but I'm beginning to feel he's pumping them for information. I've overheard a few such conversations. He also has a group of friends who call at the house and who are in a younger age bracket, which may not be significant. But there is always the possibility he could be dealing from number eight.'

Elis drank the remains of his coffee and didn't reply, as she continued to explain that she'd also noticed a developing friendship between Wilson and Felicity Fraser, adding, 'And, bearing in mind she's Charles Fraser's daughter-in-law...' she stopped, her eyebrows raised.

'I see. So, is there anything else?'

'Nothing more at the moment, but, his whole image feels fake to me and I just thought you ought to be kept up to date and it was easier to tell you face-to-face rather than put it in a file, as although it's just a feeling I think it's significant. I suppose you might call it 'a hunch?'

Elis stroked his chin saying, 'Nothing wrong with a hunch, Laura. I'll certainly bear it in mind.'

'Should I carry on watching him? What do you think?'

'Mm, I think for the moment, it might be wise if you keep a watchful eye on everyone, as we discussed, but don't focus entirely on Wilson. You might miss something more important going on amongst his neighbours.'

At the front door he made a show of carrying the tool-bag back to the car as Laura closed the door behind him.

His initial opinion of her as being a good detective wasn't changed but surveillance was a crap job on times. Feeling bad about the rest of it and being restricted by his superiors, Elis drove down The Close. As he passed number three, Emlyn Jones raised a hand and walked towards his car. Ellis stopped and wound down the window.

'Elis,' Emlyn said, 'I was just about to ring you. I'm glad I've managed to attract your attention. I'd like a word?'

'Of course. What is it Em?'

'Can I meet you on the main road? I don't want my Gwyneth to see me talking to you. I'll catch you up, if you park behind The Spar.'

Although thinking this was a bit odd, and not at all like Emlyn, Elis drove out towards the supermarket car park and waited for him to arrive. He'd felt Emlyn's anxiety rushing towards him like a speeding train. What on earth could have shaken a man like Em, who was usually so calm?

A short while later, he was parked up with Emlyn sitting in the passenger seat alongside him. The older man put his hand in his pocket and removed a plastic bag which he handed to him.

'The twins were playing with these in our front garden, yesterday. Bronwen was proud of her find on the beach and came to show me.' He shivered. 'I don't mind telling you, Elis. This is beyond a joke. What are you lot doing about the druggies who hang around the square of an evening. I don't see any difference from the last time you assured me the 'matter was in hand.' I wanted to show *you* first, rather that go in guns blazing to the station. I don't want Gwyneth or Ian to get upset and angry about their kids not being safe in Oysterbend. But this is the second time my grandkids have been exposed to this rubbish and if something isn't done soon I'm going to the press and social media. I'm serious about it, Elis. It can't go on. Newton Cross nick will be plastered on the front page of every local paper and once the news reporters get hold of the story…look out.'

Elis looked down at the contents of the plastic bag. The drug paraphernalia was a sobering sight, especially as Emlyn's granddaughters had been exposed to it first hand. He was right. Something had to be done and quickly. But first he had to cool Emlyn down and reassure him. The situation needed careful handling but somehow he'd managed to get him to agree to hold off and let his team work on sorting out the problem.

Elis had finished the conversation by saying, 'Look, we're not ignoring this, Em. You can be certain of that. I can't say more at this stage. You'll just have to trust me. We've got it! It will be sorted, hopefully sooner than later. I promise you. But if you go to the press now, it could disrupt our investigations and ruin the whole operation.'

He'd watched the elderly man walking away, his shoulders sagging dispiritedly, and came to a decision. This definitely wasn't good enough. He had to do something now, in spite of his instructions.

Back at the station he rang the Chief Superintendent at The Met who was his contact working on Operation Creeping Jenny. Afterwards, putting the phone down, he realised he couldn't escape the inevitable. A trip to London was what he'd been hoping to avoid, especially as there was so much going on locally at the moment, but it was not to be.

After booking a seat on the ten o'clock train from Newton Cross to Paddington for the following morning, he began to mull over when he would be able to make things clearer to Laura and the rest of his team. Things couldn't go on as they were, whatever his superior had to say.

Number 3

The Joneses

CHAPTER 32

With a heavy heart Emlyn told his grandchildren he had a replacement for the 'toys' they'd found on the beach. And, thankfully they didn't mention it again, having moved on to playing with their new gifts.

He'd managed to keep it from their parents which he'd felt distinctly uncomfortable about doing but now he'd spoken to Elis he could lighten up a bit as the matter was in his hands. Perhaps now something would be done at last, as this was not acceptable, especially where young children were concerned. However, he was determined to keep an eye on progress. It hadn't been a threat to Elis. It was a promise and one which he owed it to his family to fulfill, if things didn't change soon.

Gwyneth had her head bent over a magazine as he entered the kitchen. Ian was just finishing his breakfast.

'Look at this, love,' she said, passing her husband the magazine. 'A weekend trip to London, see the sights and do a show, and there are some tickets still available. *And,* take a look at the price, it's a real giveaway. It's a last minute offer.' Her face was wreathed in smiles of anticipation.

He saw his son-in-law hesitate and took the opportunity to jump in. Matching Gwyneth's smile with one of his own, Emlyn said, 'Right, now I know what to get you two for your anniversary. I'll give them a ring and book two tickets for you to go on Friday morning, as soon as Ian can fix it up in work. Don't worry about the twins. We'll have a grand time.'

Gwyneth leapt up from her chair and put her arms around her father's neck. 'Oh Dad, that's fantastic.'

Ian smiled, thanked his father in law, and said, 'I'm owed some Flexi time off. There won't be a problem in work, Em. I'll stay on for a couple of hours tonight to finish up and then take tomorrow off. It will give us plenty of time to get things ready for Friday. It couldn't have come at a better time. I'd booked next week off, a while back, as you know. I'd planned we could have a few meals out for our anniversary and do a couple of day trips to Porthcawl and Barry, but this is much better…in fact it's just perfect.' He slid his arm around Gwyneth's waist and kissed her cheek. 'So you decide what to take, love and I'll see you later.' As he passed his father-in-law, Ian laid a hand on his shoulder, saying, 'I really appreciate this, Em.'

The following day was filled with plans, arrangements and packing and on Friday morning

Emlyn drove his daughter and Ian to the bus station in Newton Cross. The twins were excited at the prospect of spending a couple of days with their grandfather and chatted non-stop in the back seat, planning what they were going to do.

There were a few people already waiting at the bus stop when they arrived and Emlyn noticed Alice and Norman Barker from Number two standing at the head of the queue, a small suitcase at their side.

As he drove away he thought how pretty Gwyneth had looked. Her chestnut hair had been left loose and was falling in soft waves to her shoulders, instead of being tied back in some sort of untidy knot at the back of her head. He felt a tug at his heart, she looked so like his Megan. It was good to see her relaxed and happy. She was a hard working mother and daughter and he was so proud of her and the family she'd nurtured. He knew he'd been right not to tell either of them about what the twins had found on the beach, at least not yet. It could wait. They hadn't been harmed, so what was the point in upsetting the whole family?

It was good that they could have a couple of days away from the village and perhaps, in the meantime, Elis would have stepped up his efforts to sort out the neighbourhood drug problem. After all, he'd stressed everything was under control, which, in the circumstances, was comforting to know. He'd just have to wait and see. But he wouldn't let it go, he'd keep watching.

'Let's go down to the beach and hunt for shells when we get back, Bampa,' Bronwen said.

'Can we, can we?' Bethan added.

'Well now, girls. I've got something better planned for us. How d'you fancy a trip to the fair? Candy floss and the Water Shute?'

'Yay,' they chorused from the back seat.

Emlyn bit his lip. It wasn't that he didn't trust Elis to sort it out but putting the girls in harm's way wasn't an option. In his opinion the beach was a dangerous place and he'd make sure he'd be watching his granddaughters more closely from now on.

Number 4
Sam Jess and Daniel Evans

CHAPTER 33

The garden room at number two had been designed by Daniel's father, who was an architect. The pool table was situated so his son could reach it from his wheelchair and the wall facing the sea had bi-fold doors which opened to give easy access to the beach and the ramp on which the boats slid into the sea. It was this ramp which Daniel used, when the tide was in. He liked to go for a swim as often as possible during the summer months, as his upper-arm strength compensated for the lack of it in his lower limbs. During the winter he swam in the Leisure Centre in Newton Cross, but it wasn't the same as the being in the sea.

In the garden room Jake said, 'Ha! Beat you at last!' He laid down his pool cue on the table. 'You're good, you're really good.'

'Yeah well I've had lots of time to practise,' Daniel answered, his grin making light of the words.

Jake sat in the armchair facing the sea as both boys watched the yachts passing by on the tide, then Daniel said, 'So how are things at home now? Any better?'

His friend shook his head. 'Not really. It's not going to be too bad this weekend though because

Wilson has gone up to London. He said it was something to do with work but I don't believe him. In fact I don't believe a word he says now.'

'You really don't like him, do you? What's he done to make you feel like that?'

'Oh, you know, he's full of himself, thinks he's God's gift. That's not all though, it's what he's like at home is the problem. When he's out talking to people he's charming and wants to know all about the person he's talking to. But when he's with us he spends most of his time up in his loft room and hardly any with mum and me. I've tried to show some interest in his hobbies. The other night, when there was a full moon, I even asked if I could have a look at it through his telescope. Guess what he said?'

Daniel shrugged.

'He said, "No. Definitely not! And I don't want you going up to that room when I'm not around either." He was angry, really angry, in fact I saw my mother give him such a look! Then, he said, all sickly sweet like, "It's just, well… you know, it's an expensive piece of equipment and I've got private things up there for work so I'll be locking it up from now on."

Jake turned to his friend. 'Is it me? Or d'you think that's a bit odd?'

Daniel thought for a bit' 'Not really, he could be telling the truth. Perhaps it *is* just work stuff and he doesn't want you to go nosing about.'

'Yeah, well anyway, I just don't like him. I can't wait for mum to dump him.'

'Think there is any likelihood of that happening, do you?'

'Your guess is as good as mine. But, they don't sleep together you know. Oh, yeah, they go upstairs and make a big thing of going into their 'supposed' bedroom together. But I got up the other night, couldn't sleep, and I heard the sound of snoring coming from the loft. So I crept up the stairs and listened outside the door and it was definitely him.'

Daniel raised an eyebrow. 'Perhaps they'd just had a tiff? I know my mum storms into the spare bedroom sometimes, if my Dad's snoring gets too bad or she's mad at him for something. Might be nothing at all.'

Jake sighed. 'You've got a point, Dan. Especially as I never thought there was any chance they'd get together in the first place. So, what do I know? But, the other night was really odd listen to this....'Jake took a deep breath. 'He's supposed to be a gardener, right? So what could he possibly have up there that is so secret? Unless of course he's growing cannabis plants up in the loft.'

Daniel began to laugh. 'You're hoping,' he said. 'Now, are you going to give me a chance to beat you this time?'

'Yeah, go on then,' Jake said, picking up his pool cue.

Number 7
Molly, the cleaner.

CHAPTER 34

Thinking about it now, the last time she'd seen him had been on the cliff path. Molly ineffectually flicked a duster over the top of a side table. She'd been meaning to confront him to let him know his pretence of not knowing her, wasn't working. But as he'd talked about the weather, the neighbours and how lucky he was to be living in Seabeach Close, she'd decided to take another tack altogether and approach it from a different angle.

Now she was convinced it had been the right decision. Bringing up the past could only get her into trouble. Playing him at his own game was the way to tackle this situation. After all, she had her job to think of and she wasn't exactly dripping in money that she could afford to lose it. And, definitely not for the likes of Ethan Brady!

Nevertheless, she would have to be careful. He was capable of ruining everything for her. He needed watching. But, where Elis Williams came into it all was a mystery. He was a cop in a small town and people like 'the new neighbour' in Seabeach Close usually wouldn't come under his radar, unless…

Sitting down on the window seat Molly thought, as far as Elis was concerned, he would only think she'd just gone up to the big city looking for fame and fortune when she was little more than a kid and had come back when she'd realised it was never going to happen, and that was all there was to it. Why would he ever think differently? But somehow she had to stop Brady talking to Charles Frazer and spoiling things. Frazer had not only let her 'clean' this place but there was the other job she'd been doing for him and between them both she was doing okay financially. She'd spent years trying to forget what went on in Ward's club and now all of a sudden, like a bad penny, Ethan had turned up and was living opposite the house where she was working. Was it just a coincidence? Ha! She thought, she definitely didn't believe in coincidences, especially where he was concerned.

Putting down her duster and peering through the window at number eight, Molly sighed. She hadn't seen him for a few days. His wife…she stopped…that was a laugh - his so-called wife and her son were in the house. She'd seen them earlier. They'd looked as if they'd been to the village shopping as they were holding supermarket carrier bags. But where *was* he? She needed to have it out with him or she'd go crazy.

Molly stood up and glanced at the clock, then came to the conclusion she'd done enough cleaning for the day. In her opinion the place was spotless anyway. Cleaning number seven was a doddle, which she usually spun out for form sake, not wanting to appear as if she was an unnecessary expense in Frazer's eyes.

In the kitchen she stubbed out her last cigarette in the sink and washed the ash away. Then, slipping the stub into her pocket she sprayed air freshener around the kitchen, just in case any of the Fraser clan decided to pay an unexpected visit, then, satisfied that her job was done, Molly walked outside and into the warm morning air.

The new occupant of the house next door, a young woman with wavy, shoulder-length fair hair, was getting out of her car and struggling with a shopping bag and a loaf of bread tucked under her arm. As she tried to point the car key fob at the lock Molly saw the bread slide from her grasp to the floor and land at her feet. Bending down she picked it up and handed it back to the woman.

'Thanks a bunch. Lazy man's load, that's me all over,' the woman said, with a smile. 'Are you my next-door neighbour by any chance?'

Molly chuckled. 'Fat chance. I'm just the cleaner, love. I'm Molly. Settling in okay, are you?'

'Yes thanks. I'm Laura,' the young woman replied. 'Don't suppose you'd fancy joining me for a drink? I'm bushed and longing for cup of tea. Besides, it would be nice to get to know you, especially as I'm new to the area. Maybe you could fill me in on a few things, so I don't go putting my foot in it with the neighbours.'

Molly wasn't sure why she'd agreed quite so quickly, but followed Laura inside number five, thinking she was probably just trying to be friendly and perhaps feeling a bit lonely after having just moved in. And, as she had nothing to do except clean her own place, she'd replied, 'Yeah, I'd like that.'

There was always the possibility that in the future she might be of some use to her, especially where keeping an eye on Ethan was concerned. You just never knew when it might come in handy, especially, as she was permanently living in full view of number eight. Although, she'd just have to play it cool for a while, maybe, get to know her a bit first?

'Why don't we sit in the back garden?' Laura said, opening the French doors. 'It's such a lovely day. Make yourself comfortable and I'll bring the drinks out. Actually, let's skip the tea. I've got a bottle of Chardonay chilling in the fridge. What d'you say? Not driving are you?'

Molly began to relax. She had a feeling she was going to like Laura, so perhaps it would be good to get to know her after all. 'No, I'm not driving. I live in the village, and thanks the wine would be good.'

They were on their second glass when Laura began to ask about the neighbours. She said she was hoping to get to know them one by one but wondered if

Molly could give her a quick rundown of who lived where.

'Well, I suppose I know most of them now,' Molly said, giving her a brief description of each inhabitant of The Close, until she reached number eight. She couldn't wait to see what Laura's reaction would be.

When she'd finished, she waited but Laura's expression didn't change as she said, 'Oh, yes, I think I've seen the guy who lives there. But then you couldn't really miss him, could you?'

Molly realised Laura was waiting for a response from her. But she'd quickly changed the subject and chatted for a while longer and then drained her glass and stood up. 'Right, it's time I got going. So, thanks for the drinks, Laura. It was nice to meet you. See you again soon I expect.'

'Certain of it,' Laura said. 'Besides, we could go for a spot to eat next time, if you're up for it?'

Walking down The Close, Molly took a deep breath. She hadn't been able to do it, she couldn't ask Laura about him, she didn't want her to think she was interested in him, not at the moment, possibly not ever. She'd even been about to confess their shared past. What a mistake that would have been. It must have been the wine and the fact that Laura was the sort of person who made you feel like confiding in her. But sense had returned just in time before she'd opened up a box which should stay firmly shut. Her mind was in a turmoil. What on earth had she been thinking? There was only one person she should talk to, one person who could give her the reassurance she needed. She had to have it out with him.

Leaving The Close behind her, Molly took the route through the village until she reached home. She'd inherited her house, which was in the middle of a row of terraced properties which had originally been built as fishermen cottages. Her grandfather had owned it first and left it to her mother who'd left it to her. It was a roof over her head and one which she owned but that was about all you could say for it. The place was run down and needed work to bring it into the twenty-first century. The bathroom had been added when her grandfather was alive and was stuck onto the back kitchen like a decaying limpet. The roof leaked when the wind was in the wrong direction, and there were roof tiles missing which made the back bedroom damp. It was nothing like the property in Seabeach Close, nothing at all!

She decided to forget about cleaning it, she'd done enough cleaning for today. Molly changed her clothes and planned to take a walk on the seafront in the hope she would bump into Ethan. She still couldn't get using the name Wilson. But as fate would have it she saw him coming out of the newsagents at the corner of her road, just as she was about to close her front door.

She waited, and seeing him getting nearer, Molly walked straight up to him, before he could turn away. 'We need to talk, and right now,' she said, firmly.

The London Trip.

CHAPTER 35

It was Friday morning. The coach was waiting for them at the junction of Market Street and Redbank Road. Gwyneth kissed her father and thanked him for taking care of the twins who were now walking to school with their best friend and her mother. Emlyn waited as Ian took the case from the boot and after they had both waved to him he started up the car and drove back into the traffic.

Ian placed their case in the loading area and followed his wife to their seat. Gwyneth breathed a sigh of relief and gripped his hand.

'We really needed this break, love. It seems ages since we've had a chance to be alone. I love Dad and the kids to bits but for the next couple of days I'm going to concentrate on my lovely husband.'

Ian kissed her cheek and the mood was set for the trip. The Courier, a short, elderly man with a shiny bald head and wearing an apron, was eager to get them all seated so he could hand out the breakfast buns and drinks.

'Right everybody, now you've all got your breakfasts, we'll be off. My name's Gordon and our driver for today is Bleddyn. We'd like to welcome you aboard Tomlyn's Ticket Tours and hope you enjoy your weekend with us.'

Gordon removed his apron, folded it neatly and stored it under his seat then standing in the aisle, microphone in hand, he began to list their itinerary for the weekend which was interspersed with asides which provoked a few titters from the passengers. At one point Ian whispered, 'I thought he was about to break into song.' And, after they stopped Gordon continued to advise his captive audience about the many shows London had to offer and for which most of them had tickets.

'It'd like to point out that Dame Shirley Bassey is at the Palladium this weekend but if any of you are thinking of last minute bookings…forget it. Unless of course you want to queue for returns. It's one of her rare performances these days…all for charity, mind you…love her.' He took a deep breath, his eyes filming over with nostalgic tears as he continued, 'I saw Shurl back in the seventies in Cardiff, before she was a Dame. And, I have to tell you, she's fantastic live. WHAT a performer! I know some of you have been lucky enough to have tickets in the draw. I only wish I'd been so lucky! Right, I'm going to sit down now and if you have any questions just shout out my name and I'll answer them, if I can.'

'Did you notice that the Barkers are sitting in the front seat?' Ian said.

'I did. I saw Alice in the Ladies when we were in the services and she asked me what show we were going to see. I wonder what our hotel will be like?'

'From what I've heard they're all pretty good so I'm sure ours won't be an exception, love. We'll just have to wait and see where it is.'

Once again entrapped in Gordon's world, they were at his mercy until they reached the drop off point outside their hotel.

Arriving, at the Bridge Hilton at midday on the dot, was a feat in itself, traffic having been heavy on the way into the city. The hotel was situated, as its name implied, near London Bridge and Ian and Gwyneth were fortunate enough to discover they had a room overlooking The Thames.

'Just look at that view, love,' Ian said, standing at the window. 'If we'd booked this on our own it would have cost us double.'

After unpacking and a short rest, they walked out of the hotel and strolled around Saint Catherine's Dock, stopping at a bar to drink wine sitting at a table outside in the sunshine. All thoughts of Seabeach Close were placed firmly behind them. They'd already checked in with Emlyn to made sure their girls were fine and could now relax and enjoy themselves.

The afternoon passed at a leisurely pace and at a quarter to seven their coach arrived to take them to the theatre. Having enjoyed the show, much to their surprise, as it was Cinderella, the only one available at short notice, they sat back in their seats and were driven back to their hotel at the end of a very pleasant evening.

Later, while relaxing in the lounge drinking coffee laced with brandy, they saw Alice and Norman Barker at a nearby table.

'Enjoy the show?' Norman asked.

'We did,' Gwyneth replied. 'What did you go to see?'

'The Mousetrap. We've seen it before, but ages ago so we'd forgotten who was the murderer.' Alice replied.

'By the way, this afternoon we took a taxi up to Covent Garden and who d'you think we saw?' Norman said, and without waiting for a reply, went on, 'Ted's wife was sitting with a couple of young men. They were listening to the Opera singers. We didn't like to interrupt them, as they were chatting, so we just waved but I don't think she'd noticed us. Seems like half of Seabeach Close is up here this weekend, I saw Elis Williams earlier too.'

In their bedroom the following morning, Gwyneth yawned and stretched out a hand but her husband was standing at the window watching the boats on the river. She took the opportunity to admire his sun-tanned, naked body. His strong shoulders and firm buttocks giving her a warm feeling of contentment. It wasn't just that she was looking forward to him joining her for a session of morning love-making, which at no point ran the risk of being interrupted by the twins, it was because she loved every bit of him, even the fine grey hairs which were starting to thread through his thatch of dark hair.

He turned towards her as if somehow knowing what she was thinking and crossing the floor in two long strides was in bed alongside her.

Afterwards, Ian propped himself up on his elbow and drawing a finger slowly down her cheek said, 'Ah, that was just great sweetheart. I'd forgotten what it was like to let yourself go without worrying about the kids or your dad hearing us.' He sighed. 'We must do this again. I'm sure Emlyn wouldn't mind looking after the girls for us to take the odd break now and then, especially as they're older and not babies anymore.'

Gwyneth's murmured reply was smothered by his chest, as he drew her to him.

Their plan for the morning had been to stop off at Covent Garden before spending the afternoon sightseeing and enjoying a leisurely evening. So, after taking a quick shower and dressing, they left their Hotel watching The Thames sparkling in the sunshine as they headed towards the taxi rank.

A short while later, stepping out of the taxi, Gwyneth took Ian's hand and steered him towards the market stalls. 'We need to get something for the girls and Dad,' she said, seeing a stall selling coloured bead necklaces and bracelets to match. Choosing a set for each of the twins, in different colours to avoid arguments, Gwyneth watched as the assistant packed them carefully in tissue paper and placed them into two separate tiny pink cardboard carriers.

'What about this for Em?' Ian asked, stoping at a counter displaying hand-painted mugs. He'd picked up one which read *World's Best Gardener* on the front.

When they'd finished shopping they made their way to a coffee bar and sat watching the entertainers. After a while Gwyneth said, 'Hey, isn't that Ted's wife sitting with those young guys? She must love coming here. Didn't Norman say he saw her here yesterday afternoon?'

'Mmm, this Danish is good. Where did you say you saw her?' Ian replied, shedding crumbs into his lap.

She looked over his shoulder and said, 'Er, not sure, either she's gone or I must have been mistaken.'

'I think their son lives up here, so you could be right. Perhaps she was with him,' Ian replied.

'Oh, I forgot to mention I thought I saw the chap that's moved into number eight, earlier too. It was when you were looking at those shirts and I left you to buy the drawing of Hampton Court for Phyllis. So you see I must be going slightly dippy. I'm imagining seeing everyone from Seabeach Close. You can tell I don't get out that often.' Gwyneth laughed.

'You're right, cariad. And, I'll have to make amends and take you out on the town more often! It's a promise.'

Tucking her arm through his, she said, 'Anyway, I hope your sister is going to love what I bought her, even if I was seeing things at the time!'

'And you hadn't even started on the wine, so that's no excuse,' Ian said, with a smile. 'Thinking of a glass of red, shall we have one in the wine bar before lunch?'

The rest of the day went as they'd planned and in the evening they ate at a restaurant overlooking the river before returning to their room to once more enjoy a session of uninterrupted lovemaking.

The next morning being Sunday most of the shops were shut until nearly mid-day. So after a quick lunch they joined the others in the foyer of the hotel as the rest of the afternoon was spent on the coach for a sightseeing trip around the city prior to their return journey home.

Gordon was in full flow explaining every place of interest they passed and even though Gwyneth found it difficult to keep her eyes open after the wine they'd drunk at lunch, she was amazed at his depth of knowledge and the amusing tales he spun to entertain his audience.

'Frustrated actor, if you ask me,' Ian muttered, looking out of the window.'

They stopped at a tea shop in Windsor and then wandered round the town until it was time to meet up again on the coach for the journey back to Wales. On the way home Ian fell into a doze so Gwyneth chatted to Alice Barker about the weekend and what they'd bought at the market.

At the bridge, someone at the back of the coach started to sing the chorus of *Guide me oh though great Jehovah,* which was soon taken up by anyone who knew the words regardless of whether they could carry a tune or not, as they crossed the border back into Wales.

Emlyn was waiting for them as the coach drew into the drop off point at Oysterbend. But Gwyneth could see his expression was grim as they drove away.

'What is it Dad?' she asked, 'are the girls okay? You said Phyllis was looking after them?'

'They're fine,' he replied, and said nothing more until he drove into Seabeach Close and stopped outside their house. Then, cutting the engine, Emlyn said, 'I think there's something you both should know.'

The Middle
Back then

CHAPTER 36

Charlie: Thirty three years ago

Miles and Ellen Roach, my parents, were unable to have children. It was the reason they adopted me when I was three months old. I grew up in a large house in Surrey, being an over-indulged, spoilt and very-much loved child, I had everything I could possibly want. My adopted father, an engineer, was wealthy and couldn't wait to spend time with me at weekends or as often as he could during the week. He was the head of a thriving engineering company which he'd created years before I was born. At weekends I'd help him to polish his classic cars, which he kept in a large garage near the house, and generally made myself useful in spite of still being quite young.

Sometimes, he'd take me into work with him and explain how the complicated machinery worked. So, over the years I learned how to please my father by being interested in everything he had to show me and I was a quick learner. As I grew he continually praised me, making me feel how much he loved and was proud of me. It was an idyllic childhood, at least… at first…before *he* came.

Seabeach Close   K.J.Rabane

I was eight when I overheard a conversation between my parents. They'd seemed excited. I could hear their laughter as I entered the conservatory. The topic of their conversation was something they couldn't wait to share with me. Their enthusiasm was infectious and I began to think that maybe my father had bought the electric car which we'd seen in the showroom. It was nearly my birthday, perhaps it was that. I know he'd said it wasn't suitable because it was for an older child as it had a real engine and not one you pedalled with your feet, but I hadn't ruled it out as a possibility.

'Come here, Charlie,' my mother said, when she saw me standing in the doorway. 'There's something we want to tell you.' She was still holding my father's hand as they both came towards me and encircled me in their arms. I remember that feeling now, it was just the three of us in our own, safe little world. And, it was the last time I would ever feel like it again.

My mother tilted up my chin, her blue eyes sparkling with delight, as she said, 'You're going to have a little brother to play with soon, Charlie. I don't suppose you remember your uncle John and your aunt Nancy. They had a son called Harrison and they lived in a place called Perth in Australia. It's a long complicated story but they died and as we were their nearest relatives…well, Harrison is coming to live with us.' She was smiling down at me. 'In fact we've known about it for a while but there were details to be finalised before we could tell you for sure. Anyway, everything has been completed and we've just heard that he should be arriving tomorrow.' She bent down to kiss my cheek. 'He's two years younger than you but still big enough to play games with. So I'm sure you'll have lots of fun together. I hope you're going to take good care of him. He's no one except us.'

I didn't know whether to be upset or pleased, part of me wanted to have someone to play with but part of me was afraid they'd loved him more than me.

'We know it's been a bit of a shock for you,' my father said, putting a hand on my shoulder. 'But we couldn't tell you until all the arrangements were made. You see we didn't want you to be disappointed if it didn't come off.'

'Is he going to stay, just for a bit?' I asked hopefully. But this was greeted with laughter and they both replied at once, 'No! He'll be staying with us forever. He's going to be your new little brother, Charlie.'

In bed that night I wondered what he would look like and whether I'd like him. I glanced around my bedroom and wondered if he would mess up my toys or want to play in my treehouse. It was mine, just mine. After all, Dad had made it specially for me. That night I dreamt about Harrison. In my dream he made a mess of everything and, in my dream, my parents loved him more than me. When I woke up, I wiped away my tears with the sleeve of my pyjamas, sat up in bed and decided that, as I was going to be the oldest child in this family, *I* would set the rules for what he could and couldn't do.

He arrived just after lunch the following day. I saw the car pull into our drive. I was in my treehouse … waiting. A short, plump lady was holding his hand and then I saw her give his suitcase to my father.

My new 'brother' was tall and thin…even taller than me and I'm the tallest in my class and two years older than him. His hair was fair, almost white, and he wore glasses with thick lenses so you couldn't see his eyes properly. I decided right there and then I didn't like the look of him. He didn't look right.

'Charlie,' my father called out when he saw me peeping. 'Come down and say hello to your new brother.'

Reluctantly, I did as I was told. I can still remember the feel of his hand in mine as my father insisted we shake hands and introduce ourselves. To be fair he looked as awkward as I did. 'I'm Charlie,' I muttered as I took my hand away and wiped it on my jeans.

His voice was high-pitched like a girl's. 'I'm Harrison,' he said. 'But you can call me Harry if you like.'

I didn't like, in fact I didn't like it at all. I didn't want him here. I didn't want him sharing my parents. I was happy on my own.

But he stayed. And it was exactly as I'd feared. My mother made a big fuss of him. She called him delicate and said we would all have to be very careful not to upset him. He was given the bedroom next to mine, which was a relief. At least he wasn't sleeping in mine. I'd been afraid they'd put another bed in my room, as it was definitely big enough. After we were both put to bed that night, I heard my mother and father talking. So, I opened my bedroom door and crept along the landing to listen.

'He's had such a bad time,' my mother said. 'Poor boy, I had to cradle him to sleep like a baby. He's so fragile.'

'Don't worry, love. We'll take care of him now. I don't think Charlie knew quite what to make of him though, but I'm sure they'll get on once they get used to each other.'

'I hope so. It will be difficult for Charlie, having to share things for a bit, but I agree I'm sure they'll be good for each other.'

'I tell you what.' My father's voice was soft, as if he were trying to comfort my mother, like he did with me if I was upset about something. 'I'll take them fishing on Saturday when you're visiting your mother. You can tell her the news in person before we all drive over to see her next week.'

'I will, love, but she'll forget it the minute I leave the nursing home. It might confuse her as she's even starting to forget we've got Charlie now. But taking them fishing will be a start. Maybe you could both show Harrison how to tie a fly properly?'

I was cross. I wanted to go with my dad on my own. I always loved it when he took me fishing. Now we had to drag Harrison along with us. It wasn't fair!

The day started badly. It was raining. Not enough that we could pack up and go home, just a fine drizzle, the type that got you just as wet as if it had been a downpour. As Dad piled the fishing gear into the Land Rover, Harrison didn't say much, not even when we drove through the woods and could see the river. He only spoke when Dad spoke to him. So, I ignored him and looked out of the window. He just sat there, his pale eyes blinking behind his spectacles. I decided, there and then, that he wasn't much good as a brother,

Dad and I usually spent half an hour threading the flies and putting them onto the rods. But today was different. He began by taking Harrison aside and showing him all the things which were special to us, while I just stood waiting, drizzle dripping from the hood of my jacket into my eyes. And that was only the start of it. All through the day I felt left out, as my father continued to praise every little thing Harrison did. I didn't like it. I didn't like it one bit.

Then, he started to call him Harry, so I made a point of never calling him anything but Harrison. I know it might sound childish, but then I *was* only a child. Nobody seemed to realise it though. They expected me to make of fuss of him but he was a stranger and the longer he lived with us the stranger he got in my opinion.

I suppose that day by the river was when my feeling of antagonism towards this cuckoo in the nest first began. Afterwards, I did my best to make him look foolish in my parents eyes but they were sympathetic and if anything it made them even more focused on him. As the years passed and I realised he wasn't going anywhere soon, I became more skilled at making him the fall guy and removing any possibility that I'd been involved in doing so.

He was a clever boy, but I was cunning. It occurred to me that my Dad seemed to have forgotten how clever I was, in favour of praising Harrison's academic achievements at length. I didn't want to go to university and neither of my parents appeared to be bothered but when I left school and started work as an apprentice electrician my mother thought it was entirely unsuitable and kept trying to persuade me to change my plans. But I ignored her. It was my choice.

When Harrison passed his exams to go to university, life at home became almost unbearable. He was the golden boy, the favoured one. They fussed around him, my mother getting his 'stuff' ready for University, my father telling his friends how proud he was of Harry. It was endless, Harry this, Harry that. During the weeks before he was due to start at Durham University I decided something had to be done about it.

Seabeach Close   K.J.Rabane

And then there was the car accident and Harrison was injured so badly that he never did go to Durham.

I'd hoped things would change then, after the accident I mean, but it was worse. All my parents' time was spent fussing over him as he needed special care because he couldn't walk. I didn't understand why they were making such a fuss. It wasn't as if they hadn't got a nurse to take care for him. It was all about him and it seemed my needs were totally forgotten in the scheme of things.

Then disaster struck. My dad's company went into liquidation and he was left facing bankruptcy. The house I'd grown up in was sold. We moved into a small terraced house on a housing estate where drugs were sold on every street corner and unemployment was rife. So, I offered to take over caring for Harrison.

After he died I had to gradually watch my parents health deteriorate and felt helpless to make things better for them. Because, in spite of their lack of attention to me since Harrison had come to live with us, I still loved them, which was basically the reason why I'd done it to Harrison in the first place.

Then, after their death, the house had to be sold and the proceeds, which weren't much were left to me. At first I moved into a rented flat in Gouge Street. From my bedroom window I had a view of the Post Office Tower, like a gigantic spaceship hovering on the horizon and from my kitchen all I could see were

Seabeach Close   K.J.Rabane

the druggies and their pushers hanging about in the lane. Nevertheless, it was a short walk to the small company where I now worked as an electrician.

One afternoon, I was taking my lunch break in a café which was near my latest job. As, I drank my tea and ate my meal the place began to fill up.

'Is this chair taken?' Someone asked, and looking up I shook my head as our eyes met. And that was our first meeting. How was I to know then it would change my life for ever?

Ten years ago

CHAPTER 37

Ethan

Looking out of the grimy window into the street below, I stretched my arms above my head and yawned.

'Well, you've really landed in it this time,' I muttered as I watched the druggies huddled in the doorway opposite and the rubbish from the Chinese takeaway blowing about in the gutter.

I'd checked my phone as soon as I'd woken up. There were no new messages, so it was business as usual. I wondered how long this was going to last before I could finish it. I couldn't expect Ash to wait around forever. I'd promised faithfully that this would be my last time but fate had a way of intervening and turning that promise into a lie.

When I'd agreed to do this job I hadn't known how much time it would involve. I should have said no from the start. But I didn't really have much of a choice. I knew it would only have gnawed away at me like a rabid dog, until I'd agreed. Ash would have to understand if we were to stay together. We'd agreed that after this time, we'd talk about it, sort it out properly. But, this was my life and there would no doubt be more of this type of stuff in the future. I should never have agreed to make it my last time. Ash would just have to accept it. I felt the rush of adrenaline spiking through me at the thought of what was to come. Stepping into the shower I washed away all traces of last night from my body. I could still smell her perfume lingering in the air long after she'd gone to work and left me to sleep in the flat which wreaked of last-night's takeaway. I dreaded the thought of sex with her but realised my excuses were wearing thin.

Wiping away a patch of steam from the bathroom mirror I sighed with resignation. Then I heard my mobile buzzing on the windowsill and checking the screen saw it was a message from Drew. I read it and pressed the delete button. Then I opened the back of the phone and removed the Sim card. After rubbing my hair dry with a towel I slid the Sim into a compartment in the heel of my shoe, replacing it with the original. Satisfied all was in order and slipping into a pair of jeans and a white tee-shirt, then pulling my denim jacket from the hook behind the door and taking a quick glance in the mirror, I spiked up my hair with gel, and left the flat.

The beard had been Ash's idea. And I had to admit it did the trick. I was almost unrecognisable from my clean-shaven self. It was too early for the usual meeting in the bar of the *Moody Pig* so we'd arranged to meet in a café at the corner of the street a short distance from the flat.

Sitting at a table away from the window, I waited.

'What can I get you, love?' asked a middle-aged waitress smelling of cigarette smoke and body odour. She stood in front of me and sniffed, her black-circled eyes speaking of a lack of sleep or a habit, both of which were signs I could recognise only too well.

'Coffee, black, no sugar,' I replied, and seeing Drew walking towards me, added, 'and a pot of tea for my mate.'

He looked as if he'd been up all night, his sallow skin appearing yellow in the harsh morning light. What little hair he had stood on end like a porcupine. He rubbed at his eyes, and yawned, as I said, 'So, what's up?'

We waited until the woman arrived with our order and when she left, Drew replied, 'Tonight - half-eleven - the warehouse on Baker's Row.'

'Understood.'

'Thought you might need this,' he added.

'O…kay,' I replied slowly, as he slid a carrier bag towards me. Feeling its weight I pushed it onto my lap. 'Yeah, got the message. At least I won't have to run the risk of her seeing it before tonight.'

Leaving Drew still sitting in the cafe, I walked to the corner shop where I bought a woman's magazine, a newspaper and a six-pack of beer. These I piled into the carrier on top of the revolver. She'd be working at the bar until the lunchtime rush was over. Then I knew she'd get her head down for an hour or two before her night shift began at Ward's club, where she'd be dancing until the early hours, leaving me to do my job uninterrupted by her constant questioning.

It was obvious I'd have to spend the early evening in bed with her, if only to make absolutely certain she wouldn't go poking around the place before she left for work later. I groaned at the thought, knowing there was no alternative. It had to be done and the sooner the better. I couldn't risk her getting suspicious and ruining things.

After opening the front door of the flat, I removed the cans of beer from the carrier, placed the magazine on her bedside table and wrapping the newspaper tightly around the rag covering the revolver hid it under the mess I'd accumulated in my bedside table drawer.

A wave of anticipation swept over me at the thought of what I'd be facing in the early hours. We'd planned it down to last detail. But I knew there was always the chance it could go tits up and either way someone would meet his maker before the night was out. I just hoped it wouldn't be my turn.

Seabeach Close   K.J.Rabane

Ten years ago

CHAPTER 38

Emmy

Sitting on the bus heading for London and leaving Oysterbend far behind me, I'd felt excitement fizzing up inside like bubbles in a glass of champagne. I'd been longing to get away from the village where everyone knew what I was doing and those who didn't made it their business to find out. I was young and wanted a life of my own filled with fun and new experiences.

A guy I'd met on the beach a couple of weeks ago had said there were loads of jobs for a young girl like me in the city. I could have one in a cafe he owned, if I wanted to…or so he'd said.

Three years later, peering into the fly-blown mirror in the club's changing room, the overhead neon strip crackling with an unforgiving, harsh light, I saw the first faint lines of crow's feet appearing when I smiled, and wished I could turn back time to the optimism I'd felt on the bus leaving my home.

The guy on the beach hadn't owned the cafe of course. He just worked there clearing tables. There *was* a job for me but it was working for a pittance every hour of the day and came with a condition… that I slept with him. But that was then, and life was very different from the one I'd imagined just a couple of years ago. So, this was where I'd ended up, working at a club in Soho, covering the bar duties during the lunch hour and working as an 'exotic' dancer on stage until the early hours. At least I was making some money.

My figure wasn't bad, I was still young, my bust was firm and my hips well rounded so I couldn't see any of the clientele in the club being bothered by a few faint lines near my eyes. They hardly ever looked further up than my nipples anyway. I turned away from the mirror, took off my blouse, hung it on a peg, and dressed in just a G-String and mini-tasselled-bra, opened the door and walked into the passageway.

I could hear my music playing as I stepped up to the podium. Then draping my body around the pole I began my routine without lowering my eyes from a point on the ceiling. Seeing their leering faces wasn't an option tonight. I had other things on my mind than attracting their beady little eyes and hungry glances. The couple of quid they stuffed into my G-String was peanuts compared to what I was going to make in the future, if everything went to plan.

I'd never liked the name Molly, it reminded me of Nancy Thomas's mangy cat. And when I'd signed on at the club I'd used my initials M.E.Johnson. For some reason I'd been known as M.E. ever since. Ironic really, Emmy *was* ME, it sounded like me and now I had Ethan, I could begin to live the life I'd always wanted. I'd soon ditch this job. I sighed…it was just a matter of time.

There was something up tonight though. I could feel it in the air. And it wasn't just in the club either. Ethan had been unusually quiet earlier. It was as if he was nervous about something. He couldn't have found out about the shipment, not from me, anyway. I hadn't breathed a word. It was more than my life was worth. Besides, this was my way of getting out of this racket with enough money to spare. I'd been told the girls weren't due to arrive until tomorrow night. But I'd guessed Marcus and his mates were into something on the side. Obviously it was to do with drugs. What else could it be? Not satisfied with working for Ward they had to get involved in their little sideline. If Ward found out it would mean the end of them, in more ways than one.

I'd wanted to tell Ethan about the girls and the money I'd make but I'd hesitated. All I had to do was be there at the venue and coax them into not causing any trouble. Besides, Ethan must have known about Ward. Most people in this business knew. Ethan couldn't have been as blind as all that and would realise it was definitely not legit.

As I thought this over I realised Ethan was a bit of a mystery himself and although he'd never said it, I'd guessed he was in the same business as Ward or something similar. It was obvious by his conversation and the people he knew, none of them on the up and up. Although, lately I'd begun to wonder if something more serious was going on. He'd seemed cagey and on edge.

Even though we'd been together for a while, I'd never really known what he was thinking. I still couldn't figure him out completely. It had been part of his attraction at first but I was beginning to think it could all blow up in my face. Much as I was attracted to Ethan it was Ward who was going to help me get in a financial position to be able to escape from the seedier side of the city with money to spare.

I knew from experience what upsetting Haydn Ward involved. It had taken months for me to get around him so he could trust me with the girls. Being in a sleazy club most nights, and getting pawed over by the punters, was better than the alternative, which was working long hours in a café or being at the beck and call of a pimp. Although some would say that that's exactly what I *was* doing. But, I'd lived on the streets for a bit, after I left the cafe and knew what it was like. Now, I could afford the rent of the flat, eat some decent food and I'd been able to attract a man like Ethan, before a life on the streets had permanently robbed me of my looks.

I'd often wondered why he stayed when he could have had just about anyone. I'd asked him once but he'd just giving me that slow smile of his and shrugged. It wasn't really an answer but it was all I was likely to get. He'd always been a man of few words.

Making the best of a bad job had been something I'd been doing ever since leaving Oysterbend. I couldn't rely on Ethan to save me. Deep down I felt certain he would let me down like all the others. There was no one waiting to catch me if I fell in London. I only had myself and my wits to depend upon.

If what I'd heard about tomorrow night's operation was right I figured things were going to change big-time. I decided to forget trying to figure out what was wrong with Ethan. I'd take his mind off it when I got home. Although, if I thought about it, that was another thing. He hadn't been so keen to have sex with me lately. So, I knew something was definitely in the wind and whatever it was, it couldn't be anything good.

The night dragged on and I tried not to think about tomorrow night. Not thinking about it made it drift away, which was the only way I could handle what I was doing. But I knew not thinking about it didn't mean it wasn't going to happen. But, I argued to myself over and over again, if I didn't do it, someone else would. It would happen with or without me.

It seemed ages until a weak shaft of sunlight cracked through the dingy windows of the club. Ricky, the barman, turfed a lone punter out into the street and closed the door behind him. A stale smell of beer and weed wafted towards me as I waved to Ricky and took the side door leading into the alley. A short taxi ride later and I was putting my key into the front door of the flat.

In the bathroom, I stripped off my clothes, washed, and opened the bedroom door, trying not to wake him. But the room was empty, the bed hadn't been slept in, and there was no sign of Ethan.

CHAPTER 39

33 years ago

Charlie

It was a quarter past five and the light was beginning to fade when I saw a van stopping outside. I took a break and looked out. It had been a long day, I'd been working since half-six that morning in order to finish the job, but it was nearly done. As I watched, a figure emerged, opened the rear door of the van and lifted out an armful of pot plants. At last, I thought. I'd been told to expect the delivery, which was to add the final touches to the shop refit and was beginning to think the firm had let us down. Carrying the plants from the van into the front of the shop took a while and in the gathering gloom I thought I recognised the guy from the cafe, the one who'd shared my table recently. And, I was right.

When he'd finished unloading, he said, 'So, we meet again! All on your own, are you? How's it going, looks like you've nearly finished? Remember me? From the cafe the other day?'

So, many questions, which one did he want me to answer? The guy was a pain. 'Yeah, thought it was you. I'm just finishing off the wiring and that's it. The painter and the plumber have already knocked off.

Won't take me long though.' That covered them all, I decided, and it seemed to satisfy him.

'What about these plants though? Do you want me to put them around the place or should I leave them here? I could sort them out for you if you want. I've finished for the day and this is my last delivery.'

I was about to say, no the owner could do that in the morning, but then I thought…why not?

'Yeah, you could do, if it's no bother, mate.' Was, mate, an overkill? He wasn't my mate. What was I trying to prove?

'Right. You tell me where you want them and I'll make a start.'

It wasn't a world shattering exchange but, looking back, I suppose it was the beginning of it all. When we'd finished, I locked the shop up behind us and was about to go for my bus when he said, 'Do you wanna lift?'

'It's not far, it's Paddington but yeah, if you're going that way, okay, thanks.' I glanced at my watch. 'I've probably just missed the seven ten and don't feel much like walking after the day I've had.'

'What's your name then?'

'Charlie,' I said, getting into the van.

'O…kay. ' He frowned. 'Call me Birdy, most people do.'

Looking back, neither of us ever called each other the names we'd given then but they were significant as with those words our fate was sealed.

CHAPTER 40

10 years ago

Emmy

Somehow sleep must have come eventually. When I finally awoke it was to hear the usual sounds of the morning sliding in through the open window, carrying with them the smell of bacon frying from the cafe next door. I shivered, then pulled the window latch shut against the frosty morning air and the smell. The central heating in the flat was inadequate to say the least and at best only worked when it felt like it. Why hadn't Ethan shut the window when he went out last night and where on earth was he now?

My head was still pounding from the sound of last night's band whose amps had been loud enough to wake a corpse. Drinking black coffee in the small kitchen and swallowing a couple of painkillers, I wondered what was going on and why Ethan hadn't phoned to let me know what had happened to him. There had been no calls during the night and he hadn't left any voice or text messages either.

It was definitely odd. So, I rang him yet again but there was only the standard voicemail reply asking me to leave a message after the beep. So I left another message wondering why he'd been ignoring all the others. Beginning to feel the first fingers of fear prodding at my chest I waited, then cupped my hands around my mug to bring some warmth into them, but there was still no reply to my voicemail. Tying the edges of my inadequate robe together with the belt, I put the phone down on the table and was making for the bathroom and a hot shower when I heard a crash coming from somewhere on one of the lower floors. This was soon followed by the sounds of heavy footsteps running up the stairs. I tipped my head back and drank the last dregs of coffee, trying to blot out the noise, before a loud crack, like the door to my flat begin forced off its hinges, made me rush into the hallway. Three police officers in flak jackets stood in front of me, one holding a small battering ram of the type I'd seen being used in films, when there was a drugs raid in progress. Beginning to feel like I was somehow still dreaming and had become a character in one of those films, I gasped.

'Emmy Johnson?' One of them asked, holding up his ID.

I nodded, initially struck dumb by the shock, until anger made me shout, 'Christ! Did you have to break down my door? Couldn't you have just rung the bell?'

'Ignoring my question, he said, 'You're to come with us to the station. You're under arrest. We're taking you down for questioning.' The words made me shiver. There were so many things I needed to ask but could see it would be a waste of time to even try.

'Get dressed, and get a move on, now. We haven't got all day,' he said.

The rest of the morning blurred into me slipping on a pair of jeans and a sweater, grabbing a jacket and being pushed into the back of a police van, which was already occupied by a group of women, some of them looking vaguely familiar and others whom I knew from the club.

'It's a raid, luv,' the one who was nearest to me whispered, 'They bust into my place when I was in bed with a punter! I only just had time to pull on a couple of things over my thong, when they threw me in here. Do *you* know what's going on Emmy?'

Not a clue,' I lied, recognising her as Shanice, one of the strippers at Ward's club.

Trying to make sense of it all, I thought it must have been something to do with the shipment and the change of date. Great! Why had no one warned me about it? Was it because they'd decided my part would come later, when the girls were in the club? And, was Ethan's disappearance and not answering his phone something to do with it? My stomach did a quick somersault and I couldn't stop my hands from shaking. I had no ready answers and was beginning to fear the worst.

CHAPTER 41

Ethan

Haydn Ward had been arrested along with the rest of the crew. The girls had been bundled into the back of a police van and I knew by now Emmy must be with them. I supposed they would be spending the night in the cells and questioned the following day, but was doubtful if any of them knew exactly what was going on, except perhaps for Emmy. She'd been working for Ward for some time and was nobody's fool, so how much *did* she know and how much was just supposition? She'd never said a word to me, however much I'd try to nudge her into it. All I suspected was she was in with Ward big time.

Later, in the station, I was questioned, and when they'd finished, was taken to a cell. Realising the cooling off period for the girls would be standard procedure, I kicked up a fuss hoping I could make Emmy hear me. Loudly protesting my innocence and generally creating mayhem, I struggled as they marched me past the holding cells. It was important… I needed her to see me. I needed her to know I was here.

As things turned out, she was discharged before me, after the twenty-four hours were up, and later that same afternoon I entered the flat we shared to find her throwing her clothes into a suitcase on the bed.

'Hey Babe,' I said. 'What gives?'

'What gives? Are you serious?'

'Hey, it's okay. I'm here. They've got nothing on me.' Crossing the room and putting a hand on her arm to stop her ramming more clothes into the case, I turned her around to face me. I could feel her anger dispersing as she rested against my chest. So, I began stroking her hair. I needed to keep her sweet.

'I've had enough, Ethan,' she said, in a tone I'd not heard before. Emmy wasn't a quitter. 'I'm going home. Ma's sick and it's time. Besides, Ward is up to his neck in it now and I've had enough.' She looked up. 'The writing was on the wall ages ago and I should have gone home long before this.' She sighed. 'Getting arrested was definitely not what I'd had in mind when I'd agreed to it.'

Emmy slumped to sit on the edge of the bed and said, 'As far as I was concerned it was just taking care of the girls who'd arrived from abroad and who wanted to work but had no work visas. Ward told me it was just dodging a bit of red tape, when I'd begun to ask a few questions. And, like a fool I'd believed him and looked the other way! '

I could tell she was furious, not only with Ward but with herself. I couldn't let her go. She knew too much and it wasn't finished. She could ruin everything.

'You can't leave now. Let me come with you.' I was trying to think of a way to stop this from happening. But short of insisting, which would do no good at all, I had nothing left to use as a bargaining tool. 'So, what d'you say if we both go to Wales to see how your mother is and when you're satisfied she's okay we can come back?' I suggested, out of sheer desperation.

'I don't know.' She slumped back on to the bed, her shoulders drooping. 'Oysterbend is no place for you. It's too quiet. You'd hate it.'

'Come on Em, it can't be that bad,' I tried to make her laugh but she was having none of it so I changed tack. 'Besides, what would I do without you?' I took her hands in mine and sitting alongside her, tipped her chin up so our eyes met. I saw her waver. It had worked in the past and looked as if it was about to again. I breathed a sigh of relief. But I was mistaken. I'd misjudged the situation.

'I've had it with London, Ethan, the club and now Ward being held by the police. It's time to go. You know what he's like. If I wait, it will all start again.'

I could feel it slipping away from me. All the months of hard work, all the contacts, everything sliding through my fingers like water from a tap.

'Don't forget there's your job to consider too, Babe.' I kissed the nape of her neck, her cheek and eventually her mouth.

'Stop it, Ethan,' she whispered breathlessly.

And I knew I'd won…at least for the moment. But maybe moving *would* be on the cards. I'd have to think about how to go about it. I'd have to make a few phone calls first. There was still so much to do in here. I'd have to see how it could all work out.

Charlie

CHAPTER 42

It was time for a move. We'd had it good up until now. We'd got on from the start Birdy and I, and sharing a flat had been a wise decision, prices in London being what they were at the time. There were always highs and lows in life but I knew he and I could make a go of living together.

We'd soon realised it could work out for us both work-wise too. He didn't interfere, he let me do my own thing and I didn't ask too many questions which suited him. And, on balance, it had worked just fine. But now we were facing a new challenge.

'It's up to you,' he said, with a smile. So, once again, I knew there would be no problem from him.

'It will be a change and hopefully for the better.' I said, thinking back to my childhood, before Harrison had spoiled it all. I'd had to make all the decisions then. It hadn't been easy but it had made me strong and it had shaped my future. I never did waste time thinking about what might have beens.

So, without a backward glance to the past we left our old life behind and headed for Brighton. It was the first step on a road which had ended with us finally deciding to retire and move to South Wales and the village of Oysterbend.

The Middle
now

Molly Johnson

CHAPTER 43

Bumping into him near my house had been unexpected for both of us. I'd been thinking how to tackle him about the lies and our shared history when I'd seen him walking towards me. From his expression he'd seemed surprised too and I was sure, from past experience, he was busy trying to think up a story which would be laced with more lies. I could see it in his eyes as Ethan gave his fake smile and slipped beneath the skin of Henry Wilson.

'Inside,' I said firmly, taking a key from my purse and opening my front door. Wondering whether he'd follow me or carry on with the charade and continue to walk towards the promenade, I turned around. But he was already passing me in the passageway and heading for the front room. When he spoke his whole demeanour had changed.

'Okay, okay Emmy, keep your hair on.'

Hearing him call me by the name I'd used in Ward's club only strengthened my determination to have it out with him immediately. There would be no more hiding from the truth. He sat in an armchair, stretched his long legs across the rug and with a sigh, said, 'Right then… spit it out, before it chokes you.'

So, I thought, let him have it, don't hold back girl. But first I had to calm down or I'd be lost. Turning away from him I stood near the window and watched as grey clouds gathered over the bay. Then before I could speak, I traced the path of a stray raindrop, sliding down the windowpane, with my fingertip.

At last I was ready, so facing him, I said, 'I'm not sure what you're up to this time but you and I both know you're living a lie. There's no way you're married with a family. I know that for a fact! I don't want to hear about what you've got yourself into or why you've arrived in Oysterbend, except to make you understand, whatever it is, I don't want any part of it.'

He raised his eyebrows and stared at me. His dark eyes dragging me in as they'd done all those years ago. But I was older now and wasn't so easily fooled. 'All I want is for you to keep your nose out of my business.' I said. 'I've started a new life here, leaving what happened back then far behind me. But if Charles Fraser gets even a sniff of my former life then everything will change.' I took a deep breath and without raising my voice, added, 'and if that happens your life will change too Ethan Brady, because I won't keep quiet, believe me!'

'So threats now, is it Emmy?' His voice was light, almost as if it were a joke.

My anger was rising, my pulse racing. 'My name is Molly. You'd be well advised to remember it if you want me to keep quiet. Emmy no longer exists. I left her in London along with you!' There was so much more I could have said but decided enough was enough…at least for now. The rest would come later if he couldn't be trusted to keep to his side of the bargain.

'Yeah, yeah, I get the message.' It was said with an air of resignation, which at least rang true.

'So we understand each other?'

'We do.'

'How do I know I can believe you? If the past is anything to go by, it will be a stretch.' My voice still had an edge to it. I had to make certain he knew I was determined to carry out my threat.

'I think you know me better than that?' His eyes never left mine. 'Besides, why would I try to make things bad for you? What happened back then was a long time ago. As far as I'm concerned it's forgotten…dead and buried. We've both moved on.'

His words made me shiver and I wrapped my arms around my body in an attempt to calm down. When I spoke the words didn't reflect what I was feeling inside but I think it worked. 'Ha! Not that long ago, and I've got a good memory. You'd do well to remember it, if you know what's good for you. But as long as we understand each other, then this conversation never happened. And, don't forget I know about Ash too! So, you don't know me and I don't know you, except that you happen to live in the house opposite where I work.'

As, he closed the door behind him, I leaned back against it my heart rate slowing. *Could* I trust him? I didn't really have a choice. There was no workable alternative as far as I could see. My only hope was that he'd stick to his word. Although, I still couldn't quite get the question of what he was doing in Oysterbend out of my head, or why he'd used a fake identity? If the past was anything to go by, you could bet your life…whatever it was…it wouldn't be anything good. But, I'd made it quite clear to him and all I could hope for was that he didn't try to involve me in any of it. I'd been down that road once before and had no intention of travelling it again.

When I was alone my thoughts spiralled like a pebble in a whirlpool. There was still the fact that I felt uncomfortable being in such close proximity to Brady whenever I went to work. I also lived only a short distance away from Seabeach Close and knew I couldn't avoid seeing him. Besides, I had to admit, in spite of knowing he was living a lie and that having a fake family was the biggest lie of them all, I was still physically attracted to him. It was impossible to forget the nights in my flat when I slid beneath the sheets and he'd been there, waiting for me.

Afterwards, thinking about it, I realised he'd just avoided directly answering most of my questions by turning on the charm and re-directing his replies. But it was some small comfort that he was now aware I had the ability to make things very difficult for *him* too.

Opening the small bottle of vodka I'd bought on my way home, I poured enough into a glass in order to stop my hands from shaking. It was the only way I could forget my previous history with Ethan Brady and to believe it wouldn't come back to haunt me.

CHAPTER 44

I sat on the rocks and watched the tide sliding towards me, like a gigantic sea serpent twisting it's way across the sand. It was nearly five o'clock and most of the locals had left to go home for tea. Only a few stragglers still hung about, stretching out their time on the beach until daylight shifted into twilight.

Felicity Fraser had been jogging along the shoreline earlier and I'd sketched an outline of her face. Now I added, from memory, the rest of her, running top, shorts and white trainers, hair tied back in a band. The twins and their grandfather had left some time ago and they too were in my sketch book. I'd spotted the three of them as they'd sat on the sand nearby. The girls busy building sandcastles in a circle around themselves as their grandfather read the paper. But even I could see that reading his paper was a subterfuge, as he never took his eyes off the girls for even a second.

The elderly couple, who lived in one of the bungalows opposite, had been sitting on the promenade for most of the afternoon but now they too were leaving. The stood and with a proprietary air hanging about them, walked away, as if that particular bench was their personal property.

Seabeach Close   K.J.Rabane

I'd taken a note of the how often they'd sat there, presumably to watch the world go by. But, I couldn't rule them out of the equation. It didn't do to make assumptions in this job.

All through history there'd been cases of serial killers, who'd appeared to be ordinary people to their acquaintances, not the monsters they actually were. I was determined not to discount anyone, no matter how insignificant they appeared, and would gently strip away the layers, until their true persona emerged.

The only local to remain, on the beach, was the woman who'd helped me with my car, not long after I'd moved in. She was still feeding the birds. I added a few extra details to my previous sketch of her, the carrier bag, the birds, and her long cotton skirt inflating around her in the breeze like a sail trying to catch the wind

As the seagulls swooped towards her it reminded me of a scene in a film where a young boy had made friends with a homeless woman who fed the birds in Central Park. But there the similarity ended as this woman was no vagrant. She had a trim figure and her pale blue skirt was topped by a tight fitting white tee-shirt. Her short fair hair had been expertly cut and was tucked behind her ears and her eyes were hidden by a pair of large, fashionable sunglasses. From where I sat it was difficult to determine her age. But before long she was joined by a middle-aged man whom I recognised as being her husband. They walked up the sand together until they reached the steps, and then stood and looked up at the roof of number eight, before climbing up and walking back into The Close.

As the sun began to sink lower on the horizon I decided to follow the couple and make my way back to number five. By the time I'd reached the steps myself Henry Wilson was standing at the top looking down at me. At last there was an opportunity to speak to him. I felt it was long overdue.

Taking the steps two at a time I hoped to catch his attention but just before I reached the top he turned away sharply and hurried in the direction of number eight. I wanted to call after him but decided against it. So, walking back to number five, with a growing sense of unease and wondering why he was trying to avoid me, I made a mental note to keep a closer eye on him. Something wasn't right about Henry Wilson. I'd thought it from the start and even though I'd mentioned it to Elis and he'd seemed to discount it, I was determined not to ignore my intuition.

Back inside the house, the windows were all closed and I felt the heat hit me as soon as I'd opened the front door. Taking the stairs to the first floor I cracked open the kitchen and living room windows. The breeze drifting throughout the house brought with it the tang of salt which was so strong I could almost taste it. Once more I realised how lucky I was to have been given this job and was able to live in a house such as this, even if it *was* only until the investigation was finalised.

After making a cup of tea and taking it to sit on the window seat in the living room, I picked up my sketch book and flicked though the pages until I came to the one where the image of Henry Wilson stared back at me.

Convinced, he was worth focusing on but not knowing to what degree, I stood up abandoning the window seat and went to sit on a chair facing the bungalow opposite. From here I was able to look out, without being seen, so it became the perfect viewpoint to observe the comings and goings of the neighbours.

Ted, who lived in number six, next door to the Wilsons, was stacking away a couple of deckchairs in his garage. As I watched I soon saw the door to number eight opening. Henry Wilson emerged, crossed his lawn and stood talking to his neighbour. From what I could tell he appeared to be keen to have a chat. So, why had he been so disinclined to connect with me?

Realising there could be a number of reasons, none of them being in the least bit suspicious, I drank the remains of my tea. Was I looking for trouble where none existed? Elis's words spun around in my ahead. Perhaps he was right and I was in danger of spending too much time on Wilson, at the risk of ignoring the rest of the neighbours. Opening my sketchpad and carrying it into the alcove where I kept my printer, I scanned the images into my laptop then set up a new file for each of them.

Charles Fraser

CHAPTER 45

Slamming the office phone down on my desk, I stroked my chin, thinking it was increasing likely that Ben had screwed up again. Admittedly it was only a small mistake this time but one which was becoming worrying. After he'd married Felicity, he'd seemed to be growing up at last. I'd sown a few wild oats myself when I was young and had indulged the boy after Grace died. Losing a mother at fourteen hadn't been easy for him.

Although, there was a pattern emerging here, which was bothering me and if I didn't know any better I'd say Ben was using again. But Joe Benson was keeping an eye on him and had been for a while now, and Joe had assured me that he wasn't visiting any of the known pushers on *his* radar, so it was unlikely.

Frustrated I stood up, wondering what *was* wrong…stress…marriage problems…overwork? Going in search of Ben, I found him sitting at his desk staring at his laptop screen. As I approached he closed the screen with a firm slap.

'Got a moment?' I asked, narrowing my eyes.

He gave me a forced smile. 'Sure, Pop. What is it?'

'I've been thinking and have come to the decision that you and the lovely Felicity should take a holiday before autumn sets in. In fact I've had a few ideas as to where you might like to go.'

'Nice thought, but too busy with the Bronteg development at the moment. Besides, we had our holiday at the beginning of April remember…the Caribbean?'

'Yeah, I know, I'm not senile yet, son. But I *am* the boss and what *I* say goes around here.' I chuckled to take the sting out of the words. 'And if *I* say you should take a holiday then that's what you should do. My advice is, take the offer now before I change my mind.'

Ben bit his lip and was about to repeat his earlier reply but seeing my expression thought better of it. 'Er, yes, thanks, but I'd have to check with Felicity.'

'Of course. Let me know if she's up for a spell in the Maldives.'

'The Maldives?'

'Remember Howard Clarke? He's got a holiday home there and it's yours if you want it. He usually spends the summer out there but he's getting over heart surgery and wants to stay put in this country for a while.'

'Er, I'm still not sure, Dad. I don't think I can just leave at a moment's notice. You know how things are.'

'Nonsense! Nothing we can't handle from this end. And I can always ring you if I need some advice. As I said, it will do you both good to get away. Let me know when it suits you and I'll get it all arranged. You don't have to do a thing.'

Leaving Ben staring at his laptop screen once more I went back to my office. There was definitely something not right. This lack of interest in my proposal was new. In the past he would have jumped at the chance of an impromptu holiday without giving this place a backward glance. What was he hiding, I wondered? And why had he slammed the laptop screen shut as soon as he saw me approaching?

Jake Wilson

CHAPTER 46

Hearing his voice drifting up from the garden below, I wondered if he knew sound travels on a hot summer's morning, especially when the windows were open and there was a breeze blowing. I slid out of bed as quietly as possible and moved nearer to the window where I'd be able to hear his conversation more clearly.

'I know. I understand. But it could still be a problem. She remembers me. There's no doubt about it. Yeah, of course I was using an alias and there's no chance she knew exactly what was happening back then. But, she knows about Ash and me and that complicates things, big time.'

Then there was silence, presumably he was on the phone and listening to the other part of the conversation. But, I couldn't stand up in case he saw me, so I lay on the floor and waited.

'Okay, yeah, just thought you should be aware of it. She could stir up trouble and you know what that would mean. I'm talking big time disaster. All our plans could be in danger of collapsing.'

Silence again. I waited.

'Right. As you say I can always shut her down if necessary. Just let me know if that's what you want.'

Seabeach Close   K.J.Rabane

There was nothing more to be heard, except the sound of footsteps going out of the garden by the back gate. Peering over the rim of the window ledge I saw Wilson standing near the sea wall. Dodgy or what? I'd always thought he was up to something. Now I was certain of it. But, should I tell Ma? No, of course not, well, not yet, not until I knew exactly what was going on with Henry Wilson, or whatever he was calling himself. It sounded as if he was used to using fake names in the past. He was a liar, that much was clear. So, now I was sure that nothing he told me was true. It was all made up…just a story. But why? What was the point of it all?

I sat and thought for a bit. I had been the only one to overhear his conversation and so I could play it whatever way I chose from now on. Thinking it over, I decided to wait and get more concrete info on him and what he was up to. It was the only sure way to make certain my mother wasn't going to get hurt. Besides, if I told her about it now, she'd only say I was jealous and not to be so dramatic. But I wasn't my father's son for nothing. Investigating was in my DNA.

There was still a week or so of the school holidays left. There was time. After a quick wash and throwing on a pair of shorts and a tee-shirt, I went into the kitchen. There was a note from my mother propped up against the bread bin. After reading it, I slid a slice of bread into the toaster and then poured coffee from the machine into my mug, just as the kitchen door opened.

'Hi Jake, awake at last. I see you've read it.'

'Yeah.' I could hardly bear to speak to the man, but if I was to avoid him becoming suspicious I had to tread carefully, so added, 'she's gone to Newton Cross shopping.'

'She'll be away for the day then, more than likely. You know what your mother's like when she's with Norma from the dry cleaners.'

I ground my back teeth together, Wilson was talking like he knew her and Norma, like he'd been around forever, like he was a replacement father, like he wasn't a fraud.

'Want to come out fishing at the point with me? We could have a pizza at that new place for lunch,' he said.

Trying to hide my true feelings, I croaked a reply as a crumb of toast stuck in my windpipe, along with Wilson's words. 'Sorry, got plans,' I managed to splutter.

'Okay, another day then?'

'Yeah, another day.' Over my dead body, I thought.

There was only one person I could trust completely in this place and couldn't wait to tell him about it. So, after finishing my breakfast, I left Wilson pretending to read the morning paper and went to find him.

Daniel Evans

CHAPTER 47

I waited until Jake had finished talking then hesitated before answering. It was possible he was making a fuss about nothing. It could be any number of things, especially as it was only a one-sided conversation he'd overheard. But, I wanted to get things clearer in my mind. Was he jealous of his mother's 'new' husband or had he stumbled on something much more serious.

'Well? What d'you think?' Jake asked, again.

'Not, sure. For a start it's odd, I can see that. But remember you only heard one side of it and it's difficult to be sure of what's going on exactly. It could mean almost anything.'

'Mm, trust you to be so sensible. Though, I am *living* with the bloke remember! He's a nightmare. He's so false it's not true. Why Ma can't see through him is a mystery. She's usually so on the ball about people. I'm telling you Dan, I know he's up to some shifty stuff. I'm sure of it.'

'O…kay…so let's say…he needs…watching.' Aware I was spacing the words out slowly, whilst thinking what to say next, I sighed, and finally came up with a solution. 'What if the two of us spend the rest of the holidays trying to find out what it's all about. Will that suit you?'

Jake sat back in his chair and let out a sigh. 'Some sense…AT LAST!'

We hooted with laughter, the tension sliding from Jake's face like honey from a spoon. Maybe he had a good reason to suspect his step-father of being into something dodgy. Only time would tell but we didn't have much time left before school started again.

'Right, well, we've got a perfect cover. He's got to have seen us working out on the prom most mornings during the holidays. So I suggest we should keep it up, and use it to see what he's up to…watch who he speaks to and where he goes for his run in the evening, maybe even follow him, if we could, without him getting suspicious.' Taking a deep breath I looked up at him. 'Have *you* thought of plan of any kind?' I asked, not really expecting him to have come up with anything workable as he was still furious about Wilson and probably wasn't thinking too clearly.

But, I was wrong. Jake thrust his hand into the pocket of his jeans and removed his phone, pressed a few buttons then handed it to me. The App on the phone showed a combination of maps and notes. I was amazed to see Jake had been logging his step-father's comings and goings for a few weeks before this.

I was confused. 'You're going to have to explain what I'm supposed to be seeing here, mate. I'm lost.'

He took the phone from me and said, 'He's been meeting that Fraser woman, from number one, a bit too often for my liking. Then yesterday, I was in the village and saw him talking to the cleaner from number five. She was angry with him, really furious, and then she went into a cottage near the square and he followed her! And that's just for starters. There's more…'

When Jake had finished explaining, he ran his fingers through his hair and waited for me to speak.

'So, let's say I'm with you on this and you might be on to something. Why or what it means is unclear, but maybe by the end of the school holidays we'll have an idea what's really going on. You've obviously made a start and like I said, we should keep a close watch on him, whenever we can.'

The door to the summerhouse opened and Mum appeared saying, 'What are you two up to now?' She was smiling and holding out a tray to me on which stood two cans of coke and a plate of pastries.

'Nothing much,' we both replied at once.

Chief Inspector Elis Williams

CHAPTER 48

Slamming down the phone on my desk I sank my teeth into my bottom lip so hard it drew blood. To a certain extent my hands were still metaphorically tied by protocol and my frustration at the restrictions this involved had mounted to the point where, once more, I'd had to make a formal request that Laura be fully informed. But Andrew Manning had refused point blank. I'd tried to explain yet again that expecting her to carry on investigating undercover, without being fully briefed could be putting her in danger, but my words had fallen on deaf ears.

Standing up, I paced the floor until I came to a decision. In the outer office Dennis Evans was ploughing through yet another pile of paperwork.

'If you want me, I'll be on my mobile, Constable, but make sure it's urgent, not something you can deal with on your own. I should be out until late afternoon.'

'No, probs, Boss.'

'Oh, and Dennis, if Manning rings, take a message and get in touch with me immediately.'

Dennis pushed his glasses up the bridge of his nose with a fingertip. 'Will do,' he replied, automatically.

When I arrived at number five with a tool-bag and sink plunger visible, she was in the garden.

'Oh, hi, I wasn't expecting you quite so soon,' she said, trying not to appear confused. Then, loud enough for the neighbours to hear, she said. 'It's the cloakroom toilet again. I think I must have put a wet wipe down it by mistake.'

'No problem. I'll soon sort it out,' I replied, following her inside.

As she closed the door, Laura said, 'Is there a problem?'

'Yes and no. Let's go upstairs and I'll fill you in.'

In the kitchen I watched as she put the kettle on and when we were sitting at the table, Laura's laptop and two hot drinks separating us, I said, 'I've been reading your latest report.'

She looked up from her coffee mug and raised her eyebrows. 'And?' she asked.

'I want you to stay well away from Wilson. Do not on any account engage with him, other than to pass the time of day or nod in his direction.'

'So I'm right then?'

'How d'you mean, right?'

'I was sure he was up to his neck in this. But, I don't understand. Surely, that's why I'm here working undercover to find out as much as I can about a suspect and to make that connection, whilst avoiding him becoming suspicious?'

How to explain, without explaining, was something I was having to come to terms with, but I'd been under instructions from The Met boys from the start, even though it was crippling me. I'd always been aware how difficult this was going to be, especially in Laura's situation, but I hadn't anticipated it would become such an impossible task. Deciding to plough on regardless, I took a deep breath.

'You are right to be suspicious of Wilson. But remember, this is an operation led by the London squad and we are in their hands. Let's just say, as I mentioned before, you are to concentrate your investigations on the rest of the locals, particularly those in the vicinity of Oysterbend and Seabeach Close. But leave Wilson to them. Is that understood?' My tone was insistent.

I saw confusion in her eyes and could sympathise. It didn't make any sense, even as I was saying it, but she was too astute to question it further.

'Whatever happens we want you to keep safe,' I said, my voice softening. 'You have a watching brief as far as Wilson's concerned, but absolutely no unnecessary engagement. You can contact me in the usual way if there's anything you are concerned about regarding him, but that's it, I'm afraid Laura.'

'I…er…' I could see she was trying to fathom it out and failing miserably. Finally, she said, 'Anything you say, of course.'

With a sigh I stood up. 'Good. Now, having fixed your toilet issues, I think it's safe to go back to work.'

As I left the house I saw Ted and his wife in their front garden opposite, I raised my hand to them as I made a play of loading my tools into the boot of the car, then drove away from Seabeach Close. How long would it take to wrap up Operation Creeping Jenny I wondered? It seemed to me The Met were no further forward than when they'd first spread their investigations to Newton Cross and as yet I had nothing I could work with or be able to pass on any useful information to Manning. There was no doubt we'd have to get a move on soon or the distribution chain could spread even further.

My conversation with Laura was still bothering me. Parking the car at my apartment building, I walked towards the station, feeling the weight of my decision pressing heavily on my shoulders.

Felicity Fraser

CHAPTER 49

There was no doubt in my mind that Ben had been getting worse lately. He was definitely taking something on a regular basis. I'd suspected it was speed and hoped it wasn't worse. My father-in-law was no fool either, he was sure to notice soon, in view of his son's history.

The sound of the shower running reassured me I wouldn't be seen, so I slid the dressing table drawer shut with a whisper. They weren't in there, nor in the pockets of his suit or jeans. Knocking loudly on the door of the en-suite I called out, 'Just taking your car keys, darling, I think I might have left my handbag under the seat yesterday.'

Hurrying downstairs and into the garage, knowing my bag was where I'd purposely left it last night, I slipped into the front seat and popped open the glove compartment. It was just as I thought, all the confirmation I needed. There they were, hidden at the back, under a couple of screen cloths and tissues. amphetamines…my suspicions had been right all along but now I had to decide how to confront Ben before his father did, and pray this wasn't just the tip of the iceberg.

In the kitchen I heard his tread on the stairs and switched on the toaster.

'How many slices?' I asked.

'Not for me. Just a black coffee then I'll be off. Got a meeting with Jackson this morning so I can't hang about.'

Jackson was the solicitor dealing with Brynteg development and I could see Ben was anxious. There was no way I could add to it by tackling him about the drugs now. I'd have to pick the right time.

'Just one slice, then?' I asked, hoping he'd at least he'd eat something.

But uncharacteristically he raised his voice. 'I said no! And forget about the coffee too. I'll grab one when I get to work.' He turned away and over his shoulder said, 'Not sure what time I'll be home. Don't bother to cook for me. I'll get a takeaway.'

I walked towards him but he left without kissing me goodbye. Feeling my cheek suddenly wet with tears, I wiped them away with the back of my hand. I was stronger than this. It wasn't as if it was anything new. I'd been here before and if the past was anything to go by I was certain it would only get worse.

After pulling on a pair of shorts, my running top and trainers, I left the house and jogged towards the promenade. My focus was on the exercise I needed to clear my head, and to think how I was going to stop this thing with Ben from spiralling into a disaster.

Inhaling the fresh, morning air and feeling the first, warm rays of sunshine stroking my body, I began to pick up speed and headed for The Point. The drugs could be a big problem. Ben could spoil everything we'd built together if he didn't get a grip. I had to do something and do it fast.

'Wow! Slow down, I'll never catch you up at this rate.' I glanced over my shoulder. It was Henry.

I slowed my pace in frustration until he reached me, part of me wanting to be alone to think more clearly about what should be done about Ben, and another part thinking, maybe a problem shared could be a problem halved. Did I believe the saying or could it be storing up more trouble than it was worth?

Emlyn Jones

CHAPTER 50

I closed the door of number three behind me and, locking it firmly, looked up at the sky. It was promising to be another fine day. Perhaps the spell of good weather would continue. I hoped so, as Gwyneth and Ian had taken the girls to stay with Ian's parents for the week. They had a cottage and a caravan in Tenby. The caravan was in a field alongside the cottage and the twins had been so excited at the prospect of a boat ride over to Caldy Island in Bob Jones's boat. They were also longing to stay in the caravan which was like a small house having every facility, right down to a shower. Bob and his wife had invited me to stay too, but I'd thanked them and said I had too much on at the moment.

It was only a little white lie. Truth was I was looking forward to a bit of time on my own. It goes without saying that I loved my family and was pleased we'd decided to pool our resources to buy the house in Seabeach Close. I did miss my Megan and hadn't relished the prospect of living alone after she'd died. So, the arrangement had worked out for us all as I was on hand to look after the girls when needed and being needed was important to me, especially now. Nevertheless, there were times when I enjoyed not thinking about anything other than myself. Selfish, I know, but most of the time I put my family first and if they knew how I felt about it, they would have understood.

The allotment club was holding a meeting at Idris Thomas's plot to welcome Ted as an official member to the group. He had been waiting for a plot to become available for years and now Bert Williams had finally met his maker the day had arrived.

Enjoying the sunshine, I walked down the lane to the promenade and stood for a while at the top of the steps leading to the beach. The sweep of the bay lay in front of me, the sand soft and unspoiled by the feet of holidaymakers and the locals, which never failed to make me smile. As I was enjoying the view a sound from behind made me turn around and glance up at number eight. Henry Wilson had opened his dormer window, a modern affair which turned into a small balcony. And there he was now looking down and staring straight at me.

'Lovely morning,' I raised a hand to him but he turned away and went inside without replying.

I thought, he's a strange one and no mistake. I couldn't quite make him out. He must have seen me. One minute he didn't stop talking to you and the next it was like he didn't know you! As I was mulling over the enigma that was our neighbour, I heard the sound of wheels and the pounding of feet.

'Morning boys,' I said, as Daniel and his new friend Jake sped past me.

'Hi Mr Jones. Can't stop, or this one will beat me,' Daniel called out.

I couldn't help but chuckle. At least the boy was happy, in spite of all his problems. Feeling my good humour restored, I walked towards the square and up the lane to the allotments.

Alice Barker

CHAPTER 51

I could hear Norman in the kitchen making breakfast and singing contentedly. Ever since he'd retired he'd been such a caring husband. But it wasn't just after retirement. He'd always been the same, even before we'd got married. I knew I was lucky. My life could have turned out quite differently if I'd settled for Bill Turner, at the bank. A smile tugged at the corner of my mouth and grew wider as I thought back over the years since we'd met.

I'd loved Norman dearly, almost at first sight. Nothing had changed for us both in that department except our looks. Gone were the two people who'd met in a dancehall in Croydon all those years ago. Back then Norman was tall with thick dark hair, twinkling eyes and a body lean and strong from playing golf and working on a building site. I was slim with shining chestnut brown hair flicking up on my shoulders my long mini-skirted legs bopping along to the beat. We were young and were determined to make the most of every day.

It was the age of Aquarius, as the song said, and every weak beam of sunshine found me soaking it up in order to have the first tan of the year. We married in the *Summer Of Love* in 1967 and were determined to visit Haight-Ashbury as soon as we'd saved enough money. San Francisco was our dream and we made it two years later.

Now, my lovely husband was beginning to lose his hair, which was almost white, and catching sight of my own image in the wardrobe mirror at the foot of the bed, I saw a face showing a roadmap of lines wrinkled well before its time. We were never told about the dangers of sitting in the sun when we were young. But it was too late for me to bother about it now. My younger self had vanished like breath on a mirror and if I was honest the years had been kinder to Norman than to me.

'Another nice day, love,' he said, holding the bedroom door open with one arm, a tray carefully balanced on the other.

'Allotment club meeting later?' I asked.

'It is. We're going to hold it at Idris's today. It's to welcome Ted in officially. He's made up to have his own plot at last.'

'I'm sure he is, love. He's been so patient all these years. I was talking to May on the prom yesterday and she said he's been like a dog with two tails ever since it became available.'

Norman handed me a napkin and placed the tray on my lap. 'Only shame is Bert had to pass away for it to happen.'

I picked up a slice of toast. 'True. And that news came as a bit of a shock I don't mind telling you.

Apparently he hadn't even been ill. Stroke, they said in the grocers. It was very sudden.'

Norman straightened the quilt cover and I changed the subject, 'By the way, I've heard some spiteful stories going around about the new family at number eight. I'm amazed people can still be so critical in this day and age. I've never noticed the colour of someone's skin, never have. Live and let live has been my mantra, as you and I know only too well!' I didn't mention Denzil. It was before I met Norman and it *was* only a summer fling as he was leaving soon to go to college. But there had been something very special about Denzil. He'd been my first. I don't mean the first man of colour I'd slept with. He was *the first*, and you never forget your first time, good or bad. Thankfully mine had been the former which was why Denzil would always hold a special place in my memory.

Norman chuckled. I could read him like a book. He was remembering all the things we did in our youth, and were still doing, in spite of the limitations age imposed. Maybe he had a few memories I wasn't privy to as well. But that was fine by me.

'You remember my dad worked on the docks?' I said, my thoughts retuning to our new neighbour. 'We grew up with all nationalities living around us. Just because Henry Wilson is mixed race doesn't mean he should be a target for every bigoted gossip in the village. You would think by now they would be more enlightened.'

'Yeah, but we both know what some people are like love. It was one of the reasons we moved down here, remember? To get away from all the talk. But then there are always a few with odd ideas still about. You can never truly escape them, however hard you try. But I'm sure Wilson's got a thick skin. He won't let that type of senseless gossip bother him.'

I nodded. He was right, of course. But then Norman usually was. After I'd finished eating, I said, 'Besides, he hasn't been living here long enough to have built up a reputation of any kind, good or bad. I remember when he first moved in and he invited us round for that party. I thought he was very pleasant *and* his wife. Not to mention the fact he's a bit of head turner.'

Norman's lip twitched, I could see he was trying to hide a smile.

'What's so funny?' I asked, raising an eyebrow.

'Not a thing love. You're just perfect in every way,' he winked before I could reply, adding, 'It was one of the reasons I fell in love with you.' He gave a suggestive chuckle and bent forward to kiss my cheek. I saw the skin showing through his hair at the crown and thought, at least we were making the most of our old age. People would be surprised if they knew what *we* got up to sometimes.

I flexed my throbbing fingers. I was suffering with the first signs of arthritis, which I was trying so hard not to think about. But then, as with most things,

Seabeach Close   K.J.Rabane

Norman had made sure he had the answer to all my aches and pains. Throughout our life he'd always made sure he had the answer, whatever situation arose. And I knew I could count on him to deal with this one too.

CHAPTER 52

Ted had his allotment at last. I was thrilled for him. It was about time, as we'd been living here for nearly five years. He'd joined the gardening and allotment club a few months after we'd moved in, on the understanding that when a plot became available he'd be next on the list. But we soon realised that everything was much slower in Oysterbend than in a big city. There were times when I found it so frustrating but I'd adapted to the new, more relaxed pace of life over the years and now it didn't bother me at all. In fact it had worked out well for us both.

Watching him hurrying towards the square, as if he couldn't wait, I turned and took the steps to the beach. The tide was out, the sand baked hard beneath my feet. As the sun rose higher on the horizon there appeared a thick bank of rain clouds hovering in the distance, threatening to spoil the day for Ted. Although, it was a just a formality, the committee meeting and official handing over of the keys to his shed, but, he'd been so looking forward to today. The plan was to sit with his friends in the sunshine and to enjoy watching the new shoots springing up, as he'd been unofficially planting and watering for over six weeks in order to make the most of the spring and early summer weather.

I turned towards the promenade and could still see his bright green tee-shirt as he stopped to talk to a couple of teenagers near the cafe. Then my attention was caught by a tall figure approaching him from the direction of the square. Even from this distance I recognised our neighbour Henry Wilson. He stopped and spoke to Ted, as the youths broke away from them and jogged towards the steps leading down to the beach. I knew they'd seen me feeding the seagulls and watched as they crossed the sand towards me, kicking a ball about and generally playing the fool.

By now Ted had left Wilson and was nearly at the square. But our neighbour had turned around and I was sure he was following my husband. Was I overthinking things? It was a bad habit of mine but one which had served me well in the past and one which I couldn't avoid. I shivered at the thought.

'Want a hand missus?' one of the youths chuckled and took his hands out of his pockets.

I delved into my carrier bag and handed him the bread. Then left them and walked back to the bungalow. Something wasn't right. I could feel it in my bones and knew I couldn't let it rest. I had to find out exactly what Wilson was up to. This feeling had been gnawing away at me ever since he'd moved in, which was partly my own fault. The Coopers, who'd lived at number eight before, had been an ordinary couple after all. They wouldn't have hurt a fly. Was it wrong to expect the same from our new neighbours?

The first drops of rain fell like darts striking my shoulders with such force I winced. Reaching the promenade I noticed the sky had darkened considerably and in the distance I heard a faint rumble of thunder. Was this heralding the last of the heatwave, I wondered, as I hurried up the back lane and into the shelter of our kitchen?

As I filled the kettle and glanced out of the window I recognised a sound coming from next door. Someone was opening the window-balcony in the roof. By this time the rain was cascading down our windowpane and puddling on the path leading towards the back gate. I was tempted to venture into the downpour and look up at number eight but decided it wouldn't be wise.

Just as I was mulling this over, the landline rang. From the display I saw it was Will. The kitchen clock showed it was nearly eleven. What on earth did Will want?

'Can't you sleep?' I asked anxiously. 'It must be nearly three in the morning over there.'

'Dad about?' Will asked, ignoring my question.

'No love, today's the day he takes ownership of his allotment. You know what he's like. He left ages ago.'

'Good. I've just spoken to Mark. Things aren't going well for him, job wise. I'm a bit worried about it in fact.'

I heard a sharp intake of breath from the other end of the line. 'I'm sure there's no real problem,' I replied. 'These things happen from time to time. I don't want you to start worrying about Mark, love. I'll give him a ring right now.'

'Okay. You'll get back to me then? I don't like the idea of things going wrong again.'

I felt a rush of love for my first born. He was still trying to look after his brother, as he'd done when they were kids. 'Of course. You just forget about Mark and concentrate on your pregnant wife.'

Putting the phone down, I sighed. The boys never brought their problems to Ted. It was always for the best. I didn't panic and they knew their father would act first and ask questions later.

I was the capable one and I'd deal with Henry Wilson too, in my own way, and the sooner the better.

Elis Williams

CHAPTER 53

Putting down the phone I frowned in frustration and made my way to the briefing room where a small band of assembled officers were waiting for me to update them. My instructions had been to inform them on how and when the swoop was to be carried out.

To say I'd been surprised by the outcome, of The Met's joint investigation into Operation Creeping Jenny, would be an understatement but I took care not to show it. There was little point in alerting them to the fact that I was not convinced about the result.

Although I'd already spoken to Andy Manning and voiced my concerns, it was obvious I was fighting a losing battle. The man, who was known as Henry Wilson, had been instrumental in their final decision and they weren't budging. It didn't help that I couldn't offer them an effective alternative. I'd always believed in 'the copper's hunch,' and like Laura could feel it now. Something didn't quite add up.

However, as the day progressed, I saw the links in the chain gradually snapping into place. The swoop by the officers in London and the south of England proved to be a successful one. So it just left the Newton Cross force to clear up things at our end. My instructions were plain and I intended to carry them out to the letter, in spite of my reservations.

There was always the possibility I was making the wrong decision. But, only time would tell.

CHAPTER 54

It was too late to stop Wilson interfering. I rang Will and told him what was going on. He listened and then said, 'Don't worry, Ma. It will work out, you'll see. You could be quite wrong about him you know.'

It was after lunch when they came for him. The sound of loud and insistent knocking on the front door was the first indication I had. After that, when I opened the door, they rushed past me and into the living room where Ted was completing the crossword in his newspaper.

Three uniformed officers stood in the doorway.

'What is it?' Ted asked, looking up. His glance swept from them to me and back again.

'Mr Edward Finch?' the taller of the three asked.

'That's me. What's going on?' His expression suddenly changed. 'Is it one of our boys?' Ted took off his glasses, stood up and put out a hand to me. I took it and started to whimper like a frightened animal.

'You might like to sit down, Mrs Finch,' the officer said, quietly. But I stood rooted to the spot, my hand still holding Ted's.

Then another one muttered something incoherent into a phone attached to his jacket and afterwards everything seemed wrapped in confusion. I heard the jumble of words as if they were speaking a foreign language and saw Ted's look of incredulity.

'Edward Finch.' The taller officer spoke again, 'We are arresting you as part of a joint investigation into the supply and distribution of drugs in the South Wales area. I must advise you that anything you say might...'

The rest was lost to me as I felt my legs buckle. The next thing I knew Laura from number five was patting my hand. There was no sign of Ted or the officers.

'What's going on? Where have they taken Ted? And what are you doing here?' I asked as tears slid down my cheeks. I quickly put my hand up to my face to wipe them away. It occurred to me I'd seen enough crime dramas to know what shock looked like and was certain Laura was thinking along the same lines.

She put an arm around my shoulders. 'I was in the garden and saw the police arriving,' she said. 'Then soon after one of them approached me and asked if I could come and stay with you. They said they were taking your husband to Newton Cross Police Station for questioning. I didn't want to interfere but I *was* worried about you being on your own.'

Grasping her hand I tried to stand up. 'If it's Newton Cross then I must go to him to explain to them. To tell them they've got the wrong person, Ted's never done anything illegal in his entire life.'

'I wouldn't think they'd let you see him at the moment. Maybe, you should wait a while?' Laura put her hand in her pocket and removing a business card, said, 'But I did ask them for the telephone number of the investigating officer and they gave me this for you.'

'This is ridiculous. Laura, you've got to understand they've mistaken him for someone else. Ted wouldn't do such a thing. It's impossible to imagine!' I gripped at my throat. 'All he's interested in is growing plants and his allotment.'

Laura tried to calm me down but I paced the floor, trying to think what should I do next. 'I'll ring Mark, he'll know what to do. He'll soon sort this out,' I said.

But she stood up and laid a hand on my arm. 'Come and sit down. You've had a shock. Although, I do think a relative or close friend should be with you. But until then I can stay for as long as you want me to.'

I nodded my thanks and asked if she'd mind making me a hot drink to steady my nerves. When she was in the kitchen I phoned Mark. But all I got was his answerphone message. I needed to tell him what had happened. Then, as I couldn't reach Mark I rang Will. But this time there was no answer from him either.

Seabeach Close — K.J.Rabane

'Look, I'm going to ring your doctor to see if he can prescribe something for you. You've had such a shock,' Laura said, handing me a mug.

I shook my head. 'No, really. It's a kind thought, but not necessary.' I took a deep breath. 'It will soon pass. I can't go to pieces, not when Ted needs me to stay strong.' I took another deep breath and let it out slowly. I found it helped. 'I'll ring our solicitor. Something has to be done to make this right. There's been a terrible mistake. I know there has. Ted would never do such a thing…never.'

Felicity Frazer

CHAPTER 55

It was the third time this week. Hanging my head over the toilet bowl I dry retched until I felt the nausea passing. *Was* it possible? Could I *be* pregnant? I splashed cold water on my face and rinsed my mouth. It was true I did feel different, but I'd assumed it was all due to my ridiculous infatuation with Henry Wilson. So the glow I saw on my face in the mirror, when I dressed each day, might be down to pregnancy? I'd noticed it was more difficult to fasten the waistband of my shorts lately but had made up my mind to eat less and exercise more. Why hadn't I considered I might be pregnant before this?

Although it had become a rarity over the past few months, ever since I'd suspected Ben was using again, we had made love occasionally. So, it wasn't impossible, surely?

In our bedroom I started to smile as I smoothed a hand over my stomach, whilst assessing my reflection in the full-length mirror. Then reality stepped in and the smile dissolved into a frown. Did I really want a drug addict for the father of my unborn baby? Sitting on the edge of the bed I wiped away my tears with the back of my hand, then bit my lip until I felt the bitter taste of blood. These should be tears of joy at the prospect of having a much wanted baby at last, but the memory of what had gone before intervened. Now things were going to be quite different I told my reflection. Steps had to be taken if I was to save our marriage. But could I go through the trauma of watching as he struggled with his addition? Could I stand to wait for another interminable round of hoping to see if he was clean and wouldn't relapse? I knew what lay in front of me and wondered if I had the strength to go through with it again. The alternative was to seek a divorce and manage on my own. The settlement would mean I'd have no money problems to worry about. But then I knew what it was like to have an absent father and had to consider what it would mean for my unborn child.

He'd left for work early as usual this morning but 'as usual' was now the new normal. Ben was wired, jumpy, and on edge and when I'd tried to get him to eat something, before he rushed out of the door and into his car, he'd snapped at me saying he had no time to spare and besides he wasn't hungry.

What could I do? From past experience I knew he'd deny it if I confronted him. Should I speak to his father first? Should I speak to Henry Wilson if only to get his opinion, or would it be a betrayal in such circumstances? Trying to make a sensible decision which might be instrumental in shaping our future, I paced the floor just as the sound of a siren disturbed my thoughts. Looking out of the window I saw a police car, blue lights flashing, siren screeching, pulling up outside number six. I stood transfixed, as the peaceful atmosphere of The Close was suddenly transformed into something resembling a scene from a movie. There were police officers in flak jackets running from the car up the driveway of the bungalow belonging to Ted and his wife. They banged on the door, then opened it and rushed inside.

As I watched, Laura, who lived in Elis's house, crossed the road, spoke to one of the officers standing in the doorway and then stepped inside the bungalow. Of Henry Wilson there was no sign, which I thought was a bit odd. I was certain he was inside the bungalow next door. He couldn't have avoided seeing the police car. I'd seen him at the window only moments before the police had arrived just as I'd rushed to finally throw up in the en-suite. So why hadn't he come outside to see what was going on?

Daniel

CHAPTER 56

It was a week since Ted Finch had been arrested for drug trafficking. Everyone I met was talking about it, but I had other things on my mind. Yawning at the interruption of a particularly enjoyable dream about Zoe White, I could hear my father calling me to come into the kitchen. So, narrowing my eyes I peered at the digital display on my Home Assistant and saw it was still only seven fifteen. With a sigh I reached for my wheelchair and went to see what was up. Zoe would have to wait for now.

Jake was sitting on a high stool at the kitchen worktop, a mug of coffee cradled in his hands. I thought it was a bit odd. He wasn't usually up and about so early. My mother had left for her morning swim, as the tide was high and lapping onto the steps. I could just see her as she swam in the direction of The Point. She loved being able to walk straight into the sea instead of having to cross over the pebbles, sand and mud at low tide. I knew from past experience she would be swimming in a straight line hugging the coast until she felt the tide pulling back as it turned, when she would start to make for home.

Dad put his hand on my arm and said, 'Dan, Jake wants a word with you. Coffee's in the pot. I'll be in the den if you need me.'

'God! Couldn't you sleep?' I asked Jake, wheeling my chair towards the lower counter and pouring coffee into a mug.

'I've got some news, mate. Couldn't wait to tell you.'

'Yeah, I got that much.'

'We're leaving! Mum said, we're going back to our old house. We're off home as soon as.'

He was beaming, his eyes shining. I wanted to be happy for him but couldn't quite manage to tell my face. 'Bit quick. When did all this happen?' I asked.

'Last night. I've not been able to sleep much since I heard. I couldn't believe it. At last! I can't wait to get back home to see my mates.' He was obviously excited by the prospect of moving, but then his expression quickly changed. 'Hey, I'm going to miss you though,' he said, the words tumbling around him in a broken promise. 'But you could come up to stay. We've got plenty of room and you could sleep downstairs…I could.'

'Yeah, I'd like that,' I replied, knowing it was unlikely to happen and that our friendship, if it continued at all, would be of the digital kind. Messages on What's App, Instagram and whatever other Social Media platform we could hook up through. It was bound to happen. Everything changed when distance was involved.

'Anyway, how come, the sudden move?' I asked, trying hard to hide my disappointment.

'Not sure really. I know I didn't see it coming. Mum just told me her and Henry were 'done' and she was glad she hadn't sold our London house but had decided to rent it out. As it happened the current tenants have left so the place is empty. We can leave as soon as we've got things sorted here. But Mum said there was quite a bit to do and maybe it wouldn't be until the beginning of next week.'

I didn't want to spoil his excitement but was starting to think it was all a bit too convenient. After all, we'd only just started to seriously investigate Henry Wilson's 'dodgy' lifestyle. Was that going to be abandoned too like the inevitable course our friendship would take, I wondered, while still trying to be glad for Jake?

Laura

CHAPTER 57

I saw his car drawing up outside and Elis was striding up the garden path. As, I opened the door I raised my eyebrows. This time there was no sign of his bag of tools. My heart sank.

'I suppose you've come to hand me my notice? Just when I was getting used to living here?' I tried to make light of it as he followed me inside. It had been on my mind lately. I'd been waiting for this day to arrive, ever since Ted Finch had been arrested.

'Well, no. What made you think I would? But I did want to discuss your future plans, which may or may not include living here.'

I could tell he was going to let me down lightly. The signs were all there. He simply didn't know how to do it.

'Coffee?' I asked, climbing the stairs to the kitchen.

'Great, as a matter of fact I picked up a few Danish pastries for us on the way,' he said, opening a cardboard carrier and placing the contents on the table.

It was just as I'd thought. He was softening me up for the final blow with my favourite snack.

We sat down at the table, the pastries and coffee mugs separating us. I didn't wait for him to explain, to apologise, to say I'd always known it was to be a temporary arrangement. 'Okay, let me have it.' I jumped in. 'I know my undercover work wasn't very helpful. I didn't have a clue it was Ted Finch and to be honest I still have difficulty believing it, even though everything points to the contrary... the stash in the bungalow, the means of distribution, the link with his son in London.' I sighed.

'Not at all. You've got the wrong end of this stick here. I've no problem with your work and neither has Andy Manning. Obviously you'll eventually be working back at the station but not for the moment. We've decided you should stay where you are until Finch is sentenced. That's if you agree. It might be useful too, if you still kept up the pretence with the neighbours. I mean with the undercover persona we created for you.'

This wasn't at all what I'd expected and neither was his follow up.

'And as far as your living arrangements are concerned...well to be honest, I'd rather have you looking after the house than the idiots I evicted before you came.'

I let out a slow breath of relief. 'So, I don't have to look for new accommodation after all?'

Elis's eyes widened in surprise. He put his mug down on the table. 'Laura, let's get this straight. I'm more than happy for you to stay here for as long as you like. Because, as you know, I've absolutely no intention of living here myself at the moment, if ever. We've agreed a nominal rent and I'm perfectly content to let things continue until you want to move out.'

'Wow, I mean, great. I thought…'

Elis raised his mug in a toast and held up the pastry.

'So that's sorted then.' His phone beeped and he read the message. 'Got to go. Keep your head down until all the loose ends are tied up then we'll get you back to station duties, okay?'

'Sure,' I replied, trying to stop myself from grinning like a fool as I followed him downstairs and closed the door behind him. Only then did I give a whoop of pure joy before going upstairs once more and accessing my computer files in order to update them.

It wasn't just because of the house, although that was my main concern. But, I still had the strongest feeling that, in spite of everything pointing to him, Ted Finch wasn't the link in the chain. And I still believed Henry Wilson was in some way connected to it all. There was the stash in Finch's house for a start. Obviously Wilson could easily have offloaded the drugs into number six without their knowledge. It was only next door, after all.

Daniel

CHAPTER 58

We shivered as a cold wind swept in from the sea. Soon school would be starting and Jake would be back in London.

'So, are you going to tell me what's going on or not?' I asked. 'What's the real reason? What's with the sudden sale of the bungalow and you and your mum moving back to your old home?'

I'd been bottling up the question ever since Jake told me of the move but hadn't been sure how to ask him. It was plain to see there was trouble in the Wilson household so it must have all come to a head, as he'd said. But why would they both move after such a short time and why go to the bother and expense of building that roof thing? None of it made any sense. Both parties in a marriage don't usually move on so quickly, unless there was a massive reason for it. It was too expensive for a start. And what was wrong with Oysterbend anyway? It was a great place to live. Then there was the feeling I had that Jake was hiding something. Previously he'd been so open about Wilson but not now.

'What d'you mean? I told you about it all the other day,' Jake said, turning his face into the wind so I couldn't read his expression.

'No. You didn't explain, just said you were going home and were looking forward to seeing your friends and that your mother said they were done. So what has Wilson done? It must be something big. It's all happened so quickly.'

'What? No…I… he's great.'   Jake's words blew back at me like a slap.

At first I thought I was hearing things. I couldn't let it go, so I said, 'Look, last time we spoke about Wilson, you told me he was definitely up to something and he and your mum weren't sleeping together. And then there was that conversation you overheard. What was *that* all about?'

'Yeah, I know, I meant to tell you…I got it all wrong see…He's cool. Really…he is! Mum said it was just that they'd discovered they were better living apart than together. Nothing more to it than that.'

I shrugged. I knew Jake wasn't telling me the truth but could see he was refusing to budge. So, I shut up. If I kept on probing it might start an argument and it just wasn't worth it.

Nevertheless, I couldn't resist asking one more question. 'Okay, so why all the hurry?'

'School. Mum wants me to be there for the start of term next week.'

I sighed, it was a reasonable answer, I supposed, Although, I couldn't quite shift my suspicion that all was not what it seemed. But I was unlikely to find out the truth and what lay behind it now, not now they were all leaving The Close.

'I'm going to miss you, mate,' I said, knowing at least that was true.

'Yeah, me too. You will come to stay in half term? I'll make sure everything is right for you. I mean…' Jake looked at my chair and hesitated.

'We'll see. I could always come up for the day and we could go for a run around Hyde Park, grab a Pizza…'

'Yeah, sounds like a plan, man,' Jake grinned with relief.

But we both knew it wouldn't happen.

The End
Now

CHAPTER 59

Striking another line through the day on the calendar I realise it is exactly six months since Ted was incarcerated in Cardiff jail. At least I can see him regularly, it's not that far, but it's not so easy to see Mark. How they found out he was involved is beyond me. I can only hope he stays strong until he's served his sentence. He's a good boy really and doesn't forget to ring whenever he can. He keeps telling me not to worry and that he'll be out before I know it. Seven years is a long time but with good behaviour he'll be out in five, well, four and a half now.

It's the way I manage. It's not easy thinking about Ted, but he assures me every time I visit that it's not so bad. He's been reading up about horticulture management in the prison library and he said he has plenty of time to think about what he's going to do with his allotment when he gets out.

He doesn't realise that the allotment committee have reallocated his plot in his absence and I haven't the heart to tell him. I'm still wondering how I'm going to broach the subject of moving. I've decided to sell up and go to live in San Diego with Will and his family. They have a massive house and grounds. It's like a mansion. I won't be in their way. I'll be living in the annex for now and Will said he is in the process of getting two bungalows built on the edge of their property overlooking a man-made lake. There's a view of the coast too. Not much like Oysterbend though. I've seen the photographs. Sail boats cruising offshore, expensive craft lining up in the Marina. There's obviously plenty of money where Will lives. I think Ted will understand, eventually. We thought it wise, considering.

I can't stay here now. The neighbours are polite but I know what they're thinking. Besides, I can help to get things ready for him and Mark when they come out. The business in thriving and Will says there'll be a place for Mark to work with him in some small capacity when he's released. One bungalow will be for Ted and me and the other for Mark. Will says he's looking forward to having us all in one place. So, the family business will continue. I'm glad. It's more than I ever thought possible when Ted and Mark were incarcerated…much more.

It makes perfect sense to me. There have been lessons we've learned along the way and, apart from a few casualties and sacrifices, we've managed to survive. I think I'll enjoy retiring properly and leaving all the decision making to our boys.

Norman Barker

CHAPTER 60

The sky looks grey this morning. The Close isn't the same as it was. Everything changes, and we, with the passing of time, do the same. Ted's in Cardiff jail and the Wilsons have gone back to London. I heard they were splitting up, which is a shame for young Jake. Alice and I had become very fond of him and were sorry to see him leave. Daniel will miss him too. They were good friends.

The cannabis plants no longer fill my greenhouse on the allotment. No one knew what they were of course. I'd fixed it up so they were well hidden behind a screen of tomato plants. But I thought it a wise move to dispose of them, after Ted was arrested. I've made other arrangements now.

As the morning wears on the rain begins in earnest and I see Alice picking up her knitting, her fingers knotted with arthritis. She doesn't know it but to me she still looks the same as she did all those years ago when we spent the summer in San Francisco.

It never leaves you, the feeling of the drugs entering your body and blowing your mind. The images returning when you least expect them, the rush, the days of love-making, and lying on the grass with the rest of us hippies, flowers in our hair.

Seabeach Close   K.J.Rabane

We've had such a full and happy life together and whatever happens in the future we intend to make sure we enjoy the rest of it to the full.

'Shall I get the book?' I ask Alice.

She looks up and gives me a slow smile. The years fall away. Her chestnut hair shines in the summer sun, her kaftan billowing around her legs in the breeze and her dark eyes showing a promise of what is to come.

'I think it's time,' she replies, packing away her knitting. 'Ted's been in jail for six months. It should be safe now.'

The door to the loft is in the small bedroom. It looks like a wardrobe. I step into Narnia and open the lid of the wooden chest. Moving aside the piles of knitting, throws, jumpers and baby clothes which make a perfect cover for what lies beneath, I remove the album and a square tin box. Inside the box is the equipment I need for the afternoon. I carry it into the kitchen, then take the album into the sitting room, where Alice has opened the wine and poured it into two large glasses which are ready and waiting on a side table.

Closing the blinds I switch on the side light then raise a glass to my lover.

Laura

CHAPTER 61

Ted Finch's case file has finally been closed. He is continuing to serve his time in Cardiff jail and I've been working back at the station in Newton Cross for two weeks now, but unknown to Elis I haven't altogether abandoned my undercover work.

As we agreed, I'm still living in Seabeach Close and hope to be for the foreseeable future. I've been able to continue keeping an eye on my neighbours. I'm certain they still don't know I'm a serving police officer, as I tell them my online business wasn't very successful and I've had to take up a part-time office job in Newton Cross. Elis has agreed that it might make things easier for me if they aren't aware I'm a detective. He says there is also the possibility of more undercover work occurring in the future if I'm interested. He says this with a twinkle in his eye so I'm not exactly sure whether he is pulling my leg or not.

The reason why I'm keen to protect a certain degree of anonymity is because I'm still finding it difficult to believe Ted Finch has masterminded a drug distribution link of such magnitude spreading over the whole of the South West Wales area. I remember seeing his expression as he was led away in the police vehicle. He was totally bewildered. Either he is an excellent actor or he is innocent and I firmly believe it is the latter.

Parking in the driveway of number five at the end of yet another busy day consisting of compiling reports and tidying up loose ends arising from the teams' involvement in Operation Creeping Jenny, I notice the For Sale sign is still in the garden of number eight.

I haven't seen the Wilsons since Ted was arrested. That's another thing…it's one coincidence too far for me to swallow. Opening the front door, I mull over the situation and believe it has all the hallmarks of a quick get-away. I can't seem to rest until I've explored every event to my satisfaction. So I begin with the new files I've compiled on my computer, and which I haven't shown to Elis…yet. I don't want to appear foolish to my boss, especially as such a strong feeling of elation still lingers in the station, at the conclusion of Operation Creeping Jenny.

Andrew Manning came up with the name. He'd been working in Vice for years before he finally made it to become Superintendent in charge of The Met's drug squad, which had mainly involved clearing up some of the clubs in Soho and the surrounding areas. Apparently he is a keen gardener and was fed up of getting rid of a particularly fast growing plant called Creeping Jenny. When he'd been asked to head the current investigation, and while thinking of a code name, he'd remembered the plant and had thought it appropriate, as the spread of drugs was as difficult to eradicate and its namesake.

A fresh smell of furniture polish hits me as I walk up the stairs. Elis has arranged with Molly, the cleaner, who works once a week for Charles Fraser at number seven, to clean number five every fortnight. When I said it wasn't necessary and that I didn't mind cleaning the house, he had wiped away my objection by replying that because I was working full time for him he didn't expect me to clean his house as well, apart from keeping it tidy of course.

I have to admit it *is* nice to come home to a clean house and it also gives me more time to carry on with my surveillance. Ted's wife bothers me. She is obviously upset about recent events. I haven't even seen her feeding the birds as much since Ted was arrested. I suppose the obvious reason is because it was how her husband had been caught. They say he'd built up quite a chain of customers, some of whom picked up their drugs on the beach under the guise of helping him to feed the birds. There was also a complicated pick up involving Mark Finch's associate, a middle aged woman, who would sit on a bench and hand over the drugs in a supermarket carrier bag. The bag varied each time and Finch had made sure he had the same type of bag ready for the swap.

Making a quick cuppa I take it into the living room. Why did Wilson move so quickly after Ted had been arrested? I still can't get it out of my mind, so putting my mug on a side table I open my laptop. Accessing the files I'd completed on my neighbours and which now are no longer required I open the one headed Henry Wilson. I've been adding to these files ever since The Met had swiftly closed down the operation. For the moment, ignoring the rest of the neighbours, except those in the bungalows opposite, I sit back and read the details concerning the inhabitants of number eight until I suddenly realise exactly what has been going on under my nose all along.

Ben

CHAPTER 62

I'm in a mess. Okay, I know it's of my own making but I'm trapped. Not only is Flick constantly at me, but now the old man is on my case in work as well. I can't avoid him. He wants a meeting, says he's got something important to discuss with me.

Reluctantly dragging my feet both metaphorically and physically towards his office, I slip a pill under my tongue to try and calm down. Uppers and downers have become part of my daily routine. I know I need help but I can't face it. I've been there before and know what's in front of me.

His office smells of extra strong mints which means he's had a liquid lunch, more than likely with Forrester. So this is going to be another headache with the new development, I can see it coming like an express train picking up speed.

He's smiling at me…always a bad sign. What's he been up to now?

'Sit down, Ben. I've just finished talking to Felicity. And, we've agreed. The time has come to do something drastic. So I've booked you into a clinic in Cardiff, and, when you are clean, you'll both take that holiday. The one I told you about…in the Maldives.'

I start to shake my head. 'It's not going to happen, Dad. I've got too much on. Besides, I haven't got a problem. It's just Flick making a fuss about nothing.'

He is still smiling.

Why is he smiling at me, with a gargantuan grin which is stretching his lips too wide? This isn't what I'd been expecting. It's not how he should be reacting. He should be ranting and raving, threatening to cut me off without a penny or… the list is endless. But still he sits there… smiling.

'Don't worry about this place. It's all sorted. Pack up and get home to your wife. She has some good news for you.'

I start to protest but can see it's of no use. Why isn't he shouting the odds at me? He knows I'm addicted and yet he's still not raising the roof. Closing the door behind me I leave work totally confused at my father's reaction to discovering I'm back on the drugs.

Throughout the journey home I wonder how I'm going to get out of this. Drug rehabilitation is the cure I'm dreading. I need the pills. I don't want 'the cure'. The road hugs the coastline like a constipated snake. The traffic at this time of the day is a nightmare. I weave in and out, overtaking when I can, then decide to hang back. Why am I in such a hurry? Felicity is bound to start on at me again. I don't blame her. But she doesn't understand the pressure I've been under.

Excuses crowd into my brain like hungry birds scavenging for food. As the road twists and turns I feel my stomach churning and stretch out an arm for the glove compartment. But, they aren't in the usual place. I pull into the side of the road and frantically search through the compartment, removing car cleaning cloths, tissues, a USB lead and a pen but it's obvious they aren't there. Someone has removed my support as effectively as kicking the crutch away from a one-legged man.

Pulling into the driveway, I feel sweat running down my forehead and trickling into my eyes. Can I get to our bedroom before she notices I'm home? Then the front door opens and Flick stands there. She, like my father, is smiling.

Felicity

CHAPTER 63

I can hear his car pulling into the drive. Charles has warned me, so I know what to say. At least I have his backing. I can't do this alone. I remember what it was like before. But now I have exactly what I've always wanted and I'm determined to fight for it.

He looks pale as he locks the car in the garage and then walks towards me.

'So, you've spoken to Charles?' I ask, as the smile slips from my face.

'He's not making any sense. What's this all about? Do you know?'

'It's no good Ben. I've known you were using for a while. I warned you over and over that if it happened again I would leave. But you just shut me down and tell me to stop nagging.' I say, making sure the words sink in this time.

He looks astonished, unable to believe I mean it. It's best if he thinks it's true…at least for a while… until I'm ready. It will keep him on his toes. I've thought it through in detail, covered every eventuality in order to protect myself and my unborn child. Charles thinks it's fine and I'll be staying with his son to play happy families once the baby is born. But he has no idea what's going on in my head. I know it doesn't work like that…once and addict, always and addict. This time there's no going back, if I can help it.

Ben comes towards me and I turn and walk upstairs into the living room. I can hear his footsteps on the stairs behind me but don't turn around and don't say another word. I'll wait to see what excuses he makes this time.

My husband sits heavily in the chair opposite me, his face in his hands.

'I'll do it. I promise. Please don't leave. You know I love you. I need you, Flick.'

'I've heard these words, or something similar, before Ben. It's the same as the last time, and the time before that. They don't mean a thing…they're just words.'

'The old man's booked me into a rehab centre. I'm not going to come home until I'm clean, for good this time. It's a promise I won't break Flick. Say you'll wait for me. Please…'

He looks so devastated I feel my resolve weakening as he pleads. But I must be strong for both of us. I rest my hand on my stomach.

'I can't do that. I can't make yet another promise, which I might be unable to keep. You mustn't ask me Ben. When…if…you are clean and can convince me this is the last time, I'll let you know my decision.'

He nods and croaks out, 'Fair enough'. He still thinks I'll let him back into my life. I can see it in his eyes. But I'm not the person I was, so I take a deep breath. Now is the time.

'This is important Ben. It's not like the last time. This time you aren't just involving me in your habit. I don't want our baby to grow up with an addict for a father. I won't have it.'

They are so arrogant, Charles *and* his son. Money spawns power, they think how foolish I would be to give up this house, the handsome husband, the wealthy father-in-law. But I'm not greedy and the settlement and maintenance for my child will be more than enough for me to break away from the ties binding me to this unworkable marriage.

As soon as I remembered, where I'd seen Henry Wilson before, I knew for certain Ben would never change. He's too close for comfort. Wilson is using a fake persona and I've a pretty good idea why. Wilson/Brady, whatever he chooses to call himself is connected to the man who nearly ruined Ben. It was Ward and his sleazy operation which sucked him into a web of drug taking all those years ago. And it's a man like Brady and the rest of his kind who will always find my husband and feed his habit. Like a hamster on a wheel Ben will keep falling off and I can't go through it all again.

He looks up from his hands.

'I…we…you're telling me you're pregnant?'

He stands up then and comes towards me but I hold out my hand and place it firmly against his chest. I won't make this easy for him, it's not been an easy ride for me, none of it. Constantly worrying he would relapse, and alternatively believing he could beat it, has taken its toll. I know he has an illness and recognise it's been hard for him too. But I feel I've supported him for years and now I've done enough. I've never shied away from it before…not until now.

This time it's different. This time I have options. If I stay I'd be living a lie. I don't love my husband anymore, his addiction has killed it stone dead. But, if I go I'll be robbing my child of its father. That's the problem…am I sure I can do it? Doubts threaten to weaken my resolve. Living in a one parent family was not easy. I grew up with friends who had stable, contented lives with parents who loved each other.

I won't be struggling financially like my mother. I can still give my child a happy life filled with holidays, posh schools, the best of everything… materially speaking. But, would it make up for the physical and emotional distance from its father?

But, I must have a life too and I mean to live it for us both. I rest my hand on my belly, and curb the smile playing at the corner of my mouth.

His question spins in the air then falls to ground at my feet.

'I am, yes, four months.' I reply.

Then I see it, as clearly as the shadows creeping over the rooftops opposite. It's the answer to the problem I've been struggling with ever since I was sure a baby was growing inside me.

I take a deep breath and say the words which will shape all our futures.

Alice

CHAPTER 64

At the time I remember saying, "I can't believe it. Not Ted Finch at number six! There has to be a mistake. He's such a nice man." And Norman had agreed.

I like both of them. May, his wife, is quiet, she keeps herself to herself most of the time, and Ted is a kind, gentle man. It just goes to show how mistaken you can be. Drugs! It doesn't bear thinking about. Well, that's what I tell everyone, should the occasion arise. I do admit to feeling a bit of a hypocrite though, after what Norman and I have been up to all these years.

When the Finches moved in…it must be five or six years ago now…The Coopers were living at number eight. They were a nice couple too. They were getting on a bit. They'd bought their bungalow when it was new, a bit like us. It was such a shock when they died. Something to do with the brakes failing on their car, at least that's what I heard.

So many things have changed in The Close lately. It's such a shame. I expect Ted's wife will think of moving soon too. It can't be easy for her living around here with everyone knowing about Ted. I

Seabeach Close   K.J.Rabane

suppose she could move to The States to be with her son and his family, as she's all on her own now. I wouldn't blame her. In some ways I would envy her such a move…California…oh, the memories we had. But, I know it's different for May. It's bad enough finding out your son has gone to prison for drug offences without knowing your husband has been suppling drugs to youngsters as well, and right under your nose. Then there's the gossip. Most of the locals are kind and sympathetic. Not all, mind you. Yesterday, in the Spar I heard the woman from the dry cleaners and Glenys from the butchers slagging her off saying she must have known about it and had chosen to turn a blind eye.

I felt like putting them right, to give them a piece of my mind and tell them not to spread such hurtful gossip. I really should have told them to be ashamed of themselves. But Norman has always told me to keep a low profile. He said we don't want anyone knowing what we've been up to over the years. So I kept quiet, but on my way home I thought about what they'd said…how they thought it odd May didn't realise. Then I began to mull it over in my mind. After all she *was* living with him and they *were* a very close couple, it's true.

I used to see them from my window most mornings, feeding the birds then going for a walk on the prom. But, I suppose appearances can be deceptive. Well, actually I know they can, you see! Norman and I know it's all a lie. Ted Finch is innocent, we know that for a fact. But if we say anything we might risk the police looking more closely at us. Perhaps it's best to keep quiet and let things pan out. Least said soonest mended, I expect.

Emlyn

CHAPTER 65

We've given his allotment to Ernie from the fish shop. We hesitated for a month or two mind you, wondering if there had been a mistake and they'd arrested the wrong person. But, the court case made our minds up in the end. Ted wouldn't be doing any gardening for quite some time, well not around here in any case. The locals would make his life a misery, just like the drugs he'd peddled were destroying the lives of the addicts he'd fed. Everyone agreed, at the Emergency General Meeting, we had to move quickly. It made perfect sense but it didn't sit comfortably on my shoulders. Because, you see, we'd all liked Ted, that was before we knew what he was up to of course.

There are still days when I find it unfathomable that he could do such a thing. By all accounts I should be angry, furious in fact, especially after what happened to Bronwen on the sea wall, because, if it hadn't been for Ted Finch my granddaughter wouldn't have ended up in Newton Cross General. But, somehow I can't believe the man I've known for years would do such a thing. He's spent so many hours with me, sitting in the sun and carefully tending his growing plants. Ted being a drug dealer, especially on such an enormous scale? Well, it just doesn't make any sense…none at all. It just goes to show how wrong I could be.

This thing with Ted has made me doubt my own judgement. I always thought I was good at reading people, spotting the bad ones and leaving well alone and making friends of the honest, good people who I enjoyed being with. I have to accept the verdict though. They don't put a man in jail without strong evidence to make a conviction. Since the trial, it's shaken my faith in human nature good and proper.

Ted's wife, May, is the one Gwyneth feels sorry for. She says she's heard some spiteful gossip about her and wouldn't blame her if she moved well away from Seabeach Close. My daughter hasn't a nasty bone in her body. She's just like her mother.

We have to move on and try to forget about it all. It's for the best. But it won't happen overnight. The whole affair will be talked about for a year or two yet I should imagine. After all it's been only six months, still quite fresh in people's minds. I suppose, like most things, it will die a death and Ted and the drugs thing will fade into history.

Number eight is still empty. The Estate Agents' boards, swinging in the breeze, tell another sad, sorry story. Why the Wilsons should have moved so quickly after Ted was arrested is a bit of a mystery too. That new loft extension of his must have cost quite a bit. It really doesn't make a lot of sense. The bungalow has lovely views, the village is only a few miles away from the town. It's a perfect place to live in my opinion. You just never know with folk. Perhaps they missed city life. But then, the other day, I did hear someone say they thought the Wilsons had split up… another marriage going belly up… it's all we seem to hear about these days. It could be just gossip though, you know what people are like. They never miss an opportunity to spread a good story, true or not.

I feel sorry for Daniel at number four too. He'd made a good friend of Jake Wilson. They'd been inseparable all through the summer and I'm sure Daniel will miss him no end.

Laura, next door, has made friends with my Gwyneth. They go to Yoga together and have a meal in Newton Cross occasionally. In fact they went out last Friday night to the new Italian restaurant which has opened up near the Police Station and Gwyneth said a funny thing happened when they were there.

It was just as they were finishing their meal and drinking their coffees. She said, Elis, who owns number five where Laura is living, came in with a few of his friends. They were celebrating something or other. Gwyneth recognised a few of them as being police officers, due to the fact that she'd been courting one of them before she met Ian. Apparently, as soon as they'd arrived, Laura had suddenly wanted to leave. It was quite obvious, apparently. She said, she seemed very agitated all of a sudden. Then one of the officers came over to their table and asked if they'd like to join them for a drink but Laura stood up and made an excuse about having to get home.

I think I know what's going on there and I put our Gwyneth in the picture. Elis Williams is a good looking young man and he's been calling at the house to fix a few plumbing issues since Laura has been living in number five. Now I come to think of it, it's been more than just a few times. *Either* he's had other reasons to call or he needs to get a plumber in to fix the problem permanently. Well, it's as plain as the proverbial nose on your face…she's got a crush on her landlord. But Gwyneth just laughed and told me I was living in the dark ages. Women of Laura's age wouldn't mess about and would soon make their feelings plain, she said.

She could be right, I suppose. All I know is it wasn't like that in our day. It was up to the man to let the woman know his intentions. I couldn't imaging my Megan being so forward. Not in a month of Sundays!

Molly

CHAPTER 66

So, he's gone. At least I can breathe more easily now. My jobs are safe, both of them, and what little reputation I have left is still intact. I don't earn much from my job at number seven but being part of the team responsible for cleaning Charles Frazer's offices is a different matter. That is permanent and the pay is good.

The days when he slept alongside me are long gone, the memory not so easy to erase. I remember waking in the late morning and watching him sleep, his body turned away from me as usual, making it difficult to see his face without moving and possibly waking him. But his long back and soft, coffee coloured skin, and his thick black hair curling at the nape of his neck, never failed to awaken a desire in me. It is these memories I've found which keep returning in spite of it all. Even after I knew the true reason why his lovemaking was mechanical and short lived. You'd think I'd know better now. Perhaps I'll never learn and will keep making the same mistakes over and over again. I'd often thought it was my fault but I know fault had nothing to do with it. There is another reason why it could never have worked between Ethan and me, one which is insurmountable.

Scabeach Close   K.J.Rabane

When he arrived in Seabeach Close with a 'ready made' family I knew it was all fake. If I hadn't seen him with Ash and understood why he could never be the lover I wanted him to be, I might have been taken in by the charade. He was aware I could have spoiled it all for him and that I was holding the trump card, although I'd never actually put it into words. I think he'd hoped I would begin to doubt what I'd seen and gradually it would fade into the past. Especially if he kept denying it and saying I'd made a huge mistake.

But, there is one question still remaining in my mind. Why? What was it all about? The fake family, the move to a backwater like Oysterbend? During the time I knew him he was very much involved with Haydn Ward and his enterprises. So when Ted Finch was arrested for drug trafficking I couldn't help laughing out loud. It was so obvious. It was why Ethan was hiding in plain sight. It was why he was desperate to stop me from destroying it all.

Now I have a decision to make. It's taken me six months to think about it. You see, I'd hoped it would all come out and Ted would have been acquitted without me having to open up old wounds. Six months when an innocent man has been in jail. I could have stopped it if I'd wanted to. So, what held me back?

The view from the window of number seven is almost the same, except for the For Sale sign in the garden opposite. As I sip my coffee liberally laced with vodka, a habit I'm determined to give up soon, it's the sight of the sign which makes me determined to give Ethan up to the police. It's about time.

He's destroying two peoples lives along with the countless number of addicts he's enabled along the way. I'm as certain as it's possible to be that he's used Finch as the fall guy. Anyone with half a brain could see he hadn't suddenly become a supplier, especially on such a monumental scale. It would have taken a different sort of man altogether. A man who'd been used to the London drug scene…a man who'd been arrested before…a man who was a personal friend of Haydn Ward…a man like Ethan Brady, who ticked all the boxes.

It didn't take a degree in rocket science to see what was going on right in front of their eyes. The Newton Cross force were out of their depths. They'd been well and truly conned by a ruthless individual with the charm and good looks of a Hollywood film star. I should know, I'd fallen for it all before but I've learned the hard way not to trust a word he said.

Turning away from the window I put down my mug and pick up my mobile.

'Newton Cross Police Station,' the disembodied voice almost makes me hesitate.

'Put me through to Detective Inspector Elis Williams. I have some information for him regarding the recent incarceration of Edward Finch,' I say.

Norman

CHAPTER 67

We like sitting in the sun, Alice and me. And even though we are old, we've still got our faculties. We don't miss much but keep most of it to ourselves. Gossip is destructive. Gossip can spread its tentacles and ruin lives.

We've known for some time the truth of the matter. There is no way Ted Finch is a drug dealer. But there are reasons why we didn't interfere. Some of them are selfish, it's true. You see, Alice and I were young when free love wasn't frowned on in the sixties, unlike the decade before, which had been full of repressed emotions and 'respectability'. So we've kept our mouths shut and carried on as before.

There was also our family to consider, our daughters and our grandchildren. It wouldn't do if our recreational pursuits were to land us in court. Drugs, even cannabis use, is still frowned upon and illegal, even if used in the privacy of your own home. That's not to say that half of today's youngsters take any notice of it, well maybe not quite half, but you know what I mean. But then Alice and me are in our early seventies and I could see the trouble it would cause if we were investigated by the police. I could imagine the headlines. The press would have a field day, not to mention the local TV news reporters clamouring for a story other than the scourge of dog poo on the cliff walk or the illegal parking on double yellow lines in the village. We'd never have any peace. And the gossips in the village...well it doesn't bear thinking about.

Most of the time, especially during the bad weather, we'd have an afternoon of 'enhanced enjoyment'. The book, is an album. We keep it hidden because it's full of photos we took in San Francisco during *The Summer of Love*. It's hidden in a chest in case the grandkids see it. But on our 'special afternoons' we turn its pages and slide back to our youth, whilst drinking wine and smoking weed.

We didn't indulge after our girls were born and only started up again a few years ago, after I discovered cannabis actually helped Alice's arthritis pain. I'd read an article in the Sunday Telegraph and hadn't forgotten how to grow and propagate the plants. Having an allotment made things easier than growing them in the house or garden. Finding a supplier in Cardiff, who let me buy a few cuttings, had been the easy part.

Most of the time we only smoked indoors. But, a while back I'd built us a small summerhouse in the garden. It wasn't much to look at, nothing like the ones in the glossy magazines but it gave us some privacy and we would spend many a pleasant sunny afternoon watching the activity on the prom and on the beach whilst getting high.

It was how we knew for sure Ted Finch had nothing to do with selling drugs. But knowing who it was and what to do about it were two different things.

Laura

CHAPTER 68

Six months have come and gone since Ted Finch was charged and is serving time in Cardiff jail. I remember it as if it were yesterday. The shock at discovering it was Ted of all people. I still feel a certain amount of guilt at not having had him anywhere on my radar, no doubt because I'd been spending too much time focusing on Henry Wilson. So, I'd watched as he was arrested and removed from number six, whilst trying to comfort his wife, guilt at my lack of expertise where undercover work was concerned sitting heavily on my shoulders.

Afterwards, at the debriefing session, Elis had been kind enough to let me off lightly, which was more than I deserved, I thought. And, after the initial euphoria in the station had died down, I'd continued to carry out routine policing. Although, it hadn't escaped my notice that most of my work was now relegated to desk bound duties.

But, it is all I deserve. I'm useless at undercover work. Nevertheless, I can't rest or leave it alone. It's the weekend and I've been working my way through online archive material concerning a woman called Charlotte Roach who had been the only daughter of a couple called Miles and Ellen Roach. I've spent the last few weeks trying to join up the dots and now I know I've been right not to let this go. The gut feeling I've always had that Ted Finch is innocent is still gnawing away at me and I'm determined to prove it one way or another.

Although there's still a big question mark hanging over Henry Wilson as far as I'm concerned. But, there's no way I can get any further in my enquiries. I've tried to discover what had happened to him after he moved from Seabeach Close, but it's like he's disappeared in a puff of smoke in a magician's trick. I'm convinced he isn't the person he'd appeared to be and moving out of the area so quickly after Ted Finch was arrested and charged is odd to say the least.

But I'll think about Wilson later. If I tell Elis what I suspect I'd only be digging a deeper hole for myself. So, I put his file into one marked pending on my laptop, until I can accumulate more information. And, for now, Charlotte Roach is the person I'm going to focus on, but with my luck I could be chasing another dead end, who knows?

I remember a day, soon after I'd taken over the keys of number five from Elis, when my car had failed to start. Ted's wife had fixed the problem for me. It often happens that the insignificant details become the pivot on which the answer depends, even if it doesn't seem to be important at the time.

I begin by concentrating on the couple who had previously lived at number eight. Their death had been another coincidence I couldn't overlook. It had paved the way for Wilson to move in next door to the Finches. However hard I try to escape from the idea of him being involved, it seems every avenue leads me back to the man. I spend two more days on this but can't find the link between The Coopers and Henry Wilson. So, I change direction and work through the night concentrating on their accident and just before dawn, I find the answer. It is so obvious I can't understand why I didn't see it before?

Sunlight streaks through the curtains I failed to close last night and fills my bedroom. I should feel tired as I've been working through the night but I'm so wired I push away the idea of catching up on sleep. It's Saturday and I'm not rostered in till Tuesday. Plenty of time for sleep later. Leaving number five I take the short cut through the bungalows and reach the prom. Ted's wife is feeding the birds. It's been a while. She'd stopped after Ted's arrest but now she is alone. The usual stream of young men waiting for a fix are absent. This would seem to point to the fact that Ted *had* been the distributor of course. But the more I think about it I'm sure it's not as simple as that. There is much more going on here than might not be obvious at first sight.

It looks to me as if May is mechanically going through the motions, still playing her part in this whole charade. It could be argued that someone who'd discovered her husband was a drug dealer would naturally be somewhat shell-shocked by the whole experience. But, avoiding the obvious has become second nature to me.

I stand near the steps leading down to the beach. I have to be careful. I don't want to arouse her suspicion. Not before I have firm evidence to support my theories. She still has no idea I'm a detective, which gives me time. I've been waiting for a message from an old friend who has promised to get back to me. He works in the cold cases unit in Cardiff. It's just a matter of tying up a few loose ends and making sure I have the proof I need before I mention it to Elis. But, there is always the chance the bird will have flown while I'm still waiting. But, It's a chance I have to take.

CHAPTER 69

I've always regretted tampering with the breaks of their car, especially now. If I'd left well alone Ted might never have been arrested. But, I did, it happened and it's too late for regrets. What happens now is what's important. You see, back then, I'd started to feel suspicious about The Coopers. They'd become far too nosy. I remember they'd been walking near me on the beach when I'd offloaded a large consignment to my contacts, the two guys from Haverfordwest. It was always risky, most transactions of this kind were, but I figured being out in the open…feeding the birds…who was going to think a middle aged women was distributing crack cocaine, heroin and amphetamines in such large quantities, right in front of their eyes? I'd come to think of my customers much like I thought of the birds. Feeding their addiction kept *my* family fed. It was the same in nature, I thought.

Then there was the time Alice Barker had seen the London distributor, a middle aged woman of course, handing over the pre-arranged supermarket carrier bag. Alice had been sitting on the bench on the prom. But, when I mentioned it to Mark he'd said, 'It's fine Ma, it's such a good cover it's worth sticking with it.' And it was. Alice hadn't mentioned it, so I must have imagined she'd noticed and had become suspicious. The process had worked seamlessly for years, that was until Henry Wilson moved into number eight.

Thinking about Ted, in jail, taking the wrap for the family business, which he'd never known existed, makes me feel sick to my stomach. But it wouldn't have happened if not for Wilson. He was the root cause of it. If he hadn't moved in next door… although in hindsight…well, no good thinking about it now. Hindsight isn't going to change things.

I'd always had my suspicions about him, right from the start. The man wasn't what he seemed and I'll never forgive myself for not being more careful. Will and I could have come up with something, if I'd only warned him properly instead of just dropping a few hints and making him think I was making a fuss about nothing. But I'd thought Wilson was a rival, trying to put us out of business by establishing a network of his own. I'd had no idea he'd been watching us both for other reasons.

It was something Mark said before he was arrested. I'd sent him a photo of Wilson some months before, but he hadn't mentioned anything about it at the time. It was later, after Ted was arrested. He told me he'd been wracking his brains to remember where he'd seen Wilson before. Eventually, something from way back re-surfaced. It was more than ten years ago. It was the beard which had complicated matters, he said. Beards have that effect on people, they are like a disguise, and apparently it had changed him, almost beyond recognition.

Mark said Wilson had been arrested during a large scale crackdown and clear up operation, which had focused on a club run by Haydn Ward. He said Wilson was an associate of Ward's and had ended up in the same police station as him.

Back then Mark had been young and new to the game, being in his late teens, but he'd been caught up in the raid. He didn't know what was going on and the police could tell he was small fry so he'd been sent away from the station with just a warning. But, not before he'd seen the guy who was now calling himself Wilson. Mark remembered him from the club but then he'd been calling himself Ethan Brady and was involved with a woman dancer called Emmy something or other.

So whoever he was, he certainly wasn't Henry Wilson. But still neither of us were able to discover his true identity, which led me to believe he was in the same game as us. As I've been pondering over it all I can't get away from the fact that if The Coopers had lived then Wilson wouldn't have been living next door to us. It was my fault…all of it…

I've rung Will and we've come to the decision that it isn't safe for me to stay in the UK. The hard part will be telling Ted. I don't know how he's going to take it. It keeps going around in my head, like a record stuck in a groove, as I get ready for my visit to the jail.

I needn't have worried though. Ted is fine about it. He says he's joined a gardening club in 'the nick' and is keeping his nose clean until he's released. I chuckle at his choice of words but Ted can't see the joke. He just gives me, his lovely, kind smile and I couldn't feel worse if I tried.

He'd never have believed it was me or that Mark and Will are also involved, so I let him carry on thinking Wilson has framed him. Then I make up a story about not being able to live with all the gossip and that Will thinks it would be nice for his child to grow up having a grandmother living nearby.

Ted has agreed. As far as he is concerned he's become used to the idea that he'd simply been in the wrong place at the wrong time and his solicitor has advised him there is nothing to be gained by an appeal. He's been quite philosophical about it all, telling me there are always miscarriages of justice in this world and if he can't do anything about it, he's just going to have to live with it. Apparently, most of the prisoners he speaks to are innocent, or so they say.

Even though he's accepted the situation, he is still confused as to where the drugs had come from and why they were in our bungalow. That's when I tell him I think Wilson is involved and has obviously planted them on us. I tell him he might be in with a group of thugs who would do us harm if we say anything to the police. Ted takes my hand, smiles and says, 'Let's leave well alone then love. I don't want you to be put in any danger.'

And, I agree. After all he *has* been caught red handed. When the police swooped, Ted's carrier bag was full of the stuff. It was where I'd put it, well hidden at the bottom underneath the bread.

Laura

CHAPTER 70

It's been a tiring day, I know I should carry on but I'm losing interest in trying to establish a link between a woman called Charlotte Roach and the drugs. I could be looking in completely the wrong direction and she might have nothing to do with Seabeach Close. It's not such an unusual name, I could just be desperately clutching at straws in an attempt to prove Ted Finch is innocent. But after having a relaxing bath, followed by a chilled glass of white wine, I sit up in bed with my laptop and search through anything I can find concerning the name Charlotte Roach. It's been niggling away at me for days now. But all my searches have hit a brick wall, which is why this will be my last attempt.

My eyes are beginning to close when I come across the name Harrison Roach. It was nearly forty years ago but I've found a report of an accident which had left him a paraplegic. He'd been legally adopted by the Roaches, who were his relatives, after his own parents had died in Australia and at the start had lived in Surrey with the them both and their daughter, Charlotte. I search and search but can find nothing more about him but just as I'm about to call it a day… I find it!

Seabeach Close   K.J.Rabane

BINGO, I say out loud, rubbing my eyes and sitting up straighter in bed. Their daughter had been known as Charlie. Her father had owned a large transport company on the outskirts of London. Searching the archives still further I find a photo of him and his family on the front page of The Telegraph newspaper. It was taken after his company went into liquidation.

On page three there is a continuation of the front page story and one of the photos strikes me as particularly significant. His daughter is dressed in dungarees, her short hair spiked up on top like a boy's and she's bending over the open bonnet of a car. The article mentions how Roach's daughter Charlotte had been following in her father's footsteps and was hoping to eventually work in the family business. However, his bankruptcy, resulting in the liquidation of his company, had changed her plans for the future.

Remembering the problem I'd had with my car soon after I'd moved into number five, I bite my bottom lip. Is it possible that such an insignificant event can be leading me to the answer I've been searching for all this time? Had it been there, staring me in the face, all along? I carry on reading, gradually forming a picture of the woman who is living opposite and whose husband has been locked away in Cardiff jail for the past six months. Yawning, I glance at the time on my laptop. It's nearly two am.

Only yesterday Molly, Charles Frazer's cleaner, told me how she envied Ted's wife. Apparently, she'd heard from a friend, who works in an Estate Agents in Newton Cross, that she is planning to sell number six and is going to live with her son and his wife in California. She said she has already put number six on the market but decided not to have a For Sale sign placed in the garden in order to discourage even more gossip about her situation.

Picking up my mobile I ring Elis's number in spite of the time. I know that he'll want to hear about this and I'm also aware that we need to act fast. I hear the phone connect and his voice, thick with sleep, saying, 'This had better be good, Laura.'

CHAPTER 71

Everything is arranged at last. It won't be long now. The bungalow has been sold to an investor, the funds transferred to our son's account in San Diego. Ted is contented and is willing to fit in with our plans once he's served his time. He likes the idea of living in America and is already doing research into what he will grow in the cottage garden on Will's estate. Beth calls the house we'll be living in a cottage, but it's larger than any cottage I've seen and Ted will have enough space to forget about having an allotment and concentrate on whatever he decides to grow in comfort. I expect he'll miss Emlyn and the rest of them though. But, Will says he'll make sure Ted gets to connect with a few people he knows, who are only too happy to talk about plants until the sun sets over the bay. There is Beth's father too. He has a boat and maybe Ted will start to share his hobby of sailing.

He's never asked about our family business, which Will runs. I think Ted believes it's something to do with online music advertising that Mark set up years ago and Will was doing all the administrating. He still believes Will only took it on as a favour to Mark as his brother had made a few mistakes when he was young and had got involved in drugs. I don't put him right. He would never go along with it…it *was* and *is* better if he doesn't know.

Seabeach Close — K.J.Rabane

He wouldn't accept it, not drugs, in spite of us all having had a decent lifestyle because of it. He would definitely hit the roof. In many ways he is an innocent abroad, my Ted, my Birdy. I'd recognised it the first time I'd met him when he'd helped me arrange the plants in the shop refit. I knew I could trust him from the start and nothing has changed. It's why I've loved him for a lifetime.

You might ask whether he's ever had the slightest inkling of what was going on? I've often considered that question since he was arrested. It's possible he might have guessed I've been up to something? After all he *was* with me on the beach most of the time. But no, I don't believe he's had a clue. As far as he is concerned I am…and always will be…perfect. It would destroy him, if I told him the truth.

I saw he has no idea by the bewildered look he gave me in court as the evidence against him was read out. He couldn't be that good an actor, not Ted.

Telling him about selling up has been hard. It still feels like I'm abandoning him. But, I've been surprised at how well he's taken to the idea of me moving to live abroad permanently.

Anyway, he's accepted the plan and where we should live and says, although he'll miss seeing me until he gets out, there are always phone calls and of course text messages and emails, even if they *are* read by the prison authorities before being sent. But he says there's nothing he could say in any message which would ever give them cause for concern. It seems he's thought it all out and come to terms with it, which is a relief to all of us.

I would hate it if he is suffering to save the rest of family. But he's insisted he'll feel better if I am with Will and Beth and he can stop worrying about me being on my own. He knows I'll enjoy spending time with the new baby as well as being with Will.

We've decided, Will and I, that we'll make it up to him big time, when he's released. We've discussed, and abandoned the idea of whether we should tell him about the business, It's better this way. Besides Will's cover is so well established in San Diego he doesn't want to rock the boat. It makes sense. We'll manage, and I know as long as Ted has his garden and his family around him, he'll be fine.

Laura

CHAPTER 72

Putting the phone down I mull over our conversation. Elis has stressed the importance of not letting May Finch think we are in the least bit suspicious of her. He's going to ring Andrew Manning and clear it with him before they make the swoop.

There's no way I can't sleep now. I'm too wired up. In the kitchen I drink strong black coffee then take it into the living room to find a good vantage point to observe number six without being noticed.

The Finches bungalow is in darkness. The street lamp outside number eight sheds an artificial glow over the roadway and the front gardens of most of the bungalows opposite, but leaves their windows still blackened by shadows. As I watch, I see the Finches' front door open a crack. Putting my mug down on a side table with a thud, I continue to watch. My phone rests alongside the mug, ready to alert Elis.

Then I see her. She's dressed in grey trousers and a black cardigan and is carrying a small suitcase. At first glance she too looks like a shadow. It's what she's been all the time of course, a spectral figure moving about the place as if invisible. She's been hiding in the guise of a respectable middle-aged lady, who likes to feed the birds, while somehow managing to spread her sickening trade of substance abuse and death right in front of us all. She's been hiding in front of us all along.

I see she's parked her car at the turnaround a short distance away from number six. I watch, as she starts the engine and cuts the lights, then the car purrs past the bungalows like a cat on the prowl.

A memory stirs of a conversation I've had with Ted Finch just after I moved into number five. He'd said, " I'm Ted, and my wife in May. You'll meet her soon I'm sure." Then he'd chuckled, adding, "I call her May but it's her middle name really. Her family always called her Charlie when she was growing up. She told me she liked it, as she was a bit of a tomboy. Her real name is Charlotte, you see."

Then he'd smiled and said, "I would never call her Charlie and I thought Charlotte didn't suit her either, which is why I call her May. It's like the month, and what could be nicer than May? It's when the trees and plants begin to bloom and…" He'd shrugged. "And it's stuck. She prefers it now and so do our boys."

If we hadn't had this conversation I would never have been able to make the connection between May Finch and Charlie Roach in the newspaper article. Once I've managed to establish a link to May Finch I carry on well into the night, until I discover that William Finch has a degree in pharmaceutical chemistry from the University of California. The fact, that he is now living in San Diego in particular, is also significant. It's only seventeen miles to the border with Mexico. From that moment on everything starts to slot into place…the route to the drugs, the distribution link to the UK…Finch's connection to the pharmaceutical industry. It's all there.

So in reality Ted has inadvertently handed me the means to save him from the rest of his prison sentence. However, whether he'll ever thank me is debatable. I ring Elis. His voice is hoarse. 'Developments?'

When I've finished explaining, he says, 'Don't do anything. I'll get things moving from this end. She mustn't get wind of you watching her or she'll find another means of escape. I'll alert the airport and have an unmarked car following her once she leaves Seabeach Close. You can relax now, get some sleep, Laura. I'll be in touch when it's done.'

Filling my mug with more coffee from the pot in the kitchen the seriousness of my discovery sweeps over me. The implication of Ted Finch being innocent is only the tip of the iceberg. There's the distinct possibility of there being an international distribution link ready and waiting to be uncovered and it hits me with all the force of a sledgehammer cracking a nut.

Any thoughts of sleep abandoned, in spite of Elis's reassurances, I continue sitting at the window cradling my mug of black coffee, my thoughts twisting and turning, like macabre dancers of death, round and round in my brain.

Seabeach Close   K.J.Rabane

It's still dark outside. Number six stands empty, but a faint grey glow of dawn is creeping over the roofs of the bungalows opposite, outlining the grey tiles with streaks of gold. It's going to be another glorious day.

Charlie

CHAPTER 73

Of course I absolutely knew Birdy couldn't have done it from the start. And now you all know why. He was innocent…was and is. Well, I've explained most of it to you now… most, but not all.

As I said, the first time I met him I just knew he was the one for me. I was certain he was someone I could trust and there hadn't been many men in my life who fitted into that category. I always thought my father was trustworthy and then he brought Harrison home.

I admit, I did make a mistake with his accident… Harrison's I mean… I know that now. I'd planned for it to be fatal. If it had been then maybe I'd be telling you a different story. At least that's how I look at it now, as I sit in the departure lounge of Cardiff Airport waiting for my flight to be called. I plan to fly to France and get a connection to LAX. It's all arranged, just incase the police try to follow. I'm determined to make it as difficult as possible for them. Not that I have any real concerns in that department. As far as I can see none of them have the slightest idea what's really been going on. I'm quite safe.

Looking back, I realise that after 'the accident', Harrison became more important to my parents rather than less. And, when he was finally discharged from hospital things became even worse than ever. I could feel his eyes following me around the room as if he knew exactly what I'd done. And so I planned a different strategy, one which wouldn't be obvious, as my parents were always in attendance, fussing around him all the time.

'Mum,' I said, one day when she looked whacked out, having just changed and fed Harrison. 'Why won't you let me help? I can share the burden. You don't need Sally to come in every day. I could do Monday and Friday so she has a long weekend. I've got the school holidays coming up. Six whole weeks twiddling my thumbs until September.' I was sixteen, not a child anymore.

'Oh, I don't know, love. It wouldn't be fair to you. Besides Harrison likes Sally.'

'I'm sure he wouldn't mind *me* caring for him. I am his sister, after all,' I replied, looking down at my hands, as if I were suddenly disappointed at not being allowed to help.

My mother reacted as I knew she would. 'Of course, no, I mean, I didn't …' She tripped over her words.

'Well, that's okay then.' I said. 'Will you ring Sally, or shall I?'

I didn't go back to school in September. Everything had changed by then. Dad's business failed, we moved into a crap house and Harrison had a relapse. He stopped breathing during the night. The doctor said it wasn't unusual as he had restricted movement and his lungs had collapsed after a period of sleep apnoea. The death certificate was written, the funeral was arranged and afterwards Dad agreed I should work in what was left of the business and train as an electrician in night school. Three years later, everything changed yet again, the business never really survived the first crash, Dad had a massive heart attack and died and mum soon followed him to the grave. Stress does that sort of thing to people.

At nineteen I had to pick up the pieces of my fractured life. With the little money, which was left to me after all debts had been paid, I moved into a shared, rented flat in Goodge Street. At least I had a job and could pay the rent.

The BT Tower loomed on the skyline as I made my way towards the next decorating assignment on my list. I'd joined DeeBee Decorators after Dad died. Derek Benton was a good friend of my father's and took care of my training on the understanding I would work solely for him. I'd already completed the course I'd started at night school and soon became a qualified electrician.

Gradually, the past faded and I began to enjoy working and living in the heart of the city rather than in the suburbs. My flatmates were okay. I didn't see a lot of them which suited me just fine.

I was twenty-two when Birdy first appeared in my life.

Seabeach Close   K.J.Rabane

I suppose I'd always managed to survive on my wits, even before the cuckoo had entered our nest. And afterwards, it became even more important. Looking back, I know it's worked out for both of us, in spite of what has happened since.

And as the years passed Birdy and I became inseparable, for good or for bad would be a matter of opinion but I believe it was for good. We moved into a rented flat and gelled immediately. But, I'd always known I'd have to be the strong one and there were times when I had to take the lead. It was more often than not to be honest, but it made things easier and it worked. He never did make any waves, not then and not now.

London was a breeding ground for enterprise, legal and not so. I made a few contacts and became involved in something which would be responsible for making us financially secure, with money to spare. It had been down to me…all of it. He never asked questions and let me get on with it, which set a pattern for how we were to live our lives in the future. As business increased I suggested it might be a good idea to move. I'd already decided how we should progress, the images we should portray, which was an unremarkable couple who were planning to start a family. So we moved to a small house in the suburbs, a tube ride away from the centre of town and life continued as normal.

And that was how things would have remained if Haydn Ward hadn't arrived on the scene. I remember the first time I saw him. He was attractive to both sexes, which was part of his charm and he made the most of that fact. He had thick, fair curly hair, and extremely pale blue eyes. He would focus on you with a look that made you feel you were the most important person in his vicinity. It was how he sucked people in and I think I'd always known he'd be trouble.

It was a while before things came to a head though. In the meantime we got married and had a tabby cat called Fred. But, I'd always managed to survive on my wits, so when things went bad, I was prepared for it. Thinking ahead was the only way I could survive. In my experience of life, there is always someone ready and waiting to spoil it all.

When I became pregnant, I knew I was going to have to take the initiative yet again. Determined that my child was to want for nothing I began making more connections. My decorating work took me to parts of the city where celebrities and the wealthy set lived. And it was when I was working on a job in Knightsbridge that I first met him. Ward had known my father and had done some business with him in the past. But unlike the legitimate business transactions he made with my dad, he also had a finger in a totally different pie.

Ward became responsible for me being able to expand the small business I'd already set up and which now involved me distributing meth-amphetamines and coke to some of Ward's celebrity contacts. He saw my potential immediately. A young, pregnant electrician/painter and decorator was sure to fly under the radar of the local drug squad. So, I worked for Ward until William was born then decided to go legit. Ward didn't like it at all and made a few thinly veiled threats, but they didn't work, threats didn't bother me and I insisted on cutting ties with him. After all we had a child now and I was determined not to take any chances with his future.

Will was in school and Marcus was a new born baby and as a family we were just about managing financially. But living so close to London was expensive.

Then Ted lost his job after an altercation with a customer. A thug in a red shirt had accused Ted of attacking him with shovel, and even though it was a pack of lies his employers decided to get rid of him.

We began to struggle financially and as the bills piled up I knew I had to go back on my decision. I rang Ward. He suggested we move to Brighton where there was a network ready and waiting for my distribution skills.

So, we rented a large flat overlooking the sea and our boys grew up with the beach as their playground. Birdy found work in a market garden and I continued to build up a network just like the one I'd created in the city. Ward took a cut but it still left enough for us to survive, in fact, as my contacts increased, I started to make some serious money. So as our boys grew up the situation changed yet again. Will went to university in California, got a first class degree in Pharmaceutical Chemistry, and began working in a temporary capacity in a Lab at a teaching Hospital in The States. Marcus studied music and drama and with the contacts he'd made began working in a music studio in Notting Hill.

Birdy and I were so proud of them both. But Ward hadn't finished with us. I was horrified when I discovered he'd been using Marcus to distribute drugs to some of his contacts in the music industry. I confronted him and he backed off…at least I'd assumed he'd backed off. It was much later that I discovered it had nothing at all to do with me. He'd only backed off because the Vice Squad had swooped on Ward's club syndicate and his whole enterprise had been locked down.

It was a while before I realised Marcus, who now liked to be called Mark, was running his own game. Then we had a phone call from Will, 'Mum,' Will said, 'I wanted to tell you and Dad in person but I'm so excited I couldn't wait until the weekend. I've got a permanent job in California! It's working on scientific research programmes in a prestigious University in San Diego. It's good, Mum. It's the best.' I could heard the excitement in his voice.

'That's fantastic news, love' I replied. 'I'm so proud of you and I know Dad will be over the moon.'

Seabeach Close   K.J.Rabane

I'd always realised that Will was more like me. And so it came as no surprise when his knowledge of the pharmaceutical industry became the means by which he was able to make more money than either Birdy or I could ever dream of. So, I suppose it came as no surprise when he called me one evening, when Ted was out, and suggested Mark and I join him in a new enterprise. Without going into too much detail on the phone he made it clear he thought we could set up a family business. I liked the idea straight away. I could see its potential a mile away.

We hadn't really settled in Brighton. I'd talked to Mark and Will about it and they'd agreed there was a market ready and waiting in South Wales. So I started to look for the sort of property which would not only suit us financially but where the area of distribution would be the most lucrative.

I liked the look of number six Seabeach Close, which had only recently come on the market, from the start and rang the Estate Agent to arrange a viewing.

It was in an ideal location. The bungalow was perfect. There was a view of the promenade and seafront from the back of the property which was an advantage. As far as I could make out, on first inspection, there appeared to be an elderly couple living in number eight which would be semi with us. Next to us, on the other side, there was a sold sign in the front garden. When I queried, with the agent, whether he could give us any idea who the new neighbours would be at number four he said they were a young couple with a handicapped son. So, the property at number six ticked all the boxes as far as I was concerned.

We both loved the look of the place and decided to move as soon as possible. I went up to see Mark on my own as Ted was busy in Brighton packing up ready for our move. Mark and I had a productive meeting, which we then relayed to Will who gave us the go-ahead. When I returned home I was in an optimistic mood about the future.

Everything started out perfectly. The move was successful. The first couple of years were profitable and we enjoyed living in The Close. Our neighbours Bill and Nancy Cooper were very friendly and, as they were getting on a bit, we'd helped them as much as we could. I did some of the shopping and when Bill's back was playing up Ted mowed their lawn.

I'm not sure exactly when I realised that Bill had been spying on us, me in particular, and I had the distinct impression he'd guessed a little of what was going on. In fact he'd hinted at it on more than one occasion. The last time he did so, I decided something had to be done…and soon.

The car was an easy enough proposition. My father had taught me well. It was a simple task to arrange the breaks in such a fashion as to fail without it being the obvious. And as it turned out everything went to plan.

But, now number eight was empty. We did think about buying it as a summer place for Mark and Will to come to visit. But it didn't appear to go on the market. I know that for a fact, because I'd looked every day. It did cross my mind it was a bit odd, but afterwards I decided it must have been because Henry Wilson had known the agent or was a relative of Bill and Nancy's. I had no idea then what the real truth was. How could I? It took me a while, but I gradually grew to suspect there was more to him than had appeared at first sight. Unfortunately, by the time I'd guessed the truth Birdy had been arrested and it was too late.

Of course, I could have easily saved him from a prison sentence by admitting it was me. But then there would be the possibility they'd look further afield and end up in San Diego. Besides, would they have ever believed Ted didn't know anything about it? There was still a degree of misogynistic feeling within the police force and I knew they'd never believe a woman could have masterminded such an operation. So, after talking it over with Will, we both knew Ted would be better off inside. In addition to which we knew he'd never get over it if he suspected the truth. He'd be useless without me, you see.

This way the business would be protected. Mark and Ted would do time and I would join Will in California. When they were released they would join us, by which time, Will had assured me, even if the law enforcers looked in his direction, they would find nothing unusual. He'd been covering his tracks for years. He was an expert at it. So all in all Ted doing time made perfect sense under the circumstances. We were all having to make the best of a bad job.

I remember, when Wilson and his 'family' moved in, I didn't have a clue about what he was up to. I suppose it was after that first party that I began to have my suspicions. Something wasn't right, but then I had no idea how much damage he would eventually cause.

I started to watch him more closely though and when Birdy told me he thought he was spying on us I knew we were in trouble. Number eight with its new extension had a perfect viewing point.

We'd decided that the distribution area was to be the bay. It was the best venue for the operation…free of suspicion. I'd operated there for years by simultaneously feeding the birds and feeding the drug habit of the inhabitants of Oysterband, and later expanding further along the West coast of Wales.

Mark and I were in regular phone contact and he would tell me when the London distributor would set up a meeting. It was always on the seafront promenade in full view. Who would suspect two ladies, of a certain age, with carrier bags, chatting on a bench overlooking the sea? The way it worked was simple. I would tell Mark what supermarket carrier bag to use and my contact would bring a similar bag. In one bag would be the drugs and in the other the money. It couldn't be simpler and worked like a dream until Henry Wilson appeared on the scene and ruined it all.

Even then he got it wrong though, it wasn't Ted. It was and had always been me, and as you now know, my kind, gentle husband had been the innocent party. So, as the months passed, I explained to Ted the reason I'd decided to sell number six and Will's plans for us all to live near him in California.

'It's the best, love. I'll miss seeing you of course. But at least I can stop worrying about you being on your own,' Ted said, squeezing my hand as we'd said goodbye, on my last visit to Cardiff jail yesterday.

My flight is about to be called. It won't be long now. I pick up my hand luggage and stand up. Then I see three tall men walking towards me. One of them is Elis Williams, the detective who owns number five. And suddenly San Diego seems a very long way away indeed.

Elis

CHAPTER 74

Laura sits opposite me. On my desk is her file. I clear my throat and say, 'Well Sergeant Davies how do you feel about your promotion?'

She starts to smile. 'I feel elated, thrilled, excited, I can't think of an adjective which will fully describe exactly how I feel, Boss.' Then, the smile slips. 'But part of me thinks I wish I'd seen it all earlier. If I had then Ted might never have been arrested.'

'Nonsense. Don't waste time even thinking about it. It's well deserved, Laura. Your work helped enormously in finding the right conclusion to Operation Creeping Jenny. If it hadn't been for you we would still be assuming Ted Finch was the main distributor. So, tell me, now the dust has settled, what alerted you to it being his wife in the first place?'

'I decided to look back at Finch's history and discovered there was more to his wife's past life than we'd realised. First she was an expert where car mechanics was concerned, having been taught by her father. Then I looked into her family life and saw there'd been 'an accident' to a family member, which had left him a paraplegic and who had eventually died a short while later. Then, I found a newspaper report of a couple who had previously lived in number eight and who had also died in a car accident, which raised alarm bells. It was a bit too convenient for my liking but I made the mistake of thinking it was connected to Henry Wilson having moved into the property.'

She stops talking when she sees me smiling. 'Sorry,' I say. 'But as you now know it couldn't have been further from the truth. I wanted to tell you from the beginning but my hands were tied. The Met had decided that in order to protect Wilson, no one should know his true identity.'

'Yes, I can see how difficult it must have been for you.'

'I did try to warn you not to concentrate on him though, without actually spelling it out,' I say ruefully.

'Yes, well, I should have taken it on board earlier. It might have saved me from hours of useless surveillance.'

'Not useless, Laura. You are learning from experience. Nothing is ever wasted. And now your promotion proves that your first class degree in Criminology wasn't wasted either.'

She begins to relax, the frown lines disappearing at last. 'Yeah, well, they made my life very difficult in Cardiff, once they knew of my qualifications. I could put up with the taunts when I cocked something up. You know the sort of thing, it's banter, par for the course. But this was different. Banter is too mild a word for it. Some of them would keep it up for weeks at a time. Even some of my superiors joined in.'

'There's a fine line between teasing and bullying,' I say. 'It might be of some comfort to know that the unit is under investigation for bullying as we speak. There have been similar complaints, which couldn't be ignored.'

She releases a slow breath. 'I only wish I'd had the guts to stand my ground before taking the easy way out and asking for a transfer.'

'Swings and roundabouts, Laura. If you had, we wouldn't be having this conversation and Ted Finch wouldn't be a free man. Besides, Cardiff's loss in our gain in more ways than one,' I reply, meaning every word.

Jake

CHAPTER 75

I watch the scenery flashing past the window and can't stop my face from stretching into a grin. I'm actually looking forward to coming back to Oysterbend. When I phoned Daniel to ask if he'd like a visitor for the half term holiday I'd been made up by his reaction. I've missed him since Mum and I came back home. But, even though we'd both known it would be impossible for him to come to stay at our place, as he still needs the adaptations his father has made to their bungalow, we've kept in touch since I left Seabeach Close. Social media, Zoom calls and What's App have helped but now I can't wait to catch up with him face to face.

I can never tell Daniel the real truth about Wilson. My mother made me promise. She'd said it could be dangerous for him. At first I'd been angry, until she explained about my dad and him. They worked in the same field and had become friends. It was why Mum had agreed to go along with the 'fake' family thing. After she'd explained, it all made perfect sense to me.

The train is pulling into Newton Cross station. I pull my backpack down from the shelf and slip my arms through the straps. Then I see him. He's waiting on the platform, as we'd arranged.

'Hi Jake,' he says, adding, 'wait till I tell you what's been going on now!'

We 'walk' alongside each other, chatting continuously until we leave the platform and see his father waiting in the car.

And I know, for sure, we'll always be friends. I knew it from the start. Disability doesn't make a scrap of difference. It never has to us and I know it won't in the future.

Max

CHAPTER 76

It's been over six months since I walked away for number eight Seabeach Close without a backward glance. To be honest I'd been more than happy to put it all behind me, never dreaming for a moment that it would raise its ugly head months later. Okay, so I'd got it wrong this time, but I'm not going to lose any sleep over it. Once upon a time yes, not now…I was jaded…the job no longer held my interest. At least that's what I keep telling myself, if not for me then maybe for Ash.

I'm not the only one who got it wrong though. Molly…Emmy…she'd shopped me in the end…and not before time. I knew it was bound to happen. I start to chuckle as I leave the office. I'd warned Drew Manning there was always the possibility of her spilling the beans but in some ways he'd been right to tell me to ignore it because she hadn't actually said a word until after Ted had been in jail for six months. Then, I think it all got to her and she couldn't live with her conscience.

She'd seen Ash and me together and I was sure she would have said something well before this. I feel bad about her if I'm honest, not a trait much use in my type of work I know. But, she's a good sort. She deserves to find someone honest to share he life. Someone who isn't a ghost with a hidden agenda.

Have I made the right decision now though? As the months have passed I'm not so sure. Ash has been at me for ages to finish it. Hearing about Ted Finch being released and his wife being charged and incarcerated has been a bit of a shock to the system, I have to admit. Am I losing my touch? Initially, it's true I'd felt the boulder of guilt resting heavily on my shoulders, but it was only there for a short time. I've managed to shrug it off quite effectively now.

Finch was the innocent party and I'd missed it. A cock up in anyone's book. At the debriefing I was told he hadn't a clue what his family were up to. It gives me little satisfaction to know I'd missed the signs and headed in the direction laid out for me by Charlotte Finch and her sons. The stash was where anyone, with a degree of intelligence, was bound to find it. It's become obvious to me my heart was no longer in it, even then, or I'd have seen it for what it was immediately.

At least the Newton Cross force have put it right and, to be fair, have been gracious enough to point out that she wasn't an obvious suspect. But the fact remains she is a seasoned and ruthless killer, who'd managed to con everyone, except Laura Davies, into thinking she was a retired lady who liked feeding the birds.

I wouldn't have accepted the job in the first place if it hadn't been for Janice. Adam and I had worked undercover for years until he was shot, taking a bullet meant for me. When she'd been approached about this job she'd agreed to take on the role of my 'wife' with Jake completing our ready made family, as long as I agreed to take the assigned role, which meant I couldn't possibly refuse. She said she owed it to Adam, in view of what had happened and reading between the lines I knew she meant I owed it to Adam too. I know he would have been proud of her *and* his son.

Although it soon became obvious Jake disliked me from the start and I couldn't blame the kid. He didn't have a clue what was going on, and it wasn't until after the case was being wound up and we moved that Janice told him a version of the truth about our work. Then he understood. He was old enough to realise how vital undercover police work could be and knew the dangers involved, having seen what had happened to his father.

It is why I'd contacted Drew and told him about Emmy. Andrew Manning was my contact back in the day when Emmy and I were an 'item'. He knew the history and was still working Vice whilst being involved in Operation Creeping Jenny. I'd told him she knew about my relationship with Ash and would realise the 'family' we'd created was a lie. But it turned out she had as much to lose by bringing up the past as I, which made the situation controllable.

Seabeach Close   K.J.Rabane

I check my watch and smile. Ash will be pleased. I've come home on time for a change. I've been working for the Metropolitan Police Force as an undercover officer for over twelve years and, although a desk job isn't as exciting, enough is enough. I've had more than my fill of constantly being someone else. Taking on multiply identities and personalities over the years has become debilitating. What I want now is an easy life with Ash. Surely, if I say it often enough I'll soon come to believe it?

Walking towards the tube station I take the short journey home and arrive at the small terraced house we share, shrugging off the last memories of Seabeach Close. I'd missed London, in spite of the lack of a view from our windows. I'd missed city life…you can keep Oysterbend and the beach. It isn't for me.

Opening my front door I lean back against it and sigh. A rich aroma of roast beef drifts towards me and I take a deep breath. I'm home and here I mean to stay.

Ash comes out from the kitchen, his face still pink from an afternoon cooking my favourite meal.

'Wow, on time, at last!' he says, walking towards me. 'Thanks for making the effort, Max.' He kisses me then heads for the kitchen.

I follow, as Ash says, 'Sit!' Then opening the fridge door, he removes a bottle of champagne.

Raising an eyebrow, I ask, 'We're celebrating?'

'Well, you promised it would be the last time. So now we're celebrating…again…and both of us know why!' Ash hands me a glass and fills it to the brim.'

'Yeah, we're celebrating.' I was as emphatic as I could be. I know I'd promised Ash, before I left, that I'd think about who was going to be the donor, and would come up with a definite solution, once I'd made up my mind to finally give up undercover work.'

Ash sits down opposite me. 'So?

'So…as I said…I agree. I know you said you want it to be me, as you were looking forward to our son having my looks.' I take my husband's hand in mine. 'But I think our daughter is going to look pretty silly with this,' I run my fingers over my beard and moustache, adding, 'don't you? Besides *you* are perfect. I'd be more than happy if you'd be 'the Daddy'. I chuckle, suddenly feeling embarrassed. This is definitely new territory for me but for once I'm certain, it *is* the right time.

'Well, in that case, I'll email Poppy and give her the good news. She's been dying to make us parents for years and so looking forward to being a godmother for the first time.'

'By the way, you didn't tell me who you were last time?' Ash says, 'You usually do…eventually.' He raises and eyebrow. 'And I think enough time has passed, especially as the case has finally been concluded satisfactorily, don't you?'

There is no malice in his words. I know Ash doesn't have a spiteful bone in his body.

'Henry Wilson,' I reply, sliding my empty glass across to him for a refill.'

'Good to meet you, Henry.' Ash raises his glass. 'To Henry Wilson then. May he rest in peace.'

I bite my bottom lip. I love Ash. He's put up with so much over the years and I'm determined to make being a father work and to forget about the offer of the latest undercover operation waiting on my desk for my reply. I only hope I can keep my promise this time.

THE END

About the Author
K.J.Rabane

In 2011, having had short stories published in magazines and anthologies of crime, I became aware that Amazon had created a means by which Independent authors could distribute their work to a wider audience via their Kindle Direct publishing route.

The first novel I published using this option was my psychological thriller *WHO IS SARAH LAWSON*. As the months passed I was thrilled to see that I was selling Kindle and paperback versions of my book, not only in the UK but it Canada, Australia and Europe. Sales increased and I entered the World Wide Amazon Breakthrough Novel award in 2012 and against fifty-thousand entries managed to reach the quarter finals. In the years following my novel reached number one in the psychological thriller genre in Spain and number two in the UK.

The success of my first novel prompted me to write five more using the characters of private detective Richie Stevens and his assistant Sandy Smith who first appeared in *Who is Sarah Lawson*. This series did well and I've continued to feed my obsession with writing by adding more books to my Amazon collection.

Seabeach Close is my twentieth publication on Amazon. Most of my novels are psychological thrillers but According to Olwen is the exception.

Three of my novels are available as audiobooks. They are W*ho is Sarah Lawson, Where is Jason Rayner and Termination Day.*

A full list of books is available by visiting Amazon sites worldwide.

Printed in Great Britain
by Amazon